No Sin To Love

No Sin To Love

Roberta Grieve

ISIS
LARGE PRINT
Oxford

First published in Great Britain 2008
by
Robert Hale Limited

Published in Large Print 2009 by ISIS Publishing Ltd.,
7 Centremead, Osney Mead, Oxford OX2 0ES
by arrangement with
Robert Hale Limited

British Library Cataloguing in Publication Data
Grieve, Roberta.
   No sin to love
   1. Poor - - England - - Fiction.
   2. Criminals - - England - - London - - Fiction.
   3. Stores, Retail - - England - - Sussex - - Fiction.
   4. Love stories.
   5. Large type books.
   I. Title
   823.9'2–dc22

   ISBN 978–0–7531–8364–9 (hb)
   ISBN 978–0–7531–8365–6 (pb)

Printed and bound in Great Britain by
T. J. International Ltd., Padstow, Cornwall

CHAPTER
ONE

Dolly Dixon jumped off the tram and almost danced down the street, dodging between the Saturday afternoon crowds. She turned off the King's Road into the maze of terraced streets and ran down the alley which separated Seaton Road from the posher houses in Carlton Road. She hoped Pete Crawford wasn't hanging about. She hadn't felt the same about her childhood friend since she'd met Tom.

As she opened the back gate to Number Thirty-Six, she smiled. Tom had said he'd missed her. She couldn't wait for next Saturday when she and her friend Janet would make some excuse to stop at his stall in Shepherd's Bush market. A week was a long time when you were seventeen and in love.

Did he feel the same about her? Dolly shook her fair frizzy curls. She knew he was a flirt, gave the eye to all the girls from behind his stall in the market, even chatted up the older women. Why should she think she was special — a skinny thing with no bosom to speak of, dressed in her prim navy blue skirt and white blouse as if she were still at school? And she did look prim, she knew it — not the sort of girl to attract a man like Tom Marchant. Hadn't Janet told her to wear more

1

make-up, to make the best of herself if she wanted to get a boyfriend?

But when she'd borrowed Ruby's lipstick at the church social everyone had stared and Pete had accused her of trying to look like her stepsister who wouldn't leave the house without her scarlet lips and matching nails. According to Pete's mother, nice girls didn't paint their faces. But she didn't want to think about Pete or Ruby just now though. Reliving her encounter with Tom was much more exciting.

At the back door her fingers tightened on the latch. Her happiness ebbed away as she heard shouting. Ruby was in full flow. What had upset her this time? It didn't take much. She hesitated, unwilling to become involved in yet another argument. Her stepsister usually won anyway.

"The cow, the selfish cow," Ruby screamed. "How could she do this?"

Fred answered quietly. "Give over, Ruby. What do you expect me to do? Besides, it's her choice." His voice rose. "And don't call your mother names. That won't solve anything."

Dolly's shoulders sagged. She should have felt relieved that for once she wasn't on the end of Ruby's savage tongue. But if it wasn't one thing it was another. Ruby was always causing trouble. She'd never forgiven her father for marrying Dolly's mother and lost no opportunity for taking out her spite on both of them.

"Ada's not my mother — how many times do I have to tell you?" A door slammed, shaking the small house to its foundations.

2

Dolly opened the door quietly, wondering what had set Ruby off this time. She put the bunch of daffodils she'd bought in the market on the wooden draining board. Their stems were bruised, the heads drooping where she'd gripped them so tightly. After hanging her coat on the hook behind the door, she went through the scullery to the kitchen.

Even without the shouting and door banging she'd have known something was wrong. There was no smell of cooking, no glowing fire behind the bars of the black-leaded kitchen range, no white cloth covering the scrubbed wooden table. Usually, her mother, wrapped in a flowered pinafore, would be stirring something on the hob, or setting the table for the family's dinner. And even if she was out, as happened more often lately, Dolly knew she could count on finding the range glowing with warmth, the kettle singing on the hob, and a pie or hotpot keeping warm in the oven alongside the fire.

On this chilly Saturday afternoon, the room was empty except for Fred Watson, her stepfather, hunched at the table, a ball of paper screwed up in his restless hands. He looked up at her through bleary eyes sunken in ashen cheeks. His sparse grey hair stood up in spikes where he'd run his fingers through it. When he saw Dolly, hope flared in his eyes.

"Dad, what's up — where's Mum?"

Fred didn't answer, continued kneading the ball of paper.

"Is she still over at Mrs Jenkins's? Mum said she was ill, but I thought she'd be home by now." So that was the cause of Ruby's tantrum. She always expected her dinner on the table as soon as she got in. But the look on Fred's face told a different story.

Her voice trailed away and she felt faint. Hadn't she known something was up when she'd heard old Mabel Atkins next door gossiping to the woman on the other side? She'd tried to ignore her, used to the gossip and taunts she'd been hearing all her life.

"Where is she?" she whispered now.

"No use asking me." Fred held out the piece of paper. "Read the note, Dolly."

Her hand shook as she reached for it. Until this moment, she'd tried to tell herself the neighbours' funny looks didn't mean a thing. They'd never had any time for Ada Watson anyway. But deep down she'd known that her mother's visits to Mrs Jenkins were just a cover. After all, they'd moved away from Battersea ten years ago, when Ada had married Fred, and as far as Dolly knew, she'd never kept in touch with the old lady. The brief note confirmed her worst fears.

"What does she mean — she wants a better life?" Dolly was bewildered, remembering the damp, smelly basement room they'd lived in for the first five years of her life, and fat, boozy old Ma Jenkins who'd "looked after" her while Mum was at work. Moving to the cosy terraced house in Chiswick when Mum married Fred had seemed the best sort of life to Dolly, even if she did have to share a room with Ruby and put up with her tantrums and bullying.

She put her arm round Fred's shoulders. His bewildered look told her she wasn't the only one who'd had no idea Ada was unhappy, let alone that she'd

4

found someone else. "Why? I gave her everything — a nice home . . ." He started to cry. "I'd have done anything for her," he wept.

Dolly had no doubt he believed his own words but she couldn't help remembering the tightening of her mother's lips as she'd begged for one of the new gas cookers instead of the old kitchen range. There'd been similar arguments over the need for a bathroom — they still had to wash at the kitchen sink and drag the old tin bath in from the yard once a week. It wasn't as if they were hard up now with Fred's promotion to foreman at the Fulham power station and both Ruby and Dolly bringing in a wage from their jobs at the Chiswick Polish Company.

But during the depression years Fred had learned to be cautious with money. Maybe Ada thought she deserved more now after the years of scrimping and scraping and bringing up another woman's children. Maybe this Gerald, whoever he might be, could give her what she wanted.

But how could she do it? Ada had been lucky to find a man who'd take on an illegitimate child and bring her up as his own. Ruby was right, Dolly thought, agreeing with her for the first time ever. It *was* selfish. What had poor Fred done to deserve this? Despite the arguments over the kitchen range, he'd been a good husband — and a good father too. Where would she and Mum have been without him?

She shivered and pulled herself together. "Let's have a cup of tea. And you'll have to light the fire, Dad. It's freezing in here."

"I don't want any tea."

"Well, I do. Come on, Dad — get some coal in, while I start the kindling off." Dolly was firm. She didn't see why she had to do everything. She took her mother's apron off the back of a chair and tied it round her waist.

Fred reluctantly picked up the coal bucket. He squared his shoulders and gave a crooked smile. "Life goes on, eh, Doll."

She watched him leave the room. Poor Fred. How was he going to cope? Come to that, how would she manage without Mum to take her side against Ruby? Then she too straightened her shoulders and bent to the job of laying the fire.

There were still a few warm embers in the grate and she nurtured them carefully, opening the damper to create a draught. Soon the kitchen began to warm up but as she fried bacon and scrambled eggs, Dolly still felt cold, an inner chill that had nothing to do with the temperature of the room. She just couldn't bring herself to believe that her mother had gone for good.

When the door into the passage banged open, she looked up. But hope died as Ruby strode back into the room.

"Tea not ready yet?" she demanded. "John'll be here for me soon."

"Won't be long," Dolly said, dying to turn round and slap her. Why was she so unfeeling? Couldn't she see how upset her father was?

Ruby pulled out a chair and sat down without offering to help. Dolly plonked the plates down on the table and watched as Ruby devoured her food, eying Dolly's untouched plate. "If you don't want that, I'll have it. I'm starving."

Fred glared at her and pushed his own plate away untouched. He lit a cigarette. "You just don't care, do you?" he said and his face crumpled again.

Ruby tossed her shiny chestnut curls. "I don't want to discuss it." She went through to the scullery.

When Dolly followed with the plates, she found Ruby examining her face in the mirror above the sink, oblivious to the pile of dirty dishes right under her nose.

"Aren't you going to help?" she asked.

Smoothing her eyebrows with Vaseline, Ruby turned to Dolly with a sneer. "That's your mother's job, not mine. Besides, I've been at work all day — and I have a date."

"I've been at work too — and I cooked the tea."

"Stop arguing, you two," Fred called. "Things are bad enough without you both going on."

"Not my fault," Ruby snapped.

"Can't you see he's upset?"

Ruby as usual had the last word. "He's better off without her. I never did understand why he married her." She snatched her handbag off the dresser and swept out of the house.

Dolly poured hot water from the kettle onto the sinkful of greasy crockery and rolled up her sleeves. Then she remembered the washing still hanging out on the line. There was so much to do and it looked as if she'd be left to get on with it. At least it got her out of seeing Pete tonight.

She'd hardly given him a thought since she'd got home, even the confrontation she so dreaded seemed unimportant now.

Besides, she needed time to think about what she was going to say. She'd been putting if off for ages — ever since she met Tom. It wasn't fair to let him think of her as his girlfriend — that she'd wait patiently for him until he'd finished university. He was a year older than her, but he was still at school, while she'd been working for two years.

Things weren't the same any more, though she'd always be grateful to him for taking her side against the school bullies when they were children. It didn't seem to bother him that she was labelled as a bastard and her mother called even worse names. She hoped he'd always be her friend. Convincing him that friendship was all she wanted would be hard though.

She smiled ruefully. At least Mrs Crawford would be pleased. Pete's mother didn't think Dolly was good enough for her only son. Because she lived in Carlton Road, she thought she was a cut above the people who inhabited the warren of terraces that backed onto her own street of bay-windowed houses with their indoor toilets and tiny front gardens. And then there was the stigma of her illegitimacy.

When Pete had moved on to the grammar school, Mrs Crawford made no secret of the fact that she wanted him to leave his old friends behind. But he'd

8

continued to befriend Dolly at church and Sunday school.

The soapy water swirled down the drain and Dolly rinsed out the cloth and hung it over the tap. Instead of starting on the drying up, she gazed at herself in the mirror over the sink. Her normally pale face was flushed a delicate pink and her blue eyes sparkled as she acknowledged to herself the real reason why she needed to make things clear with Pete. She bit her lip, wishing she didn't blush so easily. She didn't want anyone to know how she felt about Tom Marchant, wasn't even sure herself if this was the real thing.

The blush deepened as she recalled his cheeky grin and laughing brown eyes. Maybe she was being foolish but she hadn't been able to get him out of her mind since she'd met him a few weeks ago. When Janet tried to warn her off, she'd denied fancying him. But her friend knew why she was buying so much fruit in the market lately. How daft could you get? He didn't even know her name and she'd only found out his by chance. But when Tom smiled at her, things happened to her insides that made her blush to think of. And it was nothing like the feeling — or lack of it — she experienced when Pete tentatively aimed a kiss at her lips when he brought her home after the pictures or the church social.

She jumped guiltily as the door opened and thoughts of Tom fled.

Fred put his head round the door and tried to smile. "You nearly finished? I've made a cup of tea."

Seeing his defeated, broken look, Dolly felt a surge of anger towards her mother. How could she do this to us, she thought, banging the plates down on the draining board.

"I'm sorry, Doll," Fred said. "I feel as if I've failed you all. I thought marrying your mum would make us a proper family but it doesn't seem to have worked out that way — Billy running off to sea as soon as he was old enough, and Ruby always griping and getting on everyone's nerves. But Ada tried to be a mum to them . . ."

"I know, Dad. But it was hard for them too, losing their own mother at such an early age. Besides, Billy's going to sea had nothing to do with you marrying Mum. He always wanted to see the world." Dolly sometimes envied her stepbrother, who'd travelled to America and Australia and lots of other places as a steward on the Cunard liner *Aquitania*. Fred had never really forgiven him though, thinking his son would have been better off joining him at the power station down by the river.

Dolly sat down, reaching out to touch his hand. "Anyway, you've been a good father to me — and good to Mum, too. Maybe she'll realize it and come back." She was trying to comfort herself as much as him.

"She won't be back, Doll. I know your mother. She's still young you know — and I'm a lot older than her. Old and set in me ways. She wanted to go out dancing and that — I thought that's where she was when she stayed out so often. I knew she wasn't nursing that old woman — my Ada's not the type." He gave a short laugh, half a sob. "I didn't mind in a way — I was quite content with me football and the allotment and a drink down the pub with me mates. And I was content with me home and family too. I thought that's what Ada wanted as well." He sighed. "Maybe this other bloke can give her the good time she wants." He pushed his chair back and began to pace up and down the room. "I'd do anything to get her back though — if only I knew where she was."

"She'll come back, Dad — or at least get in touch." Dolly tried to instil some confidence into her voice — as much for her own sake as for Fred's. She couldn't bear the thought that she might never see her mother again. They hadn't always got on, but she was her only relative as far as she knew. She'd never known her real father, didn't even know his name. Mum wouldn't talk about him, said she'd never got over his being killed in the trenches in the Great War.

There was a knock on the back door and Dolly leapt up. She'd forgotten all about Pete.

"Ready then?" he asked as she opened the door.

"Oh, Pete, I'm sorry. I can't go out with you tonight." She lowered her voice, pulling the door closed behind her. "There's been a bit of bother — you'll no doubt hear all about it before long." News travelled fast in Seaton Road and Mrs Crawford, although she hardly left the house except to go to church, always seemed well up on the latest gossip.

"What's happened?"

Dolly didn't want to tell him. It was too painful to put into words. Besides, she still clung to the hope that her mother would be back. Maybe she was trying to teach Fred a lesson. With a bit of luck, no one would ever know. Hadn't she had to put up with enough sneers and taunting due to her mother's behaviour in the past? A little sob escaped her and Pete's arms came round her. She leaned against his chest, grateful for the comfort. Dear Pete. He'd stood up for her in the playground and stayed friends with her too, even against his mother's wishes.

As he stroked her hair, she couldn't stop it all pouring out — the grief, the anger and most of all the feeling of rejection that her mother had gone without a word to her, not even a note for her personally.

"I'm sure she'll get in touch," Pete said, when Dolly's sobs subsided a little.

"That's what I'm trying to tell myself," Dolly said, sniffing a little. She felt better for having got it off her chest. She pushed herself away and wiped her eyes.

"I must go in, Pete. There's so much to do and besides, I can't leave Dad on his own tonight."

"But we were going to the pictures," Pete said.

"Well, we'll just have to go another time, won't we?"

At her sharp tone, he blinked at her through his thick glasses. "What about church tomorrow?"

"I don't know. Depends how Dad is — I'll try to be there." She shook him off when he tried to put his arms round her again.

The back gate clanged behind him and she went over to the washing line. The clothes were still damp but she unpegged them. She must at least iron her blouse ready

12

for work on Monday. Ruby would just have to do her own.

As she tidied up before going to bed she caught sight of the bunch of daffodils she'd bought for her mother in the market. Their heads were drooping and, with a savage groan, she threw them into the waste bucket under the sink and marched up the stairs.

But she couldn't sleep and, as she lay trying to understand Ada's behaviour, she wondered if she was more like her mother than she'd thought. Pete was like Fred, quiet, solid and dependable, but really rather dull. Whereas Tom — the familiar churning leapt in her stomach. Maybe this Gerald bloke made her mother feel like that. But Mum was supposed to be a respectable married woman. Besides, she'd been in love with Dolly's father. Weren't you only supposed to fall in love once in your life — when you met the one and only?

Dolly's last thought as she fell into a restless sleep was that maybe Gerald reminded Mum of the young soldier who'd gone away to war and been killed before he ever knew he had a daughter. Mum had always said they'd have married if he'd made it back. The notion comforted her. At least it was easier to bear than the little doubt that niggled its way into her brain with the memory of the taunts she'd heard as a child — that Ada Watson was no better than she should be and probably had no idea who the father of her child was.

The next morning, when Dolly got up, Fred was already seated at the kitchen table, a cigarette in his hands. Had he been there all night, she wondered. He looked up and gave a weak smile.

"Didn't get much sleep," he said, gesturing at the over-flowing ashtray.

"Do you want some breakfast?"

"I don't think I could eat." He stood up. "I'll go over the allotment. I can't sit here listening to Ruby going on about your mother. I might lose me temper and say something I regret."

"But Dad, it's hardly light yet. At least have a cup of tea and some toast."

Fred nodded. "You're a good girl, Dolly. I can see I'm going to have to rely on you to keep the family together from now on." He got up and went through the scullery to the lavatory.

Dolly was annoyed. He needn't think she was going to do everything around here. She didn't mind doing her share, but Ruby would have to chip in as well.

But when she suggested Ruby should wash up and prepare the vegetables for their Sunday dinner, she managed to wriggle out of it.

"Sorry, John and I are going down the coast in his car. He'll be here any minute." She didn't sound sorry as she gave one of her smirks. She never lost an opportunity to rub it in that John Stokes was the only person they knew with a car. He was "in management" at the Cherry Blossom factory in Chiswick where they both worked. Like Dolly, she had ambitions to get away from the world of narrow terraced streets and outside lavatories.

14

It was about the only thing they did have in common, thought Dolly as Ruby flicked a comb through her hair and put her coat on. "I won't be here for dinner — didn't I say?" she said.

Dolly sighed. If Ruby helped, she'd have had time to go to church. She must see Pete and have that talk. Not that she'd have much chance with his mother there. Still, maybe they could have gone for a walk in the park after the service. Now it looked as if she'd have to spend the day cooking and clearing up, as well as doing the ironing. She looked resignedly at the washing, which was hanging on the rack over the range.

Before she made a start on that she'd pop over and tell Pete she wouldn't be coming to church this morning. She could just imagine Mrs Crawford's sniff of disapproval at the mere suggestion of doing housework on a Sunday. But it couldn't be helped. She couldn't afford to take time off work.

She slipped out of the back door and across the alley into Pete's garden. She could see him through the kitchen window, a tea towel in his hands as he helped his mother with the breakfast dishes. She smiled. Pete didn't mind giving a hand with the washing up. The back door flew open before she had time to knock.

"Dolly — I didn't expect to see you this morning," Pete said, his voice scarcely above a whisper.

"What's up? Have you got a cold?"

"No — I'm all right. I just don't want Mother to know you're here."

A cold finger touched Dolly's heart, but before she could say anything, Mrs Crawford's voice came from the other room. "Send her away, Peter. I don't know how she's got the nerve to show her face after what's happened. I won't have you associating with that family — do you hear?"

Pete looked at Dolly helplessly, his pale face flushed with embarrassment. "Sorry, Doll. She's a bit upset at the moment. I'll try and talk to you after church."

"That's why I came round — I won't be at church," Dolly said.

"I don't blame you. It must be hard to face people . . ." His voice trailed away miserably.

Anger sparked in Dolly's eyes. "I'm sure my *friends* will realize it's not my fault what my mother does." She turned abruptly away from Pete's stricken face.

"I didn't mean . . ."

But Dolly didn't wait to hear. She marched up the garden path, slamming the back gate as hard as she could. So much for friends, she thought.

All morning Dolly worked furiously, to dispel the sound of Mrs Crawford's voice and the helpless look in Pete's eyes. Surely he could have stood up to his mother just once? As she banged the iron down on another of Fred's shirts, she wondered how Mrs Crawford had heard the news so quickly. Pete must have said something to her, although he'd promised not to.

What hurt Dolly most however, was the assumption that just because her mother had done something unforgivable, the whole family must suffer. She sighed as she folded the shirts and unplugged the iron from the overhead socket. Hadn't it happened before when the kids at school had discovered Dolly was illegitimate? It had taken years to live it down. And now the gossip would start all over again.

When Fred came back from the allotment, he made a pretence of eating the lamb and roast potatoes Dolly had cooked, but she knew he didn't really want it. She didn't feel much like eating herself and wondered why she'd bothered just for the two of them. She cleared away and washed up in silence, then went upstairs to put the clean washing away.

As she opened the wardrobe to hang Fred's shirts she saw that it was practically empty. Ada had taken all her clothes — except for the old raincoat she always wore to go shopping. The sudden realization that her mother had really gone for good swept over her and Dolly sank down on the edge of the bed. A pair of worn pink felt slippers almost hidden under the dressing table caught her eye and hot tears welled up. How could Mum do this to her — to all of them, she thought.

She dashed her hand across her eyes and picked up the remaining clean clothes. She hung her work blouse on a hanger behind the door, glancing out of the window at the drab backyards. She could see across into Pete's garden and she smiled, remembering the signals they'd set up when they were children. Maybe he'd come round later while his mother had her Sunday afternoon nap. Surely he wouldn't abandon her completely. They'd been friends for so long. Hadn't he been the one to stick up for her all those years ago in the infants' school? Dolly knew he wasn't a "mummy's boy" as so many people thought. But Mrs Crawford was a very dominant person and he might easily give in to her.

Dolly's fears were realized when she went downstairs and saw the square of white paper on the mat by the front door. Pete's note apologized for his manner that morning but went on to say that it might be best if they didn't go out together for a while. He was studying hard for his university entrance exam in any case and would have little time for socialising. He'd look out for her at church if she felt able to face the other worshippers. He ended, "*maybe this will all blow over by the time I've finished my exams and we can start seeing each other again. Please wait for me. I will always love you.*"

If he really loved me, he wouldn't care what other people think, or what his mother says, Dolly thought as her eyes misted with tears. She'd always been fond of Pete. She didn't love him — not in *that* way — but she had hoped their childhood friendship would last. Unbidden, a picture of Tom Marchant's cheeky grin and laughing eyes crept into her mind. *He* wouldn't care what other people said. Still, the thought of him knowing about her mother sent a hot tide of shame over her. She was glad he didn't live nearby. Surely the gossip wouldn't reach as far as Shepherd's Bush. And why was she worrying anyway?

In the weeks that followed, Ruby was more unbearable than ever. She refused to lift a finger, saying she'd have her share of housework once she got married and had a home of her own. "Besides, I'm on me feet all day in that factory — not like you sitting at a desk all day," she said.

"But I'm studying for my exams as well," Dolly protested.

"Don't know why you're bothering with all that. You're bound to get married too and then it'll all be wasted," Ruby said.

Dolly knew her stepsister's remarks were prompted by jealousy. The trouble was, Ruby had never forgiven her for getting a job in the office at the Cherry Blossom factory, while she stood at a bench all day sticking labels on bottles and tins of polish. It had been a mistake working at the same place. But Dolly had seized the opportunity. The Chiswick Polish Company was a good employer, offering further education to its workers and the opportunity to better themselves.

And Dolly was determined to get on. Most girls couldn't wait to give up work. She'd rather stick to her career for the time being. Still, in the past few weeks she'd learned it was harder caring for a home and family than typing and filing invoices. And you didn't get paid for it either.

It was even harder trying to do both. She was so tired she'd almost fallen asleep over her typewriter one day. Only Janet's quick thinking, as she spotted Miss Potter bearing down on them, had saved her from being sacked on the spot. Janet had knocked a pile of papers off her desk, giving Dolly time to pull herself together and get on with her work.

She was getting really fed up. She never went out with Janet on a Saturday now, Pete was still avoiding her and Ruby couldn't stop crowing as she showed her engagement ring off.

Dolly desperately pushed the real reason for her discontent to the back of her mind — she hadn't had time to go up the market for ages and was dying for a glimpse of Tom and his devastating smile.

CHAPTER
TWO

It was a warm evening in June just before her eighteenth birthday and Dolly had walked part of the way home. She needed a little time to herself before she started tackling the chores. She sighed when she opened the back gate and saw Fred sitting on the low stone wall smoking a cigarette. He looked thoroughly miserable and she tried to summon a smile for him.

"Tea won't be long," she said.

Fred didn't answer, but he stubbed out the cigarette and followed her indoors. He sat down at the kitchen table, watching as she bustled around trying to find clean cups and saucers among the crockery piled on the draining board. She hadn't had time to wash up before going to work this morning.

"You're looking tired, girl," he said as she sat down opposite him.

Oh, he'd noticed. Dolly sighed, stirring her tea absently. She took a deep breath. "I don't know how I'm going to carry on with all this and working as well."

"But you've been doing all right up to now, girl. I've got no complaints."

Well he wouldn't have, would he, Dolly thought — there was usually a meal on the table when he came home and clean shirts hanging in the wardrobe. Aloud she said, "Dad, I can't keep it up. I get so tired. And I've got my exams in a few weeks. I'm getting on really well at work and if I pass, it'll be a chance to get out of the typing pool."

"I'm sorry about that, Doll. But exams aren't the be all and end all are they? You'll be getting married some time and having a family. Exams won't be no good to you then, will they?"

He sounded just like Ruby. "You don't understand, do you? I want to get on — get a better job. Make something of myself."

"I don't see the point. Your sister's quite happy working in the factory. And she's got herself a good bloke — landed on her feet she has." Fred looked up, grinning. "Besides, that young Pete's got his eye on you — what do they say, childhood sweethearts? When he's finished college he'll have a good job and you'll probably get married. You won't need to worry about working then, will you?"

Dolly stirred impatiently but Fred carried on talking. Why did men think getting married and having kids was the height of a woman's ambition? Maybe it was — for some — but not for her until she'd proved to herself and everyone else that she could get on and do well for herself — by herself. And why did everyone insist on coupling her name with Peter Crawford's — just because they'd been friends since childhood and danced with each other at the church socials? She'd always known he was just a friend — not even that since he'd practically ignored her since he'd sent that note. Besides, she was too young to get serious. She quickly suppressed the thought that there was one man she *could* get serious about.

Her stepfather's words penetrated her daydream and she shook her head as he said impatiently, "Well, Dolly, what do you think? Will that be enough housekeeping with a little left over for pocket money and your personal expenses?"

"What do you mean, Dad? Of course I'll handle the housekeeping money for you — haven't I been doing that for weeks anyway? But I don't need pocket money — I earn enough to pay my way and save a bit too."

"That's what I mean. I don't want you to go short. And if I got someone in to do the work I'd have to pay them anyway." Fred sat back with a smug smile as if he'd solved all their problems.

Dolly gaped at him. "Do you mean you want me to give up my job? But I can't . . ."

"You've just been saying you get so tired and you can't cope. So, pack up your job and look after the house for us."

"Supposing I don't want to?"

"You'll do as I say, my girl." Fred went from quiet persuasiveness to truculence in a flash. "I've given you a roof over your head all these years — it's the least you can do."

Dolly thought that if only Ruby would do her share, they could manage, especially if Fred would lend a hand too. But of course, he wasn't the sort of man to do what he saw as woman's work — not while he had a woman around to do it for him. And she had to admit he was right. Where would she be now if he hadn't married her mother? Still living in that horrible Battersea basement, that's where.

The thought was enough to make Dolly feel ashamed of her ingratitude and she gave in. She couldn't really do anything else — she was still a minor in the eyes of the law. But she wasn't going to give up her evening classes.

Ruby screeched with laughter when Dolly said so. "Book-keeping? Why don't you go to cookery classes instead — do you more good," she said, pushing her plate away.

Dolly had managed to bite her tongue up to now. But this time she couldn't help rising to the bait. "If you think my cooking's so awful, why don't you do it for a change."

"For goodness' sake, Ruby. Your sister's doing her best," Fred said, coming to her defence for a change. Usually, they both got told off for arguing.

Ruby stood up. "Well, I don't think much of it," she said, flouncing out. She paused at the door. "And I keep telling you, she's not my sister."

Fred sighed and gave Dolly a twisted smile. "When's she gettin' married?"

"September, she says."

"Can't come too soon for me," he replied.

Dolly agreed. She was sure if she only had her stepfather to look after, she'd be able to cope with her job as well. Ruby never lifted a finger, yet she expected everything to be perfect and her constant sniping was wearing Dolly down.

Next day during their lunch break she told Janet what her stepfather had proposed. Her friend's response was unexpected.

"You lucky thing — not having to go to work," she said.

"But I thought you were happy here at the Polish Company," Dolly said.

"It's a decent enough job — but I don't see me staying here forever and ending up like Old Potty." Janet giggled. Miss Potter, the typing pool supervisor was middle-aged and dowdy, very strict with the girls under her and, some said, "married to the company."

Dolly wasn't amused. "Neither do I," she said. "But I do want to get on — and Miss Potter said I was due for promotion to the accounts department if I pass my book-keeping exams."

"Accounts!" Janet gave a mock shiver. "The typing pool will do me — until I get married of course."

"Oh, got someone in mind, have you?"

Janet blushed. "Never you mind — we were talking about you. So — are you giving your notice in then?"

"I suppose I'll have to. Dad insists and I must admit I'm worn out trying to do everything. At least I'll have time to study."

"Surely you won't bother with those exams now?"

"Well, you never know — things might change." Dolly still hadn't given up hope that her mother would return some day. "I know you think I'm daft — but I can't help it."

Janet patted her arm sympathetically. "Come on, better get back to work or we'll have Potty on our backs."

Later that afternoon, Dolly approached Miss Potter and handed in her notice. The supervisor seemed to think she was moving to another company. "I'll give you an excellent reference but I hope it won't be necessary. I'm sure if I have a word with my superiors we can offer you a pay rise, enough to induce you to stay with us."

Dolly could hardly believe it, but she was too upset to feel any pleasure in Miss Potter's response. "I'm sorry — I can't stay. I need to look after my family," she said, choking back a sob and leaving the room hurriedly.

The rest of the week passed slowly and, now the decision was made, Dolly wished Saturday would come. Her colleagues had made a collection and presented her with a pretty dressing table set with a mother-of-pearl-handled brush and mirror. She was quite touched, it was so unexpected.

It was still raining hard when she and Janet left the office and ran across the factory yard to catch the bus to Shepherd's Bush, looking forward to browsing round the market, enjoying the bustle of the crowds, the raucous shouts of the stallholders shouting their wares, the glimpses of the dark secret interiors of the little shops under the railway arches.

As the bus came round the corner, Janet giggled and nudged her friend. "You're quiet, Doll. Wondering who we're going to bump into down the market?"

"I don't know what you mean," Dolly said, flushing. "I'm just feeling a bit sad — leaving work. I'm going to miss it — and you." But she couldn't help feeling a tingle of anticipation. She hadn't been down the market for weeks. Maybe this time Tom would ask her to go to the pictures with him.

Janet squeezed her arm. "We'll still be friends though. You can meet me from work on a Saturday and we can go round the market like we always do."

"It won't be the same. Besides, you won't have time for me now you're going steady with Norman."

Now it was Janet's turn to blush. "I'm going dancing with him tonight at the Pally. Why don't you come with us?"

"I'd love to but my stepfather doesn't approve." Dolly said. Besides, she couldn't really afford the Hammersmith Palais, which was considered the place to go on a Saturday night. If it was Tom asking now, that would be a different matter. Maybe it was just as well. She didn't have a dress posh enough for the Pally and, now that she wouldn't be working, there wasn't much chance she'd get one either.

The bus rattled to a stop at the corner of Goldhawk Road and the girls jumped down, careless of the mud splashing their stockings.

"I'm starving, let's go to Bob's," Dolly said.

It had been a Saturday ritual in the carefree days before Dolly's mother had run off, leaving her to look after the family. Bob's Café on the corner near the market was clean and cheerful. And his sausage, egg and chips with doorsteps of fresh white bread and large mugs of tea came at a price they could just about afford and still leave some over to go to the pictures later. It was also a favourite place with the market traders.

Dolly scanned the crowded café, trying to hide her disappointment when she saw no sign of Tom's dark curly head among the diners.

She finished her meal and got her purse out to pay. "I must go and get some vegetables before we go to the pictures," she said.

"I thought your dad grew everything on his allotment."

"He does, but the runner beans aren't ready yet and we've used up all the spring greens."

Janet smirked. "You just want an excuse to speak to that Tom Marchant," she said.

Dolly blushed. "Of course I don't."

"In that case, let's have another cup of tea." Janet peered at the rain through the steamed-up windows of the café. "Besides, it's horrible out there. I don't fancy fighting our way round the market today. Why don't we go to the first house instead?"

"But I've got to get the shopping . . ."

"You can do it on the way home. Come on, it's Ronald Colman in *Clive of India*," Janet said, rolling her eyes in ecstasy.

Dolly couldn't help giggling. She gave in and took her friend's arm. "Oh, all right. But give me Clark Gable any day."

As the lights went down on the red plush interior of the Silver cinema, Dolly tried to concentrate on the dashing Ronald Colman and his wooing of the lovely Loretta Young. But in the enveloping darkness her mind was on another tall, dark and handsome man, his warm brown eyes lighting up in a heart-stopping smile. And it wasn't Clark Gable either.

Tom Marchant shifted his feet and thrust his hands into the pockets of his navy blue donkey jacket, shoulders hunched against the cold trickle of rain which crept down the back of his neck. The bloody awning had split again. Usually he loved running the stall. It gave him the kind of freedom that most working men didn't have, cooped up in factories and offices at the beck and call of the bosses. But wet Saturdays made him question his choice of career. Not for the first time he thought how nice it would be to have a proper shop — maybe, one day.

A girlish laugh caught his ear and he stretched over the heads of the drab housewives threading between the stalls, slumping back in disappointment when he realized it wasn't her — the tall, fair girl who until recently had stopped at his stall every Saturday with her friend. He wondered why she'd stopped coming — probably got herself a boyfriend and was even now snuggled up in the back row of the Silver.

The thought depressed him and he told himself not to be so stupid. He'd only spoken to her a few times, didn't really know her, wasn't even sure of her name. What made her so different from all the other women he chatted up every day? But there was something about her and he longed to see her again. Just a glimpse of her shy smile would be enough to keep him going for the rest of this miserable day. It was the only thing that stopped him packing up as the crowds started to thin out. But she wouldn't come now, he was sure.

Another cold trickle found its way past his collar and he sighed. That's it — he'd had enough. He started filling bags with an assortment of tired vegetables — a few spuds, carrots and onions, topped off with a yellowing cabbage or cauli. "Come on, ladies — threepence a bag. Let's be 'avin' yer."

His voice galvanized the tired shoppers into action and they crowded the stall, holding out their threepenny bits eagerly for the bargains they'd been waiting for.

The last coin went into the pocket of his leather apron and the crowd melted away. At last he could pack up and go home. Not that going home held much appeal these days. Still at least he'd be warm and dry.

He turned to throw a mouldy carrot into the box behind him, his shoulders tensing as he heard her voice.

"I told you everything would be gone."

"I'm sure if you ask him nicely, he'll be able to find something for you," the other girl said, a hint of laughter in her voice.

Tom turned to face them, feeling sorry for the fair girl whose face was bright red with embarrassment. He knew how she felt. He'd been thinking about her all afternoon, telling himself she was sure to be here this week. And now that she was here, he was as tongue-tied as a schoolboy. He was usually ready with a spot of cheeky repartee with his women customers. Now he just stood there, a foolish grin on his face.

The dark girl nudged her friend. "Go on then — tell him what you want, Dolly."

"Dolly. Is that short for Dorothy? Pretty name." Tom was stammering. What a stupid thing to say. He expected her to start giggling. Instead she looked up at him from clear blue eyes, her pink cheeks flushed an even deeper crimson. She smiled. "I'd like some spring greens please, if you have any left."

Tom nodded and reached under the stall for the vegetables he had packed away — still fresh and all right to keep for Monday. The rubbish had all gone — but he wouldn't sell her rubbish anyway.

As Tom handed Dolly her change his fingers brushed hers. She snatched her hand away hurriedly, feeling the blush returning hotter than ever. Now that she'd seen him again, she couldn't think what to say.

Janet was no help. She was still giggling. "There, Dolly, I told you. He's sweet on you — I can tell."

"Don't be silly. He gives the eye to all the women — even the old ones. It's part of his market patter," Dolly whispered, stifling the stab of hurt which pierced her as she realized the truth of her statement.

She turned abruptly away, bumping into someone. "I'm sorry, Miss Spencer. I didn't see you." It was her old school teacher. They'd become quite friendly since Dolly started helping with the Sunday School. At one time, Dolly's highest ambition had been to become a teacher like Miss Spencer.

"Dorothy, my dear. You're quite a stranger. I haven't seen you in church lately."

"I've been busy, Miss." She avoided Janet's eye.

"Are you coming to the social tonight?"

"I'm not sure, Miss," Dolly said.

"It's Jessie, my dear. You're not in school now — and I did think we were friends."

"Oh, we are, Miss — Jessie. And I would like to come to the social. I meant to help you get the hall ready but I don't have much time these days. I didn't mean to let you down." Dolly felt guilty now for keeping away from church. She shouldn't worry about gossip, especially as Jessie Spencer didn't seem too bothered.

Jessie smiled. "Just try to come, dear. You should have some time to yourself." She started to walk away, then turned and touched Dolly's arm. "By the way, I saw you talking to Tom Marchant — the young man on the vegetable stall. I hope you won't take this amiss — but I feel I ought to warn you. He has a very bad reputation — quite the ladies man." She coughed delicately. "I'm sure you know what I mean, dear."

Jessie hurried away, leaving Janet collapsed with giggles and Dolly feeling embarrassed. She forced a laugh, pretending to share the joke. After all, she knew it wouldn't come to anything. As she said to Janet, it was a bit like drooling over the film stars they saw at the cinema each week. And she hadn't needed Janet or Jessie Spencer to point out that Tom sweet-talked anything in skirts. Why should she think she was so special?

It was still raining as Dolly hurried up the alley, the bag of vegetables bumping against her leg, reminding her of the latest encounter with Tom Marchant. She was fumbling with the latch of the back gate when she heard a voice behind her.

"Dolly, where have you been?"

She looked into Peter Crawford's anxious freckled face, his ginger hair sticking up as usual.

"I've been to the pictures with Janet," she said.

He flushed and pushed his glasses up his nose. "You are coming to the social tonight?" he asked, stammering a little.

"Yes, of course. I saw Miss Spencer in the market and she reminded me."

"Will you be my partner?" he asked.

"If you want me to. You only had to ask."

He flushed. "I wasn't sure — we haven't seen much of each other lately."

"Whose fault is that?" she said sharply.

He had the grace to blush. "I'm sorry, Dolly. Things haven't been easy for me — mother's not well, and I've been studying for my exams."

"Well — I've been busy too," she said, pretending to accept his excuses. Mrs Crawford had probably forbidden him to see her.

His freckled face creased in a frown. "You haven't got yourself a boyfriend — one of those chaps from the factory?"

"Don't be silly. I don't want a boyfriend — I'm too busy for all that." Dolly felt herself growing warm, remembering the recent encounter with Tom Marchant. She hurriedly said goodbye to Pete and agreed he could call for her later. She felt guilty for being so brusque with him. At one time, dancing with Pete at the church socials had been the highlight of her life. But that was before she met Tom.

Fred was sitting at the scrubbed table in the middle of the room, reading the evening paper. "Oh good, you got the shopping then," he said. "What's for tea?"

Is that all he ever thinks about, Dolly wondered. "Sausage and mash," she said shortly. "Will Ruby be wanting some?"

"Don't ask me. I've not long got in from the match. Fulham won today — two nil — so me and me mates went for a quick drink to celebrate."

"Good," Dolly tried to sound enthusiastic, thankful that Fred seemed to be regaining some of his zest for life. She filled the kettle at the cold tap in the scullery, put some coal on the range and poked the glowing embers into life. How she wished they could get rid of the blasted thing and get a gas or electric cooker instead. "So, has Ruby gone out with John?" she asked.

"How the hell should I know?" Fred sounded irritable. His pleasure in his team's victory had evaporated since coming home to find no meal on the table. He screwed his face up and rattled his evening paper.

Dolly peeled potatoes and put the sausages under the grill. As she prepared the meal, she felt a fleeting sympathy for her mother. Was this what her life had been like, waiting on her family like a servant, never knowing which of them wanted a meal or what time they'd be in? Would she be able to fill her mother's shoes? And if so, could she do it without going mad?

CHAPTER
THREE

Dolly dropped the handle of the heavy iron mangle and bent to catch her breath. The heatwave showed no sign of abating and, although it was still quite early, sweat trickled down her back. She'd been keeping house for her stepfather for only a couple of months, but already she was fed up. Fred showed no appreciation for her hard work and Ruby treated her like a skivvy.

The euphoria of passing her book-keeping exam had soon faded as she asked herself, "Where do I go from here?" Handling the household budget certainly didn't need a certificate of competence in double-entry book-keeping. Making sure the bills were paid and there was food on the table was easy compared to working in an office.

It would be different if she was running her own home. Unbidden, the thought of Tom Marchant popped into her head. She tried so hard not to think of him these days. But sometimes, as she cleaned and dusted, cooked and ironed, she allowed herself to daydream that it was his shirt she was ironing, his dinner she was cooking. She knew that if she were doing all this for him instead of for her ungrateful stepfamily, it would make all the difference in the world.

But she hadn't even had a glimpse of him for weeks. Since she'd been forced to give up her job, Fred insisted she didn't need to spend money on tram fare when there was a row of shops just round the corner that filled all their needs. And this time of year they had all the fresh vegetables they could eat from Fred's allotment.

She sighed and bent to take a sheet from the basket at her feet. As she pegged it on the line she wished she could find an excuse to go up to Shepherd's Bush. If Fred was in a good mood maybe he'd give her the money for the pictures this week.

The sheets hung limp in the still air and Dolly's hair clung in damp strands to the back of her neck. But she couldn't stop yet. There was the copper to empty and the beds to re-make with clean linen. Then she'd have to get some coal in to keep the range going so that she could cook Fred's dinner. They should call me Cinderella, she thought. Only there was no handsome prince waiting in the wings.

She had her hand on the back door when a voice came from the other side of the fence. "It's dry almost as soon as it's on the line this weather."

Is she talking to me, Dolly wondered. Mabel Atkins had never had a good word for her mother, even timed her visits to the lavatory at the end of the yard to avoid the other woman. She hadn't spoken to Dolly since Ada had left and Dolly certainly didn't want to talk to her.

"Yes, it is hot, isn't it?" she replied, for politeness' sake and put her foot on the back step.

"No word from your mum, then?" Mabel's thin face appeared round the edge of the sheets pegged on the line. The words were sympathetic but there was malice in the narrowed eyes.

"No."

Mabel wasn't deterred. "Course, I never did believe that story about her nursing the old lady. The way she used to go out — all dolled up. I could've told Fred. But would he listen . . .?"

Dolly's hand tightened on the doorjamb. "That's my mother you're talking about and I'll thank you to keep your nose out of it."

"Well, really. I'm only stating what everybody round 'ere knows. There's no need to get all hoity-toity. Still, you always did think you were a cut above the rest of us, though God knows why . . ."

Dolly went indoors, slammed the door and leaned against the stone sink, her breath coming in short gasps. She shouldn't have answered the old bag, should have pretended she hadn't heard. Tears welled up in her throat and she gripped the edge of the sink. Would it never end, this constant striving to rise above her mother's reputation? And she'd tried so hard, always kept herself neat and tidy, worked hard at school, gone to church, got herself a good job. And for what? To end up as a skivvy for the Watsons and the butt of the malicious gossips of Seaton Road?

Tears fell on to her white blouse, making dark streaks. She groped in her pocket for a hankie and wiped her eyes, blew her nose hard. "No good feeling sorry for yourself, Dolly," she muttered. "There's nothing you can do about it at the moment."

She started to empty the copper. The washing might be finished but there was plenty more to do. She'd try to keep busy, stop the depressing thoughts from taking over. As she put clean sheets on the beds, started preparing vegetables for the evening meal, she wished she had something to look forward to. Even the coming Sunday school outing held no appeal. Pete would be there and she still felt awkward with him, even though they'd danced together at the social. He spoke to her at church, but she noticed he made sure his mother wasn't around. She was still fond of him in a way. But she hadn't really forgiven him for rejecting her when her mother first left. And she couldn't help comparing him with Tom. Perhaps she'd make an excuse not to go.

It was another hot still day and Dolly felt quite sick with the heat and the swaying of the tram. As usual it was packed tight with sweaty bodies and, unable to bear it any longer, she jumped off one stop early and walked the rest of the way. She had decided that the ironing could wait. She was entitled to a bit of time off and if Fred didn't like it, he could lump it.

She was on her way to the Cherry Blossom factory to meet Janet. She'd packed up some sandwiches to share with her friend. They'd go into the grounds of Chiswick House and sit under the trees. Janet could always make her laugh and a good old gossip was just what she needed.

"It's not that I mind helping out really," she said as they found a shady spot and sat down. "It's just that I can't see any end to it all. And I get so fed up being in the house on my own all day. It's like being in prison."

"You should go out in the evenings, meet me on a Saturday like we used to," Janet said.

"I'm too tired most of the time. I even cried off the outing to Margate. I was supposed to be helping Jessie with the little ones."

"Wasn't Pete coming too?"

"That's part of the reason I don't want to go. Don't want him getting ideas." Dolly sighed.

"You should go. Do you good to get away from the house for a bit," Janet said.

"You're right — but Dad gets a bit shirty if I'm out all day. He expects his meal on the table when he gets in from work. I don't get any help from him or Ruby. They think 'cause I'm not working I should do it all. Can't blame them really I suppose."

"Maybe it'll be easier when Ruby gets married. Have they set the date yet?"

"I don't know, she keeps changing her mind. I can't wait. She drives me mad, treats me like her personal servant. And as for that John . . ." Dolly shuddered.

"I don't know what she sees in him," Janet agreed. "No one at the works likes him."

"Well, it's her funeral." Dolly shrugged and took a bite of her meat paste sandwich. She glanced across as her friend started laughing. "What?"

"Sorry — her funeral, her wedding you mean." Janet collapsed back on the grass, spluttering.

Dolly started to laugh too. It wasn't that funny, but for a few moments the girls lay back on the brittle brown grass, giggling like children. Then Janet sat up and glanced at her watch.

"Heck, I'll be late. I'll have old Potty after me if I'm not careful." She jumped up, hastily brushing shreds of dry grass off her skirt.

At the park gate the friends agreed to meet after Janet finished work on Saturday.

"We'll go round the market and then to the pictures. It'll be like old times," Janet said.

The day after the outing she went to church for the first time in weeks. Despite Jessie Spencer's continuing friendship, she still felt embarrassed when she confronted the staid matrons of the morning congregation. Mrs Crawford still didn't speak to her and, Jessie had told her, had tried to stop her teaching at the Sunday school.

After the service she tried to slip away. But Pete caught up with her and pulled her round the side of the porch. "Why didn't you turn up yesterday? The vicar was very annoyed."

"I was too busy. Besides, I did tell Jessie I couldn't make it."

"You've changed, Dolly. You don't seem to have time for me any more."

Dolly was annoyed. "Of course I don't have time. There's always cooking, cleaning and stuff to do. I never get a minute to myself and I'm always tired."

40

"You have time to go out with Janet though," Pete said, his mouth twisting in a grimace.

Dolly almost gave in. She didn't want to hurt him. But as she put her hand on his arm Mrs Crawford came towards them. "Peter, where are you?"

He didn't reply but looked at Dolly, blinking through his thick glasses. "I hoped things could go back to the way they were. You know — you and me."

"I don't think it will ever be the same," Dolly said.

"They could be. I love you, Dolly."

Before she could reply, Mrs Crawford's voice came again. "Peter, it's time to go."

He hesitated. "Coming, Mother," he called. He turned to Dolly. "I'm sorry, maybe we can meet later."

"No Pete. It's obvious you don't love me enough to stand up to your mother. Besides, you hardly spoke to me for months. Then you expect to carry on as if nothing's happened . . ." She was going to come right out and say it. She didn't love him, never had. It had all been in his mind, a childhood fantasy. And she'd gone along with it when she was too young to know better.

But his mother appeared round the side of the porch. "Oh, there you are. Come along." She ignored Dolly completely and Pete, with an apologetic shrug, walked away.

Once Pete had gone up to Cambridge, Dolly breathed a sigh of relief. Now she wouldn't be bumping into him all the time.

Things were easier at home too, despite Ruby's continuing bitchiness. Now that she'd got into a routine she found she quite enjoyed having the house to herself while Fred and Ruby were at work.

But she still wasn't happy. She missed Janet and her office colleagues, missed the mental stimulation even more. It hadn't been so bad while she was still studying but now that she'd passed her exams, there didn't seem much point in carrying on with evening classes.

Ruby sneered of course, and Dolly couldn't wait for her to leave home. Still she wouldn't have to put up with her for much longer. After several delays, the wedding date was set at last. They'd intended to get married in September but had decided to wait until John's promotion was settled and they could afford a place of their own. Ruby was determined to have everything just so and John, now firmly under her thumb, had agreed. They had finally decided to get married next Easter — only a few more months, Dolly thought with a sigh.

But first she had to get Christmas over with — the first without her mother. She wasn't looking forward to it. But at least Billy would be home. She'd always got on well with her stepbrother and was sad that lately he hadn't taken the trouble to visit them when his ship docked in Southampton or Liverpool.

On Christmas Eve she was busy making mince pies when the doorbell rang. She wiped her floury hands on her apron and went down the narrow passage, throwing her arms round her stepbrother.

Billy hugged her and stood back to look at her. "Well, Dolly, you're all grown up I see." He grinned.

"You don't look so bad yourself." A movement in the shadows caught her eye and she looked over his shoulder.

Billy drew his companion forward. "This is Annie — my wife," he said, smiling.

Dolly stared at the tiny, waif-like girl. If Billy hadn't said she was his wife, she would have thought her a child. She pulled the door wider, gesturing them down the passage to the warmth of the kitchen.

Billy tenderly helped the girl off with her coat and pulled out a chair. Dolly found herself staring again. The loose-fitting dress could not disguise the swell of her stomach — clearly the reason for Billy's hasty marriage.

Dolly looked away and busied herself at the stove, pushing the tray of mince pies into the oven and the kettle over the hotplate. She cleared away the pastry scraps and wiped the table with a cloth before sitting down herself.

"So, why didn't you tell us you were getting married?"

"I knew what they'd say, that's why." Billy took Annie's hand. "You can see how things are, Doll. We didn't want any fuss. It was bad enough Annie's dad carrying on." He leaned forward. "Do you think it'll be OK — us staying here, I mean?"

"Of course it will. Where else would you go at Christmas?"

Annie bit her lip and seemed about to speak. Billy pressed her hand. "How's Ruby?" he asked, "Still flouncing around and putting on airs and graces?"

Dolly laughed. "Not so bad now she's engaged. Oh, Billy, you should hear her — it's 'my John' this and 'my John' that."

"You'll be next, Doll."

"Not me — I've got more sense." Dolly caught the expression on Annie's face. "Sorry, I didn't mean . . ."

"That's all right, Dolly," Annie said. "You should have heard the names my dad called me." She turned to Billy and a smile transformed her plain features. "Not that I'd change anything now," she said.

"Me neither," Billy said.

Dolly couldn't help smiling. They were so obviously in love. She hoped Fred would accept the situation and not spoil things with useless recriminations.

"Where is everybody?" Billy asked.

"Dad and Ruby are still at work." As she spoke it occurred to her that he might not know about her mother. She couldn't imagine Fred sitting down to write to him and Ruby was so selfish she wouldn't even think of it. Mum had always been the one to write and send birthday cards.

As she was about to speak, Billy said, "And where's Mum? Is she working too now?"

Dolly swallowed and closed her eyes. "A lot's happened since you were last home," she said carefully. There was no way to break it gently and Billy gasped as he took it in.

"Poor Dad. How's he coping?" He reached out for Annie's hand and she gripped it tightly. "Some Christmas this is going to be," he muttered.

"He's OK — well, he seems to be. He doesn't say a lot, but I think he's getting over the shock a bit now. After all, it's been months. I'm surprised no one told you. I would have written, but . . ."

Dolly was laying the table when Ruby and Fred came in. Billy introduced his wife to them and his father gave a short laugh. "Well, son, no need to ask what you've been up to. Still, you've done the right thing at least."

Annie blushed and Dolly felt herself colouring in sympathy, especially when Ruby gave a coarse laugh. She took the empty saucepans through to the scullery and ran cold water into them, listening through the open door as Billy told how he'd met his wife. His ship had docked in Southampton late one night and he'd literally bumped into Annie hurrying home with fish and chips for the family supper. She'd shied away in fright, but reassured by his gentle manner, confided that she thought someone had been following her. He'd seen her safely to her front door and walked away, thinking he'd never see her again. But he'd made a note of the street name and number where she lived and on returning to his ship had written to her.

"She wrote back and it carried on from there," Billy said, sitting back with a big grin.

"Now we know why you haven't been home lately," Fred said.

"I stayed in Southampton whenever we docked. And last time I was back we got married. Her mum and dad weren't too pleased — chucked her out they did."

Annie gave a sob and Billy patted her hand. "I'm sorry, love. But we've got each other, haven't we?"

Again that blinding smile, full of love. Dolly's heart contracted. Fond as she was of Pete, she would never feel that way about him. And Ruby and John never looked at each other like that. Maybe it was possible to find that sort of love outside the fantasies of the movies after all. Was that what she felt for Tom, she asked herself, mentally kicking herself for her stupidity. She sometimes didn't see him for weeks on end and when she did, she was too tongue-tied to say much.

It was a good Christmas, despite the shadow of Ada's absence hanging over them. You couldn't help liking Annie and it was a delight to see the young couple's obvious devotion to each other. Ruby didn't even grumble too much about giving up her room to the newlyweds.

CHAPTER
FOUR

A couple of days after Christmas Billy came into the kitchen where Dolly was doing the ironing.

"Annie's having a lie down. She's a bit upset — not looking forward to going back to Southampton," he said.

"But her family's there," Dolly said. "Surely her parents will come round. She can't be on her own while you're at sea."

"Her mum might give in, but her dad won't have her in the house." Billy sat at the table and dropped his head in his hands. "It's my fault, Doll. Why are they punishing her? Anyway, we got married, didn't we? I'm sticking by her — we would have got married some time anyway."

"I understand, Billy. She's lucky to have you." Suddenly she remembered those playground taunts and at last understood what her mother must have gone through, trying to bring up a baby on her own. And it was always the woman's fault, wasn't it. She felt a little spurt of anger at her stepbrother. Why didn't men ever stop and think? But he was obviously head over heels in love with Annie.

"How will she manage while you're away?" she asked, returning to practicalities.

"We've rented a place — but it's only temporary. The landlady won't have kids there. But Annie's not strong you know. I can't see her traipsing around the streets looking for lodgings in her state."

Dolly bit back the retort that he should have thought of that before.

Billy hesitated. "I was wondering if she could stay here — in my old room," he said.

"I suppose so. But Ruby will gripe. She didn't mind giving up her room for a few days but she won't like sharing with me again — and to be honest I wouldn't like it either." Dolly pulled a face. "You know we don't get on."

"But she's getting married, isn't she?" Billy said eagerly.

"Not till Easter," Dolly said. "Anyway, sound Dad out first. After all, it's his house. It's up to him really."

As Dolly had expected, the only one to raise any objections to Annie staying was Ruby. What a selfish cow she could be sometimes.

Billy, in his usual quiet way, withdrew from the argument. Annie, looking pale and frightened, clung to her husband's arm. "We'll manage," she said, biting her lip bravely. "I don't want to cause any trouble."

Ruby paced up and down the small room, taking furious drags on her cigarette and looking like Joan Crawford in *Rain*. "Haven't you caused enough trouble already, getting yourself pregnant and then expecting everyone to feel sorry for you?" she spat.

That was too much, even for Billy. "Don't talk to my wife like that."

But Ruby had slammed out of the house. Dolly put her arm round Annie. "Don't take any notice of her. I'm sure she doesn't really mean it." She turned to her stepbrother. "Go back to your ship, Billy. We'll manage till the baby comes. Ruby will have to put up with sharing with me for a bit. After she's married Annie can have our room and I'll take over the small one." Dolly turned to Fred. "That'll be all right, won't it, Dad?"

"I suppose so," Fred said, going back to his football results with a sigh.

After Bill left, Annie seemed very down. She was quiet at the best of times, but some days she hardly spoke, except to wonder when she'd hear from him and when he'd be home.

When she got a letter saying that Bill hoped to be back for the baby's birth and if not would definitely be there for Ruby's wedding, she perked up and began to help around the house. She turned out to be a good cook and Dolly was pleased to let her do it.

It gave her a bit more time to herself and, best of all, she was able to resume her Saturday outings with Janet knowing that there would be a meal ready for Fred when he came in from work.

There was a hint of spring in the air this February afternoon as the girls strolled arm in arm between the packed stalls of Shepherd's Bush market. There were even galvanised buckets full of daffodils in tight bud and Dolly thought of the last time she'd bought them. How naïve she'd been. A year later the pain and anger were still with her and she found it hard to concentrate as her friend pulled at her arm. "Did you hear me, Dolly? Are we going to see *Mutiny on the Bounty* or *The Lady Vanishes*?"

"I really don't care one way or the other."

"But you like Clark Gable." Janet sighed. "And you can stop craning your neck like that, he's not here."

"I don't know what you mean," Dolly said, flushing. She thought her friend hadn't noticed her straining for a glimpse of a dark head above the crowds of shoppers, listening for his voice shouting his wares above the racket of the market.

"You're looking for that Tom Marchant on the vegetable stall. Well, he's gone — someone else has taken over his pitch," Janet said.

Dolly felt a sick churning in her stomach and she realized how much she'd come to look forward to even the briefest of encounters with him. She knew she had no right to feel this way. She hadn't seen him for months and he'd never indicated that she was any more important to him than the rest of his customers. She was just another girl to laugh and flirt with.

"What's so special about him?" she said, trying to sound as if she didn't care. But she knew by Janet's expression that her friend didn't believe her.

As the new stallholder tipped potatoes into her bag, Dolly was tempted to ask what had happened to Tom. Janet quelled her with a look and the moment passed.

They were passing the little shops under the railway arches on their way to the cinema when a voice hailed them. "Nice day, ladies. Off to the pictures then?"

Dolly whirled, her face aflame. "Hello," she stammered.

He was leaning against the doorway of the end shop, his hands in his pockets. He nodded towards the bag Dolly was carrying. "Missed me at the stall, did you?"

"I heard you'd left the market," Dolly said, biting her lip as she realized she'd betrayed her interest.

Tom didn't tease her about it as she'd expected. "Got fed up with standing in the rain, didn't I?"

Dolly wanted to ask him what he was doing now, but Janet pulled her arm. "Come on, Dolly. We'll be late for the pictures."

She was still looking over her shoulder as the market crowds closed round her.

Dolly gave a last tug to her frizzy curls, pulling her blue hat over them. Since Annie had come to live with them, she had gone up to the market every Saturday, hoping to see Tom. Although he no longer manned the vegetable stall, she knew he was still in the area. Janet had seen him unloading a van near one of the shops under the arches so he'd probably changed his job.

"You sure you're all right, Annie?," she asked as she prepared to leave the house.

Annie smiled and rubbed her bump where the baby was vigorously making its presence felt. "I'm fine. Anyway, the others will be home soon if anything happens. Go on, enjoy yourself."

Dolly pulled the front door shut behind her and ran down the road to catch the tram. It was late and she shivered in the cold March wind. She felt a bit guilty as Annie's baby was due any day. Maybe she should have stayed home. But she couldn't miss the chance of seeing Tom.

But he wasn't there and Dolly had to put up with Janet's teasing once more as she tried to hide her disappointment.

She was still feeling depressed as she put her key in the lock and walked into the passage. And she was even more fed up as she realized there were no appetising smells wafting from the kitchen and the fire was almost out. Dolly was reminded of her mother's departure a year ago. But this time Annie was sitting at the table, doubled over in pain.

Dolly helped her up the stairs and into bed. Fred came in a few minutes later, closely followed by Ruby. They both looked put out when Dolly ignored them and dashed out of the back door to call over the fence. She didn't like their neighbour but everyone called on Mabel Atkins at times like these.

"I'll be round straight away," Mabel said.

Back indoors Fred was sitting at the table while Ruby was touching up her lipstick in front of the mirror.

"Where's Annie — and why is there no dinner?" Fred asked.

A scream from upstairs answered him and Dolly paused at the kitchen door. "Baby's coming. You'll have to see to yourselves." Without waiting for a reply she ran upstairs, followed a few minutes later by Mabel.

It was some hours later when Dolly finally came downstairs. "It's a boy," she said.

Fred looked up and smiled. "I'm a grandad," he said.

"And Ruby's an auntie." Dolly looked round. "Where is she?"

"Gone out. Can't let a little thing like her brother's first child mess up her plans," Fred said. "At least she went and got some fish and chips before she went gallivanting off." He gestured towards the oven. "Yours is in there."

Dolly knew she wouldn't be able to eat. "Later, Dad," she said, and went upstairs again.

Annie was sitting up in bed nursing the baby and smiling. "I'm going to call him Steven," she said.

The poor girl looked exhausted but there was a glow about her that Dolly couldn't help envying as she clutched the baby closer to her and whispered, "I wish Bill was here."

Annie was up and about within a few days. But instead of helping with the chores as Dolly had come to expect, she gave all her attention to the baby. Even when little Stevie was asleep she would spend hours leaning over his pram in the corner of the kitchen as if frightened to let him out of her sight. It didn't help that the weather turned wet and windy and she wouldn't take him outside in case he caught cold. It was true he was a sickly baby, constantly grizzling and, despite her affection for the girl and the child, Dolly was getting fed up.

She had decided that once Annie had recovered from the birth she would persuade Fred to let her go back to work. She was sure to get her old job at Chiswick Polish back. But she couldn't leave her sister-in-law to cope, the state she was in.

As she tried to sleep, Stevie woke with a wail and Dolly heard Annie getting out of bed, then soft footsteps and murmurings as she tried to settle him down again. The crying seemed to go on all night and Dolly tossed and turned. Maybe it was just as well she didn't have to get up for work in the morning.

And so it went on. Stevie's fretful wailing night after night was beginning to set Dolly's teeth on edge. She loved the little chap and he couldn't help it, but knowing that didn't help when you woke up feeling heavy-eyed and listless.

Annie was suffering too. She missed Billy and seemed to spend most of her time hanging around the front doorstep waiting for the postman. Billy wasn't much of a correspondent though. Thank goodness he was due home on leave next week.

With the bulk of the housework still falling on her, Dolly felt she couldn't broach the subject of going back to work. It wasn't really Annie's fault that Stevie was such a sickly baby and needed constant attention but she couldn't help wishing her sister-in-law would pull herself together.

As usual, Ruby was no help, implying that Annie had only turned up in order to mess up her wedding arrangements.

54

When Billy's ship docked in Southampton, he came straight up to London, relief written all over him when he saw that Annie and Stevie were well settled and that Dad seemed happy for them to stay.

Annie, delighted to have him home, blossomed, the baby stopped crying and they had a few blessed nights of uninterrupted sleep. Even Ruby seemed pleased that her brother was home for the wedding. And Dolly made up her mind that, once it was over, she'd insist on going back to work.

CHAPTER
FIVE

Ruby and John got married on Easter Saturday and Dolly had to admit she made a beautiful bride. The cream satin dress with its tight bodice and flowing skirt made the most of her buxom figure and her hair, confined in a circlet of flowers with a short veil, glowed like ripe chestnuts in the spring sunshine. Fred, ignoring the speculation concerning his wife's absence, held his head proudly as he led his daughter down the aisle of St Nicholas's Church where John waited, accompanied by his brother, the best man.

John's sister was the only bridesmaid, demure in a pink satin dress. Dolly had refused her stepsister's belated invitation to be bridesmaid, realizing that she'd only been asked out of a sense of duty. Besides, someone had to slip back to the house during the signing of the register to put the kettles on and make sure all the refreshments were laid out properly in the front room.

Dolly smiled cynically to herself as Ruby, serene and smiling, joined John at the altar. She was remembering her stepsister a couple of hours ago, screaming like a fishwife as she got ready.

Stevie had been asleep in his pram outside the front door while Annie dressed in a pretty print dress and a white hat adorned with yellow daisies. Dolly smiled proudly as Billy, smart in his Merchant Navy uniform, joined them all on the doorstep. He'd bent over the pram and touched Stevie under the chin, at which the baby let out a loud wail.

A shriek from upstairs reached them through the open window. "If that brat's gonna bawl all through the service and spoil my wedding, I don't want him there," Ruby screamed.

Annie's face went white but she said nothing, lifting Stevie out of the pram and trying to soothe him. Billy stormed indoors, shaking off Dolly's arm. She followed him, pleading. "Let it go, Billy. She's nervous that's all, she didn't mean anything."

Fred barred his way at the bottom of the stairs. "Dolly's right, son. You and Annie get off to the church now. I'll calm her down."

"I'm not having her talk to my wife like that, calling my son a brat."

Ruby's face appeared at the top of the stairs. "I don't care, I'm telling you, if I turn up at church and that kid's grizzling, I'm gonna turn right round and walk out again. I'm fed up with it, morning, noon and night. No one's had a wink of sleep since he was born."

Dolly started up the stairs. "Ruby, don't be like that. It's not Annie's fault the poor child's sickly. Besides, you'll be out of it after today."

"And thank God for that," Ruby snapped. "Anyway, who asked you to poke your nose in?"

Dolly didn't answer. She turned away and put her hand on Billy's arm. "What's the use? Let's just get to the church and leave Dad and John's sister to calm her down."

Outside the house a group of neighbours who'd gathered to pass comments on the bride and the dresses, were goggle-eyed at the commotion and Dolly blushed on Ruby's behalf — not that she'd care what the neighbours said.

After the bad start, everything went off well and Ruby for once didn't find fault, smiling throughout the proceedings and hanging on to John's arm. Maybe she really did love him, Dolly thought, and wasn't just looking for security and a home of her own. John, too, seemed quite besotted with his bride. Dolly sincerely hoped they'd be happy, but she couldn't help thinking that poor John didn't know what he was letting himself in for.

There was another sour moment when someone shouted that the taxi was waiting and they all crowded to the front door. The newlyweds were going to Paris for their honeymoon — unheard of in Seaton Road — and the neighbours were out in force to see them off. As Ruby climbed into the taxi, Mabel commented loudly on Ada's absence.

"You'd think she would've waited till after the wedding before running off with her fancy man," she said.

Dolly could see that Ruby — proud, independent Ruby — was close to tears. She took a step towards her,

58

intending to offer comfort but the other girl pushed her away.

As the taxi drove off, Ruby sat up tall, shoulders back, glaring defiance at the gossips. Dolly couldn't help feeling sorry for her and, with a venomous glare at the lingering watchers, she went back into the house. To her relief the guests were gathering their coats preparing to leave.

When they'd all gone she went into the front room, staring aghast at the mess of leftover food, overturned glasses and empty bottles. There was no sign of Annie or Billy and she guessed they were upstairs putting Stevie to bed. She closed the door firmly, deciding to make a cup of tea before starting on the clearing up.

In the scullery she groaned at the sight of the sink overflowing with dirty crockery. That could wait till later too, she thought. As she filled the kettle she glanced through the window and saw Fred sitting on the low stone wall, a glass of beer in his hand and smoking a cigarette.

He looked thoroughly miserable and Dolly opened the back door and called out, "I'm just making a cuppa. Why don't you come in out of the cold?" Despite the sunshine earlier a chill wind had sprung up, reminding her that summer was still a long way off.

"Have they all gone?" Fred asked.

"Yes. Auntie Flo was a bit upset you disappeared just as she was getting ready to leave. But she had to catch her train and John's brother offered to take her to the station."

"I got fed up with them all chattering away like magpies and giving me funny looks. You could tell they were all thinking about your mother going off and wondering what I'd done to drive her away," Fred said bitterly.

"I'm sure they weren't thinking any such thing, Dad. If you must know they were too taken up with Ruby and her going away costume and the honeymoon in Paris to worry about you," Dolly said, embroidering the truth a bit.

"Paris," Fred said with a snort, draining his beer glass and stubbing out the cigarette in the flowerbed. He followed Dolly indoors and sat down at the kitchen table, watching as she bustled around clearing up the debris of the wedding party.

Two days later, Billy was packing to go back to his ship. It had taken all day Sunday to rearrange the bedrooms. Ruby's stuff was stacked in boxes in the front room ready to go to her new house when she got back from Paris. Fred had been persuaded to let Annie have the large front bedroom with its double bed and room for Stevie's cot. It hadn't been easy to talk him into giving up the bed he'd shared with Ada for so long and Dolly realized he'd been clinging to the hope that she'd come back one day. But it had been more than a year now and he seemed to have accepted that she'd gone for good.

Dolly was sitting on her bed sewing a button on her jacket, when she realized Billy and Annie were arguing.

She couldn't help overhearing, although Annie didn't raise her voice.

"But, Bill, you promised. You said that would be the last long trip. I can't stand it when you're not here. How will I manage without you?"

"I told you, Annie love, we need the money if we're to get a place of our own. If I went on the short runs I wouldn't earn as much — and I wouldn't get the tips neither." Billy spoke patiently but Annie wasn't mollified.

"You promised," she said, her voice rising.

"That was when we were in Southampton. But I thought, with you being here amongst family, you wouldn't be so lonely. I could carry on doing the transatlantic cruises for a bit longer."

"How much longer? How many times are you going to say — just one more trip?"

"All right, all right. I'll see what I can do next time I'm home."

Annie ran downstairs crying, and Dolly heard Billy's sigh of exasperation. He paused on the landing. "What can I do, Doll? She's always like this when I go back to sea. But I've got me living to earn, haven't I?"

Dolly smiled sympathetically. "Did you mean that — about saving for a place of your own?"

"Well, we can't stay here forever. What about when Stevie gets bigger, he'll need a room? And suppose we have more children?" He smiled bashfully.

"We'd manage. Other people do. There's the front room downstairs that's hardly used. Don't you think it would be better to do what Annie wants?"

"I want to please her — of course I do. But I don't want to give up my job. It's what I always wanted, travelling the world. We're off to Australia this trip."

"Perhaps you should've thought about that before you got Annie into trouble then," Dolly said tartly. She regretted her words instantly but it was too late to take it back. He brushed past her and followed Annie downstairs.

But Dolly knew she was right. Annie was the sort of woman who needed her man near her. She seemed incapable of making decisions on her own and Dolly dreaded that, as soon as Billy went back to sea, Annie would return to her state of depression, rocking little Stevie in her arms and crooning to him for hours. Worst of all, Annie's unhappiness seemed to communicate itself to the baby, who continued to be fretful, grizzling by day and wailing by night.

It seemed that Dolly's hopes of returning to her old job were doomed. How could she expect Annie to cope with running the house when she seemed incapable of looking after herself and the baby?

CHAPTER
SIX

Dolly had finally accepted that her mother wasn't coming back. She'd never even got in touch to let them know she was all right. The scandal of Ada Watson was almost forgotten. Even Mrs Crawford now acknowledged Dolly at church, possibly swayed by Jessie Spencer's continuing friendship.

Although she exchanged occasional letters with Pete, Dolly tried to avoid him in the holidays. Besides, they had little in common now. He was full of the friends he'd made at University and often went to stay at their houses, leading the sort of life Dolly had only read about in books.

Mrs Crawford encouraged him in his aspirations, hinting that it was their natural station in life. "If my poor husband hadn't been killed in the war . . ." she would sigh. And, "Of course, my Peter's mixing with a much better class of person now."

Dolly suspected that Mrs Crawford only spoke to her at all to warn her that her son wasn't considered a suitable spouse for someone who'd been brought up in Seaton Road, especially a girl whose mother was "no better than she should be" as the people round here were so fond of saying. Useless for Dolly to protest that she didn't want to marry anyone, least of all Mrs Crawford's precious Peter.

She'd no intention of suffering as her sister-in-law had, the months of sleepless nights with Stevie, the constant worry about when her husband would be home.

If only she could go back to her old job. She was so fed up with washing and ironing and cleaning. But Fred wouldn't hear of it. And if anything, Dolly's life was harder now. Annie wasn't strong, lapsing into depression whenever the slightest thing went wrong. And it fell to Dolly to look after Steven as well as everything else. Every time she thought things were going well enough for her to broach the subject of going back to work, some new crisis with Annie or the baby would crop up. And although Dolly sometimes got impatient with her sister-in-law, she loved little Stevie and besides, she told herself, she was doing it for Billy.

And when Annie was feeling well enough, she was glad to help out, leaving Dolly free to go dancing or to the pictures with Janet. Then there was the church and Sunday school and her friendship with Jessie.

Thinking about Annie's tears every time Billy went back to Southampton, Dolly decided that marriage definitely wasn't for her.

"You'll change your mind when you fall in love," Janet told her, laughing.

A picture of Tom Marchant's twinkling eyes flashed into her head. But she didn't rise to the bait. "Of

64

course you would say that," she replied as she waited for Janet to get ready to go to the pictures.

Her friend was now going steady with Norman Huish, a foreman in the packing department at Chiswick Polish. Dolly liked Norman but she wasn't so keen on the friend he had invited along to make up a foursome a couple of weeks ago. She'd spent the evening removing the young man's wandering hands and, as he kissed her on her front doorstep, a wet sloppy kiss that left her feeling faintly disgusted, she had resolved not to get lumbered with him again.

When she'd told Janet why, her friend laughed. "He's obviously not the right one, Doll. If he was, you would have enjoyed it."

Dolly had made a face, at the same time wondering if she'd ever meet the right one. She firmly pushed the thought of Tom Marchant and his heart-stopping smile out of her mind. She told herself she'd forgotten him, didn't care if she never saw him again. Tom was a flirt — he gave the eye to all the women, especially the young pretty ones. There was no reason to think he'd singled her out as being more special than the others. Besides, she hadn't seen him for ages.

That didn't prevent the sneaking hope that they would bump into him as she and Janet ran down Uxbridge Road arm in arm, laughing. They didn't want to be late for the film — *The Prisoner of Zenda* starring their hero Ronald Colman.

As they settled in their seats with a bag of toffees between them, Dolly found herself thinking of Tom again. As if in answer to her thoughts, Janet whispered above the swelling music as the red silk curtains parted to reveal the screen, "You don't still fancy that Tom Marchant do you — the one down the market?"

"Of course not — don't be silly," Dolly whispered, glad of the darkness which hid the blush creeping up her neck.

"Only I thought I ought to tell you — I'm sure he's married. I saw him with a woman and a little boy the other day."

"That doesn't mean she was his wife," Dolly said, louder than she intended.

Someone leaned over the back of the seat and glared. "Shhh — the film's just starting."

Janet, careless of the mutterings behind them, said, "Why should you care — if you really don't fancy him like you said?" And she popped a toffee into her mouth and turned to face the screen as the opening titles rolled up.

Dolly sank down in her seat and folded her arms tightly across her breast fighting to hold back the tears which threatened to well up. Janet was right. Why should she care? He'd never said or done anything to indicate a special interest in her and only this evening she'd firmly told Janet she didn't want to get married. So why this tight feeling in her throat, this pain across her chest?

She tried to focus on the film. But now, all she could do was mutter, "It's not true, it can't be true."

When the lights came up at the end and everyone stood for the National Anthem, Dolly whispered, "You must have made a mistake. He can't be married."

Janet laughed. "I thought you weren't interested." Her laugh died away and she looked concerned. "You do fancy him, don't you? Oh, Dolly, even if he isn't married, he's not right for you. Promise me you won't do anything silly."

"Of course I won't." Dolly was indignant. Her face crumpled. "What's the use anyway — he doesn't even know I exist."

As they hurried through the dark streets towards the tram stop, Janet chattered about the romantic adventure story they'd just seen. But Dolly couldn't join in. Her mind was full of Tom Marchant and the realization that, married or not, she was in love with him and had been since the first time he'd smiled at her in the market all those months ago.

As they waited for the tram, Dolly asked, "Why don't you like him?"

Janet knew who she was talking about. "I don't dislike him, but he's not the right one for you, Doll. There's just something about him — and don't forget what your friend Jessie said, about his reputation with women. And then there's that woman with the baby . . ."

"It could have been anyone — a customer probably." Dolly attempted a laugh. "I'm sure you've misjudged him."

Janet rolled her eyes. "You're so naïve. Look, I just don't want you to get hurt."

Dolly kicked the edge of the pavement, avoiding her friend's eye. But it would be a relief to tell someone. "I can't help it — I'm crazy about him. I know it's stupid and you're probably right . . ."

"Oh, Dolly."

"Funny, I always thought I'd fall for a steady bloke with a good job, not necessarily good-looking, but nice — you know — someone like your Norman. I wanted a nice respectable house in a nice respectable street." Dolly laughed. "Don't know why I'm getting all het up — it's not as if he's asked me out or anything."

"Well, if he does, you really ought to say no."

Dolly should have felt resentful of Janet poking her nose in. But it was only because she cared. Now that she was almost engaged to Norman, she wanted everyone to be as happy as she was.

"Maybe you're right," she said, resolving to put Tom out of her mind and reminding herself of her childhood resolution — to be respectable and respected. No one would ever taunt her again, the way they had when she was a child. If she ever had children of her own, no one would taunt them either, or hear that their mother was "no better than she should be." She changed the subject, turning the conversation to the film they'd just seen and how unrealistic such romantic stories were.

"Pure escapism," Janet agreed, laughing.

Dolly's resolve held until a few days later, when she turned the corner of Seaton Road and came face to face with Tom. He stopped and smiled that slow, lazy smile. "Hello, Dorothy. Long time no see." He always called her Dorothy and the sound of her name on his lips turned her insides to jelly.

She felt herself colouring. "Hello, Tom." It was hardly more than a whisper. She looked up at him and met his frank, open gaze. She should confront him, ask him outright if he had a wife and child. She deserved to know where she stood. But she couldn't just blurt it out.

As she hesitated, he grinned and said, "I haven't seen you down the market lately. Not the same now I'm not on the veggie stall is it? Still, you could always come to the shop."

"What shop?"

"Got me own shop now — under the arches. I thought you knew."

Dolly remembered the day she'd seen him standing outside one of the little lock-ups but she hadn't realized it was his. "What made you give up the fruit and vegetables?" she asked.

"I took over from me dad. But I knew I wouldn't be a market trader for ever. When the shop came vacant, I snapped it up. Took all me savings mind — but worth it."

She couldn't think what else to say and she felt her body grow warm as his brown eyes caressed her.

His voice deepened and he said, "I've missed you, Dorothy. I thought maybe you'd got yourself a boyfriend."

"No — no I haven't." She wished she could stop stammering and think of something sensible to say. Like, "how's your wife and child?" she thought. Don't be stupid, Dolly.

"No boyfriend, eh? Well, how about coming to the pictures with me some time?"

"I don't know, Tom. I have to help out at home." She longed to say "yes" but how could she? Suppose she went out with him and then discovered Janet was right?

To her dismay Tom didn't seem put out by her refusal. He just laughed and said, "Well, if you change your mind, you know where to find me."

He jumped onto a tram that was just pulling away from the stop, leaving her standing on the edge of the pavement.

Tom stood on the platform watching her until the tram turned the corner. That was stupid, asking the girl to go out with him. Suppose she'd said "yes"? As if he didn't have enough problems.

He went over their conversation — if you could call it that — in his mind. She must think he was a right twerp. It wasn't like him to run on like that, but it had given him quite a turn, coming face to face with her, though of course he shouldn't have been surprised. He'd knew where she lived, had made it his business to find out everything he could about her. And it was true he'd missed her, had hardly realized how much until that moment.

He found a seat and gazed out of the window, not taking in where he was going as he tried to tell himself she was just another pretty face, to be chatted up for a laugh. Besides, there was no future in it — not with a girl like her, especially if she ever found out the truth.

70

But there was no reason why she should find out. He didn't come from round here and once he was settled in his new lodgings he could make a fresh start. His resolve not to get involved with her wavered as he realized that now he was living nearby, he could be bumping into her quite often in the future. He'd ask her out again, he decided. But not before he'd sorted things out with Freda and her brothers.

Dolly danced on air all the way up Seaton Road. Tom had asked her to go to the pictures with him. He must like her then. But you turned him down, she thought, her steps slowing as she neared her back gate. Why had she done that when all her senses had been crying out to say yes? She knew the answer really — she still wasn't sure of him. So why not ask him outright if he was married? Because you didn't really want to know, came the answer.

Well, he hadn't seemed too upset by her refusal. In fact he'd laughed. Maybe it was just as well, Dolly sighed. But her heart sank at the thought that she'd blown her chances. He probably wouldn't ask her again. There were plenty of other girls who'd say yes — married or not.

CHAPTER
SEVEN

Tom stood in the doorway of the little shop under the railway arches, wishing he was anywhere but here in Shepherd's Bush. He should be happy now, away from Freda's constant nagging, the business getting off the ground and, he told himself, the follies of his youth well and truly behind him.

For the hundredth time he cursed the day he'd ever got involved with the Rose brothers and their shady dealings, not to mention their sister. He'd been going straight now for three years, but it was hard to put the past completely behind him, especially with Freda to remind him of his folly every day of his life.

He glanced over the heads of the market crowds. The Roses were sure to make an appearance soon — especially when they heard what he'd done. And Freda was bound to tell them. He might have given up the stall but they only had to ask round the market and they'd find him.

Well, they could bully and bluster all they liked. They had nothing on him now. The shop was his, all legal and above board. No one could take that away from him. And, so long as he supported Freda and the kid, they couldn't force him to live with her. Besides, if all went according to plan, he'd be moving on soon — away from the constant reminders of his stupidity. And when he did, he'd make sure no one knew where he was.

The shop was filling up and he couldn't expect Ma and young Sid to cope on their own. As he ground his cigarette out on the ground and turned to go inside, he spotted the two girls. It was a dull cloudy day, but in their flowery summer dresses he could almost imagine the sun had come out.

They were giggling, arms linked, just as they always were. Why were they always together? If Dorothy was on her own he'd be able to talk to her properly. The other one — Janet was it? — always gave him that cool little smile as if she knew what he was thinking. Did she know about Freda? And had she told her friend? If she had, surely Dorothy would have said something when he saw her the other day. She wasn't the sort of girl to go out with a married man. Could he take a chance on her not finding out?

Maybe he should go inside before they saw him. His attraction to Dorothy was threatening to get out of hand. It would be so easy to chat her up and treat her like all the other girls. But that's not what he wanted from her. She was different and, until all this business with Freda was sorted out, he wouldn't do anything to hurt her.

He turned away, his shoulders stiffening as he heard Janet's amused voice. "Oh, look, Dolly, there's Shepherd's Bush's answer to Clark Gable."

"Janet, don't," Dolly protested.

Tom looked round as if he'd only just noticed them. "Hello, Dorothy, Janet. Nice day." There I go, he thought, stupid comments again.

"So this is where you've been hiding yourself," Janet said. "Is this your shop?"

"All mine. Told you I didn't like standing around in the rain," he said.

Dolly smiled at him. "I do hope it will be a success." She was blushing again.

Janet pulled at her friend's arm. They always seemed to be in a hurry. But Tom was gratified when Dolly hung back. "Come and have a look," he said.

Dolly stepped into the tiny shop and, after a brief hesitation, Janet followed.

Behind the counter, a skinny youth was weighing out a penn'orth of dolly mixtures for a little girl, who was holding a toddler by the hand. An elderly woman showed a selection of briar pipes to another customer.

"Sid, Ma," Tom said, waving a hand in their direction. "Sid usually works on his dad's fish stall but he's giving me a hand today as we're busy." Pride shone in his eyes as he surveyed his new empire. "This is just a start. I'm gonna have a proper shop before long," he said.

On the counter stood a tray of shiny toffee apples, a box of penny chocolate bars and a set of scales. On the wall at the back were shelves of sweet jars — striped humbugs, dolly mixtures, clove-scented cough drops and jewel-like wine gums. Another shelf held pipe tobacco and packets of Woodbines, Capstan and Craven A.

74

"Ambitious, aren't you?" Janet said.

"Nothing wrong with that. What do you think, Dorothy?"

"I think it's very commendable," Dolly told him, her cheeks still pink.

"Well, my — my family didn't think so. Thought I was taking a chance, sinking my money into something new. Stick to the fruit and veg like your dad, they said."

"Well, best of luck to you." Dolly turned to her friend. "I think we ought to buy something, don't you?"

"No, ladies — I insist. On the house — to celebrate my new venture." Tom plucked two toffee apples from the tray on the counter and handed them to the girls with a little bow. "Ma's speciality," he said.

His mother looked up from serving her customer and gave the girls a sour look as they giggled and thanked him. Even Janet was a little pink now and she grabbed Dolly's hand. "Come on, we'll be late for the big film," she said.

After they'd gone Tom avoided his mother's eye and busied himself serving. She was bound to say something but he couldn't get the tall fair girl out of his mind. He was captivated by the sparkle in her cornflower blue eyes, the rosy flush on her cheeks. She wasn't a stunner like her friend, but there was something about her. And he couldn't help comparing her with Freda. She was blonde and blue-eyed too, but there the resemblance ended.

He'd found Freda's brassy good looks a real turn-on when he'd first met her four years ago and she'd been more than ready to have a fling. He wasn't the first and, he now knew, he wouldn't be the last. That's what he couldn't understand. She didn't care about him, so why wouldn't she let him go? Of course, getting married had been the worst mistake. But at the time, it had seemed the right thing. Besides, with Derek and Arthur practically frog-marching him up the aisle and standing over him while he signed the register, he hadn't really had a choice.

In the darkness of the cinema, Dolly's resolve to concentrate on the film and not think about the disturbing young shopkeeper was easier said than done. As the titles for *The Thirty-Nine Steps* rolled up, she licked the toffee apple absently and a smile crept across her face as she lost herself in thoughts of Tom Marchant. She knew he was a ladies' man; she probably shouldn't have any more to do with him. But he'd shown another side of himself that afternoon — an ambitious man, not content to run a market stall forever, a man who was going places. Not to mention possessing a heart-stopping smile and a warmth in his velvet brown eyes that made her weak at the knees just thinking about it. She bit into the flaky toffee, tasting the sourness of the apple underneath.

Janet was meeting Norman after the pictures so Dolly made her excuses and left her friend outside the cinema.

"You could come with us," Janet said. "You might meet someone at the dance hall."

Dolly knew her friend was trying to distract her from thoughts of Tom. "No, I must get home. Annie hasn't been too well and I promised not to be late."

She smiled all the way home but thoughts of Tom fled as she entered the kitchen at Number Thirty-Six and found herself in the middle of yet another domestic crisis. Her brother-in-law, immaculate in a grey suit and white shirt, leant against the mantelpiece with his hands in his pockets, while little Stevie lay in his pram bawling his head off.

"Where the hell have you been?" John snapped. "Never mind — you're here now. Perhaps you can do something with him. He's been crying ever since we got here."

Dolly bent and picked up the baby, whose screams turned to snuffles and hiccoughs as he nuzzled his wet face against her cotton dress. She carried him over to the sink and wiped his face with a damp flannel. "What's going on? And where's Annie?"

"Ruby's upstairs with her. She's not fit to look after a kid if you ask me. Good job we came round as you weren't here."

"I was shopping," Dolly snapped, interpreting John's remark as a criticism.

Stevie had stopped crying and she put him in his high chair. She pushed the kettle over the hob and turned to John. "Keep an eye on little'un. I'm going up to see what's wrong."

"Thought you were going to make me a cuppa," John said.

"Make it yourself," Dolly snapped.

Annie lay on the bed clutching a sodden handkerchief.

Ruby stood in the doorway, tapping her foot impatiently. She turned to Dolly, eyes flashing. "How could you go out and leave her alone in that state?"

"She was perfectly all right when I left," Dolly protested.

"Well, you're here now so we can go. We only popped round to ask you all over for Sunday dinner to celebrate John's promotion."

"That's nice," Dolly said absently, sitting on the edge of the bed and taking Annie's hand.

"Bye then."

"You're not going? Can't you give Stevie his bottle while I see to Annie? Poor little chap's hungry."

"If I wanted to look after screaming brats I'd have one of me own," Ruby snapped, clattering down the stairs on her high heels. The front door slammed and little Stevie started to cry again.

Dolly sighed. "Come on, Annie, pull yourself together and tell me what's wrong."

Annie gave a big sob and dabbed her eyes again. "It's Billy — he's not coming home. He doesn't love me any more . . ."

"Don't be silly. What does he say?" Dolly noticed the screwed up paper on the floor. She picked it up and smoothed it out. Surely he wasn't abandoning his wife and child. She sighed with relief when she read that Billy had signed on for an extra trip. The ship would dock in Liverpool instead of Southampton and then go

78

straight off to Australia. There would be no time for a visit home.

She gave Annie a shake. "You silly girl, of course he still loves you. He's earning extra money for you and Stevie. Now wash your face and come downstairs. Poor Stevie's hungry."

It took some persuading, but she did as she was told and, to Dolly's relief, the baby was sleeping peacefully when Fred came in from the allotment. She wasn't the only one getting fed up with Annie's depression and the constantly crying baby. She couldn't cope with his bad temper on top of everything else. But it wasn't poor Annie's fault — lots of women got the baby blues and found it hard to cope.

Dolly sympathized; her annoyance was really with Billy. He had the chance of a job which wouldn't take him away from home for so long, but he wouldn't give up the work he loved — even for his wife and child.

Annie fed the baby and even managed to bath him. When Dolly went upstairs later, he was tucked up in his cot by the window fast asleep. Annie sat beside him, tears streaming down her face.

Dolly put her arms round her, feeling the thin shoulder blades through her night-dress. "He'll be home soon, Annie. And you've got your baby — and me and Dad. It's not as if you're on your own."

"I know — I should be grateful." She sniffed and attempted a smile. "Everything always seems to fall on you, doesn't it, Dolly? I'm glad you're here instead of Ruby."

Her head dropped back on the pillow and she sighed. Dolly got up. "I'll leave you to rest. Just shout if you want anything."

Annie stretched out a hand and gripped the blanket which covered her son. She closed her eyes and Dolly crept out of the room.

CHAPTER
EIGHT

Another wet weekend, Tom thought, looking up at the leaden sky; a typical English summer. He reckoned to make most of his profit on a Saturday but today looked like being completely dead. He'd even sent Ma home when he'd noticed her looking a bit tired. If things picked up, he'd call Sid over. The lad was always glad to get away from his dad's fish stall.

He went inside and began unpacking a box of Mars bars. Maybe it hadn't been such a good idea after all, branching out like this. At least the stall had been steady — everyone needed vegetables. Still, he did quite well on cigarettes and tobacco. And if everything worked out as he planned, he'd be doing even better before long.

At least he was inside in the dry and, with so few customers he'd maybe find time to sort out his paperwork. He hadn't realized quite how much extra work there was in running a shop instead of a market stall, even if it was only a lock-up under the arches. Of course he'd have to work even harder if his plans for the future were ever to be realized. He was only waiting for the right premises to become available and he would say goodbye to Shepherd's Bush market forever.

He'd probably get some stick when he told Ma and Freda. But he was ambitious and he wasn't going to let anyone stand in his way. And how could they object, so long as he continued to meet his obligations by providing for Freda and the kid? Tom Marchant wasn't a man to go back on his word.

He was so engrossed in his thoughts that he didn't realize someone had come into the shop until he heard a little cough. He looked up and his heart started to hammer. He swallowed and summoned his usual cheeky grin. Wouldn't do to let her see how just the sight of her affected him.

"Changed your mind about going out with me then?" he said, wishing he'd kept his mouth shut as the smile disappeared.

"I don't know what you mean," Dolly said. He loved the way she pursed her lips like that, pretending to be prim. But he could see the barely hidden mischief in her blue eyes. Still, he mustn't put her off.

"Never mind," he said. "To what do I owe this pleasure, then?"

"I want a pennorth of jelly-babies please."

"Jelly-babies? For you?"

He was rewarded with a smile and Dorothy pointed to the big black pram outside on the pavement, the baby invisible behind his storm-cover.

His heart almost stopped. Surely it couldn't be hers? He realized she'd read his thoughts when she burst out laughing. "He's my brother's child — little Stevie. I thought I'd buy him some sweets to keep him quiet when I go out this evening."

"Where's his mother then?"

"Annie's not well. Besides, I love taking him out."

"You shouldn't have left him outside in this weather. Bring him in for a minute? You can wait until the rain eases up." Tom was gabbling. He just didn't want her to go.

"You sure? There's not a lot of room in here for a pram," Dolly said. She laughed. "It wasn't raining when I left home."

"Do you mean to tell me you walked all the way up here from Seaton Road?" he asked as he came round the end of the counter and held the door open for her.

She manoeuvred the pram inside and bent over to take the storm cover off.

"I needed to get out of the house. How did you know where I live?" she asked, reaching into the pram and sitting the baby up. The little boy gazed round the shop with wide blue eyes and Tom bent over and tickled his chin, pretending not to notice her blush.

"I have my spies," he said, laughing.

When Dolly didn't answer, he said, "You were on your way home when I bumped into you that time. I've not long moved into lodgings down that way."

She smiled and pulled the soaking wet scarf off, shaking her head. Her fine hair had gone frizzy and stood out round her face like a silver halo. Tom thought she looked gorgeous. He looked away and cleared his throat.

"What's up with his mother then?" he asked in what he hoped was a normal voice.

"Just the baby blues — but it's taking her a while to get over it. My brother's away at sea and she misses him, so that doesn't help."

"So you're left holding the baby — literally?" Tom started to weigh out the jelly-babies. "A young girl like you should be out enjoying herself, not minding someone else's kid." It was none of his business, he told himself. He shouldn't get angry. But he'd seen how Dolly was used by her family. She always seemed to be shopping for them and he hadn't seen her out with her friend for some time.

Dolly smiled her dazzling smile. "I *am* going out. Janet and me are going up the Palais dancing. It's my birthday." She put her hand over her mouth and he grinned.

"Sweet sixteen, eh?" He wished he'd kept his mouth shut.

"I'm nineteen if you must know." Her voice was frosty again as she handed over the penny for the sweets. He just stood there feeling foolish while she tucked the blankets round the baby and fastened the cover back in place. She didn't look at him as she struggled to open the door.

Oh hell, he'd managed to annoy her yet again. With a muttered exclamation he dashed round the counter again and made a grab for the door. The pile of invoices he'd been working on went flying and he swore under his breath.

Dorothy turned and with one of her quick changes of mood she was laughing again. She let go of the pram and bent to help him gather up the scattered papers.

"Blasted paperwork," he said.

"Not too keen on it, eh?"

"Hate it," he answered.

"Maybe I could — no, perhaps it wouldn't be . . ." Dolly stammered.

Was she offering to help? What an opportunity to spend more time with her — legitimately. His heart started thumping so loud he was sure she would hear it.

"Do you mean it? Could you really sort this lot out for me? I'd pay you, of course." He clapped his hand to his forehead. "No, forgive me. Of course you couldn't. You've got your job and looking after the kid. And it was me who said you should be enjoying yourself. Look, Dorothy, forget I said anything."

"But I wouldn't mind. Besides, I don't have a job any more."

"They didn't sack you, did they?"

Dolly explained that she'd left work ages ago to look after her family. "I was hoping for promotion when I passed my exams. But then Annie was ill . . ."

Tom admired her dedication but felt sorry she'd had to give up her job. He knew what it was like to have your ambitions thwarted by the demands of family.

"So, although I can't take a full-time job, I'd love to help out. I do have a certificate in book-keeping, you know. It shouldn't take long to sort out," she said.

"Dorothy, you're an angel." He grabbed her shoulders and bent his head to kiss her. But she pushed him away.

"If I'm going to be working for you, Mr Marchant, there'll be no hanky-panky," she said.

"Sorry." He ran his hands through his hair. "It's just that it's such a weight off my mind. OK — fair enough. No hanky-panky." He grinned as her expression melted into a smile.

"So long as we understand each other, Mr Marchant."

"Right, but what's all this 'Mr' business. It's Tom, remember."

"Tom, then — but I meant what I said . . ."

"No hanky-panky," they said together.

Laughing, she agreed to come to the shop on Monday afternoon. He held the door open for her as she pushed the pram outside, looking up at the grey sky. Was it his imagination or was there just a patch of blue showing, a gleam of sunshine?

Dolly finished her shopping and began the long walk back to Seaton Road. She could easily have bought the sweets at the corner shop. But, after being cooped up in the house all week, she'd needed the fresh air. At least that's what she told herself.

By the time she reached home she was worn out but she was glad she'd given in to her impulse to walk up to Shepherd's Bush. It had been worth it just to see Tom. And she'd be seeing him again next week — she couldn't believe her luck.

Indoors, she hung her wet coat and scarf over the back of a chair in front of the range and stuffed her shoes full of screwed up newspaper to help them dry out.

Annie came downstairs and helped unload the groceries from the bottom of the pram, while Dolly put the kettle on. Maybe, after a sit-down with a cup of tea she'd feel like getting ready to go dancing.

"You're looking better, Annie," she said.

"I had a good sleep. Thanks for looking after Stevie for me. I hope he didn't play up."

"Good as gold — no trouble at all."

Dolly turned at an exclamation from her sister-in-law. "What's this? Another birthday present?" Annie was holding a large box of chocolates decorated with a red satin bow. "Got a secret admirer, have you?"

After a moment of confusion, Dolly managed a little laugh. "I suppose I must have." She took the box and put it on the dresser. How had Tom managed to slip it under the pram cover without her noticing? If she'd seen him she'd have refused it — or would she? A little smile played round her mouth as she made the tea and gave Stevie his food while Annie got their meal ready.

Three hours later she was on the tram going back towards Shepherd's Bush. The rain had stopped and it had turned into a lovely June evening. She looked eagerly out of the windows as the tram rattled along, wondering if she'd catch a glimpse of Tom. To her dismay she realized she knew nothing about his family and friends, other than that his mother sometimes helped out in the shop. But she knew he now lived near her and her heart lifted at the thought of bumping into him more often.

The tram jerked to a stop and she jumped off, hoping Janet had already arrived. She didn't like hanging around on her own. To her relief she and Norman were waiting outside the glittering entrance to the Hammersmith Palais de Dance, known affectionately to its patrons as "The Pally". She'd hate to have to go in on her own.

Norman had brought a friend along — not the one she'd met some months ago who'd made such a nuisance of himself, thank goodness. Janet whispered that Dennis was a perfect gentleman and had promised to behave.

The dance floor was crowded but they managed to find a table near the band. While the men got their drinks, Dolly looked round at the lavish interior of the hall with its glittering chandeliers and highly polished floor. It was the first time she'd been here and it certainly lived up to its reputation as being *the* place to go for a posh night out.

"What about Dennis — do you like him?" Janet whispered as she spotted the men coming towards them.

"Janet, I've only just met him. But he seems nice. I just hope he can dance," Dolly said. "I need someone who knows the steps to lead me round until I get into the swing of it."

Dennis wasn't a brilliant dancer, but he was competent. He held her firmly but easily and once he lost himself in the music and rhythm he seemed to lose his shyness as well. Dolly was enjoying herself, even if

88

from time to time she closed her eyes and tried to imagine she was dancing with Tom.

Halfway through the evening, they were enjoying a breather after an energetic foxtrot when Dolly's breath caught.

The man who'd been occupying her thoughts for most of the evening stood in the doorway, searching the crowded dance floor. Her heart leapt and she half-raised her hand. Although she'd told him she'd be here tonight, he couldn't be looking for her. But he was threading his way through the crowd towards their table, reaching them as the band started up a slow waltz.

"Dorothy — not dancing?" He grinned at Dennis. "Do you mind if I whisk your young lady off — just for this one?"

"Not at all," Dennis said politely.

Before Dolly could protest, Tom led her on to the dance floor. His hand came round her waist, pulling her towards him as his other hand took hers. "Thought you didn't have a boyfriend," Tom said.

"He's not my boyfriend — I only met him tonight," Dolly protested.

He laughed, holding her closer. She wanted to pull away but she couldn't help it — her feet had a life of their own. With a sigh of resignation, she melted into his embrace and gave herself up to the moment. His cheek rested against hers and she closed her eyes wondering what it would be like if he kissed her.

Her eyes flew open and she jerked away. Tom smiled as if he'd guessed what she was thinking. She expected him to make some teasing remark, but instead he pulled her towards him again and they picked up the rhythm of the dance once more.

When the music ended, Dolly stood still for a moment, willing him to ask her to dance again. But he led her back to the table and pulled out the chair for her.

He grinned at Dennis. "Thanks mate. I might borrow your girlfriend again later on — if you don't mind."

Dolly's mood changed. "*I* might mind," she snapped. "And I told you, I'm not his girlfriend."

Dennis looked embarrassed but before she could say anything a voice interrupted. "Well, if it isn't Tom Marchant — up to your old tricks again, eh?"

Two burly men loomed over them. One of them took hold of Tom's arm and turned to Dolly, smiling through broken teeth. "Excuse us, love," he said with feigned politeness. "Got a bit of business with your friend 'ere."

He led Tom away, keeping a firm grip on his arm, the other man following closely behind. Dolly watched them go, her face pale with anxiety.

"What was all that about?" Janet asked as she and Norman returned to their table.

"Search me," Dennis said helplessly. "They didn't seem too happy with him."

"That was Tom Marchant, wasn't it?" Janet said. "I told you not to get mixed up with him, didn't I?"

"It's nothing to do with you. Besides, he's offered me a job."

90

"You must be mad. Don't you know he's been in trouble with the law? I didn't want to tell you — thought you'd have come to your senses by now."

"What sort of trouble?" Dolly didn't want to believe it.

"It was ages ago, something to do with a warehouse robbery. I don't think they proved anything at the time. But Dolly — those two he went off with are notorious crooks. He's obviously still involved . . ."

Dolly nodded miserably but she was worried about Tom. It didn't look as if he'd gone willingly. Surely he wasn't mixed up in anything shady. Most of the market traders were honest enough but some of them were a bit dodgy. She just hadn't thought Tom was one of them though. The unpleasant incident had taken all the sparkle out of the evening and Dolly wished she hadn't come. What an ending to what had promised to be her best birthday ever.

CHAPTER
NINE

Last Saturday night, as Tom whirled her round the dance floor, Dolly had been the happiest girl at the Pally until those thugs had come along and spoilt everything. Now she entered the shop hesitantly, not sure if she was doing the right thing.

She'd been so excited at the thought of working for Tom but now she wasn't so sure. Did she really want anything to do with a man who might have criminal connections? Her head said no, but her heart said a definite yes as he looked up from the counter and smiled.

"I wasn't sure if you'd turn up, after that business the other night," he said.

"I might not stay. I need to get a few things straight first," Dolly said.

"Quite right too," he said. "I'll get young Sid to mind the shop and we'll go in the back room to talk." He rushed across to the row of market stalls, leaving Dolly still unsure what to do.

"What was that all about — Saturday night?" she asked when he came back.

He glanced at Sid. "I suppose you've a right to know." He led her through to the windowless room at the back. In the corner a single tap dripped into a stone sink. "I meant to get this place fixed up — I can't expect you to work in here," he said with a nervous laugh.

He offered her the only chair and pulled up a box to sit on.

"You were going to tell me about those two men . . ." Dolly prompted.

"They're crooks — I expect you know that. Everyone's heard of the Rose brothers. Well, I helped them out once — when I was just a youngster. And they've been holding it over me ever since."

"So what do they want with you now?"

"Doesn't matter — I told them no. I'm going straight. Besides, I don't need their money now I've got my own business and doing all right for myself."

Dolly played with the strap of her handbag. "You really mean it? You won't have anything more to do with them?"

"I promise. Everything above board. Please stay."

He looked so anxious that she had to believe him. "Well, what needs doing?"

He picked up a cardboard box full of papers. "This is it — take some sorting out, I bet. You can't do anything today — I'll get a table in here and some shelves put up. Anything else you need?"

They chatted for a while, Tom explaining where he got his supplies from and telling her of his ambition to expand if he could get larger premises. He agreed that Dolly would work when she could, coming in a couple of times a week.

"Just till I've got your books straight," she said. "My stepfather says there's no need for me to work but I'm going mad stuck at home all day. He's a bit more agreeable now Annie's there to get his dinner — that's when she feels up to it."

She'd already told Tom about the depression that left Annie unable to do anything but sit at the kitchen table smoking and staring into space.

"I can't leave her when she's like that — for Stevie's sake," Dolly said. "She doesn't seem to know the poor little lad's there sometimes."

When she left the shop she danced down the street, vowing that Marchant's Tobacconist and Confectioners would have the neatest, best-kept set of books in the whole of London.

A few days later she was hard at work in the storeroom at the back of the shop. Tom had wedged a table and chair into a corner between the piles of stock. On the table was the box containing the jumble of paper — invoices, receipts, scribbled notes — that made up his business records.

"If you can make sense of that lot, you deserve a medal," he said, laughing.

"I'll do my best," Dolly assured him.

But it was harder than she'd anticipated. Tom's idea of book-keeping was to throw everything in the box to be sorted out when he had time, which wasn't often. Like most of the market traders he'd always dealt in cash and he confessed that dealing with banks and keeping proper records terrified him.

"Don't worry, once it's sorted out, I'll show you how I do it and you'll soon get the hang of it."

"I don't know why I have to bother, but the man at the bank said I've got to."

"You're a businessman, Tom. Of course you must. Besides, if you want to expand, you'll need the bank manager on your side — and a neat set of books is the best way to do that."

"I'll leave it to you then, Dorothy," he said, shrugging his shoulders.

She had bought a new ledger and was painstakingly copying everything from the scraps of paper. Later, she would add up the columns of figures and see if they made sense. It was ages since she'd taken her book-keeping exam and she thought she'd forgotten everything she'd learnt, but as she worked it came back to her and she began to enjoy the challenge.

As she concentrated on the figures, she was vaguely aware of the shop door opening and closing with satisfying regularity. Trade seemed to be good, she thought, as she put down her pen and flexed her cramped fingers.

She bent to her work again, looking up sharply at the sound of raised voices.

"What's *she* doing here then?"

It was Tom's mother. Dolly had a feeling Ma Marchant didn't like her, though she hadn't a clue why.

She heard Tom's murmured reply, then Ma again. "Well, there won't be any hanky-panky, I'll make sure of that."

Dolly smiled as the woman echoed her own sentiments. Her hand gripped the pen and the smile faded. Did Tom's mother think that was why she'd been installed in the back room? She was obviously a respectable woman and was probably embarrassed by her son's reputation. But Dolly relaxed when she heard Tom's deep voice, reassuring his mother — and her — that she was there to do a job, nothing more.

"I told you before, Ma. Those days are over. I don't go chasing skirts any more. All I want is to build up my business, be respectable."

"I'm sorry, son. I shouldn't go on at you."

The door opened and Tom and his mother came in. "How's it going, Dorothy? You've met Ma, haven't you?"

"I'm getting on all right — but it's a bit of a muddle. It'll take me a while to sort it all out." She stood up. "Hello, Mrs Marchant. How are you?"

The older woman came over and glanced at the ledger on the table. "Hard at it, I see."

Dolly met her eyes steadily. "That's what I'm here for," she said. She wasn't going to be intimidated by this little dumpling of a woman with her fierce scowl.

"Call me Ma — everyone does."

The scowl relaxed into a smile that didn't quite reach her eyes — Tom's eyes, Dolly noticed, but without the familiar twinkle. Mrs Marchant clearly resented her.

The older woman went back into the shop but a moment later popped her head round the door. "I'm going to Bob's for some tea. I expect you'd like some . . . ?"

"Ta — yes," Dolly said and turned back to her figures, acutely aware of Tom still standing there. She glanced up and met his eyes, a slow blush stealing up her neck. He knew she'd heard what his mother had said.

He laughed. "Don't take any notice of Ma."

"Don't worry, I won't. Like I said, I'm here to do a job and that's all. So if you just let me get on with it . . ."

He held his hands up and backed away. "OK, no need to get all prickly. But you did say you'd explain it to me, didn't you."

"I will, but I need to understand it myself." It wasn't the only thing she wanted to get straight and she wished he'd go away. How could she concentrate with him looking at her like that, the little smile playing at the corner of his mouth, and his eyes, which a moment ago had been twinkling with mischief, now holding something else — something which caused that trembling in the pit of her stomach. Yes, she wanted him to go away — but she wanted him to stay too.

The door banged open and Mrs Marchant appeared carrying a wooden tray with three cups on it. She plonked one on the corner of the table where Dolly was working and thrust another at Tom. "Haven't you got anything to do? There's customers waiting, you know."

Tom took his tea through to the shop without a word. Ma took a slurp of hers, slapping the tray against her thigh and watching Dolly through narrowed eyes. "You like my son, don't you?" she said.

Before Dolly could reply, she went on. "He's not a bad boy. Oh, yes, he was a bit wild when he was a lad. But he's settled down now — since his dad died. He looks after me a treat, does his best for his family. And he's got big ideas too — wants a bigger shop, a proper business. He's got his good points, but . . ." She paused.

"I know what you're trying to tell me, Mrs Marchant." Dolly forced her voice to remain even. "Ever since I met Tom, people have been warning me about him. But you don't have to worry. I can assure you, he's never said or done anything untoward with me. Besides, I'm not the sort of girl to . . ."

"Oh, I'm sure you're a good girl, Sunday School teacher and all. Yes, I know all about you." She smiled grimly. "It's the good girls who have to watch out. He's got a way with him, has my Tom. Well, don't say you weren't warned." She finished her tea and went through to the shop.

Dolly put her pen down and pushed the ledger away. Maybe she'd made a mistake coming here. Could she put up with his mother and her innuendos? And was everyone else in the market thinking the same thing?

She picked up her pen and drew a neat line under the column of figures, put the ledger, together with the bundles of invoices and receipts into a cardboard box and pushed it back against the wall. She'd have to ask Tom to buy a proper filing cabinet, maybe even a typewriter if he really wanted to expand his business. With that thought Dolly acknowledged that, despite his mother, she would stay.

On the tram going home, she recalled the conversation with Mrs Marchant, pondering the cause of her hostility. Tom was a grown man, he didn't need his mother to watch out for him. Maybe Ma Marchant was like Pete's mother, one of those possessive women who didn't want their sons to have a life of their own, fearing the loneliness of old age. But Ma was a strong capable woman, nothing like the delicate Mrs Crawford. No, Dolly thought, there must be another reason for Ma's barely hidden hostility.

Tom was disappointed when Dolly came through from the back room and announced that she was going home. He'd been hoping to travel home on the tram with her so that he could talk to her without Ma constantly interrupting. He couldn't complain though. She'd only agreed to take the job if she could work the hours that suited her.

He picked up the ledger, running his hand over the page, staring at the neat hand-writing, the columns of figures. Surely this wasn't necessary; none of the other shop-keepers and traders in Shepherd's Bush market kept proper books. Like them, he'd always carried everything in his head and he'd done all right up to now. Ma was right of course when she said he'd only taken Dorothy on so that he could see more of her. But he meant it — he wouldn't do anything until things were sorted out with Freda.

"Does she know you're married?" Ma demanded, as they closed the shop. He might have known she'd raise the subject again. Before he could reply she swung round on him. "I thought so — you haven't told her, have you?"

"There's no need. As far as I'm concerned I'm not married — not any more. I tried to make a go of things but she's just impossible, Ma. You know that — I'd probably end up doing her a mischief if I stayed."

"And what about my grandson, eh?"

"Do you think I haven't thought about Tony?" Tom ran his fingers through his hair. "The kid's better off without me. It's not good for him to see his mother shrieking and carrying on like a harpy every time she thinks I'm out of line."

"Kids need both parents."

"Normally, I'd agree with you — but not in this case. Anyway, it's got nothing to do with you. Me and Freda will sort out our own problems."

"Of course it's got to do with me — it's my grandson we're talking about." Ma was in full flow now and Tom sighed and let her carry on. "It's bad enough my only daughter moving to the other end of the country so I never see her and the kids, and Dick's in the Army and never comes home."

Her voice broke on a sob and Tom put his arm round her shoulders. "I know how you feel — and I'm sorry. But I'm not going back to Freda and that's that — not even for you, Ma. Besides, you still see Tony — they only live round the corner from you and Freda lets you see him whenever you like. In fact, I'll bring him over on Sunday to spend the day with you."

She smiled but he could tell she wasn't happy. He sympathized, really he did. Poor Ma, struggling to bring up her family, respectable, hard-working. He felt bad that he'd let her down yet again. She and Dad had stood by him when he'd got into trouble with the Rose boys and believed him when he said he was going straight.

Then he got Freda pregnant and had to get married in a hurry, but at least he'd done the right thing as they saw it. Now, he'd done the unforgivable by leaving his wife and child and falling in love with another woman. Not that Ma knew how he felt about Dorothy; she thought he was just messing about as he'd done in the past.

As he made his way home to his lonely digs in Chiswick, Tom realized what a mess he'd made of his life. His youthful follies were catching up with him now. If only he could wipe out the past and start afresh. Well, he couldn't do that until he'd come clean with Dorothy.

Maybe she'd go out with him on Sunday — a trip on the river or a walk in Kew Gardens. There'd be no one to interrupt them and he could tell her about Freda. She deserved to know the truth — and if she didn't want to know him after that, he'd just have to live with it. Then he remembered he was taking Tony to visit Ma on Sunday. The talk with Dorothy would have to wait.

CHAPTER
TEN

Christmas had come and gone and still Tom hadn't plucked up the courage to tell Dorothy he was married. Every time he came into the little back room and saw her talking to his mother, his heart leapt into his mouth. Had Ma said anything?

It was even worse when her friend came to meet her and they went off gossiping and giggling together. He was sure if Janet found out she'd delight in passing on the news.

If she had to be told, it must come from him. Today would be a good time. It was a dull February day with few customers and he'd persuaded Ma to stay home for a few days to try and get over the cough which had lingered since the new year. When Dorothy arrived, he'd pluck up the courage to talk to her.

The door opened and one of the market traders came in for his usual packet of Woodbines. "Not much doin' today, mate," he said. "It's perishin' out there."

"Don't envy you," Tom said, handing the man his cigarettes.

"All right for you, in the warm. How's Ma — any better?"

"Still coughing — I made her stay home. No point coming out in the cold if you don't have to."

"Give her my regards." The stallholder went and Tom returned to his gloomy thoughts.

If only Freda would divorce him. He'd agreed to provide the evidence — without involving Dorothy of course. But she'd dug her heels in once more. After seeming to accept that the marriage was over, she'd turned nasty again. Had her brothers told her about Dorothy? Not that there was anything to tell.

Tom replayed their last conversation — row more like it — in his mind. Surely if she had an inkling he was in love with someone else she'd have thrown it at him. But this time she'd harped on about divorce being against her religion. He gave a short laugh. Religion! Freda — who only went to Mass when the priest called round and bullied her into it. Still, it was her most powerful weapon and Tom lived in dread of Father Malloy collaring him and reminding him of his duties and his vows.

Well, he could tell the priest a thing or two about Freda and her vows. He had ample grounds for divorce. But, in consideration for Tony, he refused to blacken Freda's character. He couldn't have his son thinking his mother was a whore.

But he couldn't carry on like this either. Seeing Dorothy every week was torture. How much longer could he keep his feelings to himself?

The bell over the shop door jangled and she came in, shaking her umbrella and laughing.

"What a day," she said and her smile was like the sun coming out.

She hung her coat behind the door, sat down and pulled the ledger towards her. He watched for a while, admiring her neat efficiency, and, he had to admit, the way her hair curled softly at the back of her neck, the curve of her cheek.

She looked up suddenly, her face reddening as she saw him staring. She gave a nervous giggle, waving her hand at the row of black box files stacked against the wall. "I'm impressed. You're a fast learner," she said. "I've got everything up to date now, and if you carry on like this, you won't need me any more." She quickly looked down at the ledger, twisting the pen in her fingers.

He moved towards her. "I'll always need you, Dorothy." He loved saying her name — it was like a caress. This wasn't the conversation he'd planned, but he couldn't help himself. She looked up and he saw an answering need in her eyes. His hand reached out, jerking away as the jangle of the shop bell broke the spell.

Cursing under his breath, he went through to the shop. The Rose brothers stood there, Arthur's hands balled into fists and Derek grinning through his broken teeth.

Tom glanced behind him and pulled the door closed. "What the hell are you doing here? Didn't I make it plain I want nothing to do with you?"

Derek stepped round the end of the counter and put his hand on the inner door. "Got your little bit of fluff in there, 'ave yer?"

Bile rose in Tom's throat and he almost leapt to Dorothy's defence. But that would be playing into their hands, another weapon to beat him with. Striving to keep his voice even, he said, "I asked what you want."

"We want you to treat our sister right, that's what we want," Arthur said, raising his clenched fists.

"That's between me and her — nothing to do with you."

"That bint in there know about your wife and child? What's it worth to keep her in the dark?" Arthur said, grinning.

Tom was beaten and he knew it. "What do you want?"

"We need a bit of storage space for a while — only a couple of days," Derek said. "We'd make it worth your while."

"I don't want your money."

"No — but you wouldn't want her to find out . . ." He nodded towards the back room, the threat unmistakeable.

"She only works for me."

"Well, if you do what we want . . . It's only a couple of boxes, just for a few days."

"All right then. Just a couple of days." Tom sighed. He'd promised Ma — and himself. No more shady dealings. But what could he do? The Rose brothers were quite capable of hurting Dorothy if he didn't comply. And he'd never forgive himself if anything happened to her.

Dolly's heartbeat slowed to normal and the tide of pink gradually receded but she couldn't focus on the figures in front of her. Had she imagined that look in Tom's eyes? Had he meant what she thought he'd meant? If only they hadn't been interrupted. Surely he'd been about to tell her what she'd been longing to hear. Why had he held back for so long?

She knew the answer of course. He wanted to prove to her that she was special — not just another of his conquests. Hadn't she heard him saying so to his mother?

She listened to the murmur of voices from behind the closed door, willing whoever it was to be gone so they could take up where they'd left off. It was so rare for them to be alone like this. Why not make the most of it?

The door opened abruptly and she bent her head to the ledger, longing to fall into his arms, but afraid she'd misread him. When she heard him say, "Put them over there," she was glad she'd checked her impulse. She turned and almost let out a gasp. These were no ordinary deliverymen. She recognized them from that night at the Pally those months ago, and since then she'd learned a lot about the Rose brothers.

She was disappointed in Tom. Hadn't he told her he was going straight now? He caught her eye and gave a little shake of his head. She looked away and started to write, jabbing the pen into the ink bottle, careless of the blots and smudges she made. This was the last time she'd believe his smooth promises.

Tom was busy for the rest of the day and Dolly avoided him, afraid she'd say something she'd regret. She finished sorting the invoices and slipped out while he was talking to a customer.

As she waited for the tram she wondered if she should have given him a chance to explain. She couldn't really believe he was dealing in stolen goods.

"Dorothy, I'm glad I caught you. Why did you rush off like that?"

Tom's voice startled her and she shied away as his hand caught her arm. "You know why," she said.

His hand dropped to his side. "I know what it looks like, but . . ."

"You promised — no more shady dealings. And I know those two are crooks."

Tom sighed. "They also run a perfectly legal garage up Acton way. They need storage space for a few days — someone sent too many parts and there's no room at their place."

It sounded plausible and she'd read the words "spark plugs" on the side of the boxes. But she still wasn't sure. "It's none of my business, is it?" she said, trying to sound offhand. The tram rattled up to the stop and she jumped on, disconcerted to find Tom right behind her.

"We need to talk, Dorothy," he said, sitting beside her.

"You've already explained about the boxes." She held her breath. She'd been dying to hear him say he loved her. But now, although she loved him, she wondered if she could entirely trust him. And surely trust was an important part of any relationship.

She tried to ignore him, staring out of the tram window and leaping up as soon as they reached her stop. She hurried down the back alley and as she reached the gate, he caught up with her. "Please — don't go like this. I'm sorry you're upset." He grabbed her hand and pulled her towards him. "You know I'd never do anything to hurt you."

"I thought you meant it when you said you'd cut yourself off from your old life."

"I did — I do. But it's not so easy. I've known the Rose brothers since I was at school and they've helped me out in the past. I'm just returning the favour. But this is the last time — I swear, even if Derek is family."

She looked at him sharply. It was the first she'd heard of it. "Family?"

"He's my brother-in-law." Dolly flinched as he almost spat the words at her.

"I didn't realize your sister still lived in London. I thought your mother said she was up north somewhere." Tom was gripping her hand hard and she put her other hand over his gently. "I'm sorry, Tom. I shouldn't be interrogating you. As I said before, it's none of my business. I just work for you after all." She looked up at him and a small smile trembled on her lips. "I didn't want to get involved — but I am, aren't I?"

"I'm afraid you are." He pulled her towards him and kissed her gently. "I love you, Dorothy," he said and he kissed her again, this time, deeply, passionately.

She responded with an ardour she hadn't dreamed possible, opening her lips to his.

He pulled away, leaving her breathless and bewildered. She leaned towards him again but he stepped back at the sound of a door opening. "You'd better go in or I'll have your dad after me."

"I don't want to," she whispered.

He pushed open the gate. "I don't want you to either. But I don't want to rush you. We've got plenty of time."

Tom walked away, cursing himself. He'd had the chance to confess and he'd mucked it up. Assuming Derek was married to his sister was a natural mistake. But instead of correcting her, he'd jumped at the chance to put off telling her the truth. He shouldn't have said he loved her. Life was complicated enough already.

But the knowledge that she loved him put a spring in his step and he told himself that was all that mattered. Now he'd have to tell her about Freda. It was only right. "Oh, God, suppose she ditches me once she knows. Can I bear it?" he asked himself. His jauntiness evaporated and he slouched along lost in thought.

All that summer Dolly sang as she did the chores around the house, her cheerfulness brightening up the dull little terraced house. She was in love and even the news of Hitler's latest outrages couldn't dampen her spirits. She refused to believe her stepfather's gloomy predictions of war — or maybe she just didn't want to believe it — she was too happy.

She hardly noticed when Fred, spluttering through a mouthful of cottage pie, waved his fork in the air. "It's only a stop-gap — that's what it is. "Peace in our time"

— poppycock. Buying time, that's what Chamberlain's doing. This time next year — just you wait and see . . ." He bent his head and carried on eating.

Dolly ignored him, busy with her own thoughts. She no longer minded looking after Steven and doing all the cooking and cleaning at home. It didn't seem such a chore when she knew that a couple of times a week she'd be off to Shepherd's Bush and the little shop under the railway arches.

She still had moments of doubt, though — usually when she hadn't seen Tom for a few days. He said he loved her and, to her, the next logical step was marriage, or at least mention of an engagement ring. Because of her family commitments, she sometimes didn't see him for days. And when she did, the shop was often busy and there was no time to talk.

Since that magic moment in the alley behind her house, there were times when she wondered if she'd dreamt it.

And on the rare occasions when he had time to see her home, she felt embarrassed to be kissing and cuddling in the alley outside her house. He always made an excuse not to come in and maybe it was just as well. She never knew how Annie would be. Besides, some instinct told her it was better to keep her family and her love life separate.

How she wished he'd take her dancing, or to the cinema. Much as she enjoyed being with him in the shop, it was hard to be businesslike and maintain the fiction that she was just an employee. But that was

110

what he seemed to want and if she said anything, he always said he didn't want to rush things.

"I won't always have a little lockup under the arches. I want something better to offer you," he said once.

When she said she didn't care, he'd pushed her gently away and she had to admit, she admired his integrity, even if she did find it frustrating. It was hard to concentrate, sitting at the small table crammed behind piles of boxes in the partitioned-off stock room at the back of the shop, knowing he was close by.

At least he never took liberties like the other lads she'd gone out with. And if sometimes she wished there were more than just kisses, she stifled the thoughts, telling herself that nice girls didn't feel that way — not until they were married at least. And surely Tom would ask her to marry him before long, wouldn't he?

CHAPTER
ELEVEN

Dolly couldn't believe the change in the dingy little shop once the alterations were finished — just in time for Christmas.

"What a difference these new display cabinets make. It's a proper shop now," she said.

"And it's all thanks to you," Tom said, pulling her into his arms and kissing her. "I'd never have thought of selling this sort of thing." He waved a hand at the cabinets where cigarette lighters and silver cases were displayed, as well as the usual pipes. There were fancy cigarette holders too and leather tobacco pouches.

"It seemed the obvious thing," Dolly said, pleased and proud that he had acknowledged her contribution. "They're sure to sell well with Christmas coming soon."

"Let's hope we're busy now that I've taken young Sid on full time."

Sid Pearson, the youngest son of Big Sid, the fish merchant, had been helping out more often since Ma took ill. She'd never really recovered from the flu last winter and seemed to have aged over the last few months. Now Tom had persuaded her to give up work.

The shop bell jangled and, as Sid came in, Dolly pulled away from Tom's embrace. "I'd better get on with some work," she said, going through to the storeroom.

Immersed in Tom's scribbled figures, her concentration was disturbed by the sound of raised voices. She put down her pen and crept past the stack of boxes, peering cautiously round the door.

Tom, his hands flat against Derek Rose's chest, was pushing him out of the shop. His brother had already backed down.

"I told you, I don't want you in here," Tom said, his voice dangerously quiet. "Just keep away from me and there won't be any trouble."

Dolly bit her knuckles. Why wouldn't they leave him alone?

Derek thrust his face forward. "You know what we want."

"I've told you, I'll do it."

"It's Tony we're worried about," the other man said.

"I'll see Tony all right — you have my word," Tom said with a final push.

"You'd better," Derek said, clenching his fist under Tom's nose, before following his brother and disappearing among the market crowds.

Tom straightened his jacket and sighed. He came towards Dolly, hand outstretched. "Nothing for you to worry about. Just a bit of business, that's all."

"I thought you didn't do business with that pair."

"It's family business, nothing to do with you. It's all sorted now anyway."

Dolly was frightened. But, despite the mysterious boxes, she'd found nothing in the books to indicate anything unlawful. Surely she'd know if there was? She clutched Tom's arm. "Please tell me what's going on," she begged, dying to know who Tony was.

But before she could ask, Tom sighed and pulled her towards him. He brushed her hair away from her face, gazing into her eyes. "Dorothy, please believe me — it's nothing to do with you. Just trust me, eh?"

She looked into his eyes, desperately wanting to. "I'm scared, Tom. Suppose they come back when I'm on my own?"

He pulled her close, crushing the breath from her body. "I wouldn't let anyone hurt you. I love you, Dorothy. Whatever happens, remember that." He kissed her gently. "Look, it was just a bit of family bother — nothing to do with that other business. Now come on, girl, you've got all that bookwork to do before we close." The familiar twinkle was back in the nut-brown eyes. "How about I take you to the pictures tonight, then for a meal — it's time we celebrated."

However hard she tried, Dolly couldn't concentrate on her work. Half of her was still worried about the Rose brothers. But the other half was dancing inside. They were going to celebrate — and surely that could mean only one thing — he'd bought her an engagement ring.

Dolly hadn't been out in the evening for ages — Janet was usually with Norman these days and to be honest she wasn't sorry. They always seemed to argue lately — usually about Tom. And Annie had been depressed again. Still, she seemed a bit brighter today and was looking forward to having Bill home for Christmas so Dolly didn't feel guilty about going out this evening.

In the back row of the stalls at the Silver, she snuggled down next to Tom and he put his arm round her shoulders. Tonight the Marx brothers didn't seem as funny as usual. Or maybe she just wasn't in the mood. She was acutely conscious of the warmth of Tom's hand on her shoulder, his other hand clasped in hers, his breath on her cheek as he leaned closer to whisper in her ear. She couldn't wait for the film to end so that they could go somewhere quiet and he would ask the question she'd been waiting to hear for so long.

The anticipation was mingled with apprehension. She couldn't get the earlier incident in the shop out of her head. She loved Tom and trusted him. But suppose he'd lied to her? He'd said it wasn't business this time. A family matter? What could that mean? All she could think of was Tom's reputation as a womaniser. Had he got some girl into trouble — not while he was involved with her of course? She was confident in his love. But there had been girls in the past. He'd confessed that the day he'd first kissed her. "But there's only you now, Dorothy," he'd murmured, kissing her again. "I knew as soon as I laid eyes on you that you were the one I'd been searching for all these years."

She'd believed him then — and she believed him now, she told herself as she snuggled closer. Tom's hand tightened on her shoulder and he pulled her towards him. He didn't seem to be interested in the film either

115

and it was easy to ignore Groucho's manic wisecracks as well as the little voice of doubt in her ear, as she gave herself up to the blissful sensation of Tom's lips on hers.

They went to a small restaurant in Earl's Court and she was restless with anticipation. But when the wine came and he lifted his glass, the toast wasn't what she'd been waiting for. "To the business — and to you, Dorothy, for all your help."

She swallowed her disappointment and managed to smile as she raised her glass. Had she really expected anything else?

Outside her front door Tom pulled her towards him and she felt her legs turning to jelly as she returned his kiss. As always, she felt she'd have done anything he asked. The feelings that crept over her body, filling her with a delicious warmth, made her question her intention to always be a "good girl". Her earlier doubts and disappointment fled away as she surrendered to Tom's searching hands and lips. Then he was pushing her away, his voice hoarse. "No, Dorothy, we mustn't."

She opened her eyes to look into his but she couldn't see his expression in the dim light from the corner street lamp. Her breathing steadied and she realized she was leaning against the front door. A hysterical giggle bubbled up in her throat. Suppose Dad heard them and opened the door?

Tom let her go. "I'm sorry — I shouldn't have got carried away like that," he said. He grabbed her arms, his fingers digging into her flesh. "It's so hard, Dorothy. I want you so much." He let go of her again and fished in the letterbox for her key. "You'd better go in before I really lose control," he said, pushing the door open.

She nodded miserably and whispered "goodnight". All the lights were out and she groped her way upstairs to the little back bedroom, anxious not to disturb anyone. She threw herself down on the narrow bed and hot tears ran down her cheeks. Why was she crying? She should be pleased that he respected her and had let her go before things got out of hand. There weren't many men like that, as her mother had so often impressed on her. It was the girl who had to stay in control, if she wanted to maintain her dignity and respectability.

But Dolly felt angry and let down. Was there something wrong with her? Was that why he'd pushed her away? She sat up and wiped her face on a corner of the sheet. There was another explanation — one she was reluctant to face up to. Suppose Tom wasn't free to love her?

She'd never had the courage to come right out and ask him if he was married. Surely his mother would have said something right from the start. But although she'd warned Dolly not to get involved with her son, she hadn't said he already had a wife.

As her tears dried, Dolly knew she couldn't carry on like this. She must know the truth. However much she loved Tom, she just couldn't be the "other woman" in a relationship that could only end unhappily. Next time she saw Tom, she'd confront him. It was the only way to ensure peace of mind — even if it broke her heart.

★ ★ ★

Tom walked home through the empty streets to his lonely lodgings, taking deep breaths of the cold night air. But nothing could cool the heat coursing through him as images of Dorothy filled his mind. He shouldn't have told her he loved her. Things were getting out of hand and he didn't need any more complications.

What a fool he'd been to think he could get rid of Freda so easily, that if he carried on supporting her and the boy she'd leave him alone. It was over a year since he'd moved out and taken lodgings in Chiswick. He might've known she'd catch up with him. He should have moved out of London altogether.

Maybe it wasn't too late. But he couldn't leave Dorothy. The hours spent with her were all that kept him going. Dare he ask her to go with him — to start afresh somewhere else?

Lost in thought, he didn't hear the footsteps behind him. As he put his key in his door, two hulking shadows loomed out of the privet hedge and set about him with boots and fists. He recognized Derek Rose's voice through a mist of pain. "He can't say we didn't warn him." His last thought before passing out was that he should have been prepared.

CHAPTER
TWELVE

Thick fog reduced the tram to a crawl and Dolly's fingers tightened on the back of the seat. She hadn't seen Tom for a week but she still tingled at the remembrance of their last passionate embrace. But he'd pushed her away. Was he having second thoughts? Did he really love her at all? She bit her lip, determined to have it out with him. She must know where she stood. And if he wasn't serious, she'd pack the job in and go back to housekeeping for her family.

She'd already tried the shop door before she saw the closed sign. She peered through the window but there was no sign of Tom or his mother.

"Been closed all week," the neighbouring shopkeeper said as she turned away in confusion.

"What's wrong? Is Tom's mother ill?"

The man shrugged.

Unsure what to do, Dolly pushed her way through the crowded market until she reached the fish stall. Young Sid was helping his father stack empty kipper boxes. Her legs went weak at his reply to her anxious inquiry.

"Tom's in hospital," young Sid said.

Dolly grabbed his arm. "What happened?" She felt like screaming at him.

"Got beaten up — so I heard. The word round the market is he got what he deserved." Sid pulled his arm away and rubbed it resentfully.

"Why hasn't Ma kept the shop open?"

"She's hardly left the hospital. Said she didn't trust me on me own." Sid lost interest and returned to stacking boxes.

"Which hospital?" Dolly demanded. Sid looked at her blankly and she felt like shaking him. Oh, God, where would they have taken him? The nearest one, she thought.

No one at the Hammersmith Hospital had heard of Tom Marchant and Dolly was on the verge of tears. Why hadn't his mother let her know? Choking back a sob, she realized she had no idea where Ma or Tom lived, although she knew he'd grown up not far from the market. Besides, he'd moved out to take lodgings in Chiswick some time ago. When she asked him why, he'd laughed and said, "Chalk and cheese, me and Ma. I like to do things my own way."

He got on all right with his mother while they were working together, but Dolly could understand that sometimes you need some independence.

She'd try Chiswick Hospital, she thought. As she approached the main entrance she saw Mrs Marchant walking away, a small hunched figure holding a handkerchief to her face. Dolly's heart skipped a beat. Tom must be in a bad way for Ma to be so upset. She called out, but the older woman didn't seem to hear. At least this was the right hospital.

She ran up the steps and asked to see Mr Marchant.

"Are you a relative?" the receptionist asked.

When Dolly shook her head she was told that only family visitors were allowed.

"But I must see him." She was near to tears.

"Sorry, love. Hospital rules."

Dolly walked away. If she couldn't see him, she might as well go back to the shop. She'd keep it running until Tom was fit again. He was so proud of his business and, if it stayed closed, he'd lose money, especially so near Christmas. Annie and Fred would just have to manage without her.

The shop was open when she got back and Ma was serving one of the stallholders with his daily ration of Woodbines. She gave the man his change and turned to Dolly, scowling.

"Turned up like a bad penny then."

"I didn't know, otherwise I'd have come before. How is he?"

"I don't know how you've got the nerve to ask."

"I don't understand. What happened?" Dolly was puzzled. She knew Ma didn't like her but they'd always managed to rub along well enough — until now.

"My son's lying in the hospital, barely conscious — because of you. Get out — I don't want to see you again — and I don't suppose Tom does either."

Dolly tried to protest but Ma kept screaming at her to leave. She really had no choice. But she wasn't going before she found out what had happened to Tom.

Sid slipped away between the stalls when he saw her coming. But his father, Big Sid, was more helpful.

"Ma's giving it out that he was run over by a lorry down Lillie Road way — on his way home, he was, late at night. He'd been drinking apparently and stepped into the road without looking — hurt pretty bad, they say."

"Sid told me he'd been beaten up."

"Don't take any notice of our Sid — he's seen too many gangster films." Big Sid laughed.

"When did it happen?" Dolly asked.

"Last Friday night I believe."

Friday — the night they'd gone to see the Marx Brothers, the night he'd kissed her so passionately before leaving her at her front door. As Dolly walked away, she realized that must be why Ma thought it was her fault. If he hadn't seen her home that night, if they hadn't lingered over their meal, he'd have been home in bed.

So, it is my fault in a way, Dolly thought and her eyes welled with tears. She walked away from the market. She might as well go home, but she couldn't face Annie or the demands of her nephew today.

She needed to talk to someone. She'd go and meet Janet from work. Her friend didn't approve of Tom, but, being in love herself, she might understand.

The Cherry Blossom workers were pouring out of the factory gates and Janet waved as she caught sight of Dolly. "Come to ask for your old job back?" she asked with a grin.

Dolly summoned a smile. "I thought we could go and get a cup of tea somewhere."

Janet hesitated and looked closely at her friend. "Have you been crying?"

Dolly nodded and felt tears well in her throat again. Janet took her arm. "Come on, I know just the place."

The café was small and clean, and almost empty. Janet pushed Dolly into a chair by the window and went up to the counter for two cups of tea. "What's wrong? You know you can tell me," she demanded as she sat down.

"I'm so worried, Janet. I don't know what to do."

Janet stirred her tea and eyed her friend in concern. "You don't mean . . . Oh, Doll, you're not in trouble are you?"

"Trouble?" Dolly stared, then realized what she meant and laughed shakily. "Not that sort of trouble. How could you think . . .?"

"Sorry. That's the only thing I could think of." Janet leaned back in her chair. "Well, what is it then?"

As Dolly still hesitated, Janet jumped to yet another conclusion. "This is to do with Tom, isn't it? You've found out he's married. Well, Dolly, I did warn you."

Dolly put her cup down with a clatter. "Just listen — it's nothing like that. Tom's in hospital, badly hurt."

She poured out the story of her arrival at the shop, her desperate tour of the hospitals, and her encounter with Tom's mother.

"I don't know what got into her. I know she doesn't like me much. But to blame me . . ." Dolly bent her head and let the tears come.

Janet leaned forward, speaking quietly. "Do you think it's possible he was beaten up — not run over like she's saying?"

"I do know he wasn't drunk. We only had a couple of glasses of wine with our meal. What makes you think . . .?"

"Well, he's been involved with the Rose brothers. Maybe he's upset them . . ."

"Tom told me about that. But he swore he's going straight now — and I believe him." Dolly set her cup down defiantly. But she couldn't help wondering if the Rose brothers could be responsible.

"Maybe they've got some hold over him . . . I don't know." Janet sighed. "You really shouldn't have got involved with him, you know."

Dolly smiled. "I couldn't help myself. Besides, whatever he's done in the past, I'm sure there's nothing going on now — selling stolen goods or anything like that. I should know — I do the books." She straightened her shoulders and picked up the almost cold tea. "Maybe I'm getting het up over nothing, it could've been an accident like Ma says. All I know is, he's hurt and I want to see him — and no one's going to stop me."

It was harder than she'd anticipated. Visiting hours were strictly controlled and for the first few days it was "close family only".

At last she was told she could go in for five minutes only. Nervous now, she peered through the round window at the rows of beds. A blonde young woman waiting in the corridor with a little boy on her lap smiled sympathetically. "They won't let kids in but I hate hanging around out here. Be OK if they let you smoke," she said. "My brother . . ." The door swung open and she stood up as two men came out.

"Oh, there you are, Derek. Can we go now?" The girl stood up and set the toddler on the ground.

Dolly recognized him and realized she'd been talking to Tom's sister. Hoping Derek Rose hadn't noticed her, she quickly slipped through the door into the ward. A starched nurse sitting at a table looked up. "Visiting time's nearly over I'm afraid. Who did you want to see?"

"Mr Marchant — I work for him." Dolly said, reluctant to admit that he was her boyfriend.

"You have a couple of minutes. He was badly hurt, as I expect you know — but he is improving slowly." She pointed at the bed nearest the door.

Dolly's steps faltered as she neared the bed. This couldn't be her handsome Tom. What little she could see of his face through the swathe of bandages was yellow and puffy, one eye almost closed. His left arm was in plaster, suspended from a pulley contraption in the ceiling, and there was a cradle over his legs. Dolly pulled up a chair and sat down shakily.

She touched the hand that lay on the white counterpane. It too was bruised and puffy. "Oh, Tom," she whispered.

He turned his head painfully, moving his lips in a caricature of a smile. "Dorothy, you're here — at last."

The words were forced out through cracked, swollen lips.

"I've been here every day — but they wouldn't let me in. Didn't anyone tell you?"

"I haven't been taking much in, completely out for three days they tell me. Thought I was a goner." He inhaled sharply and his good eye closed against the pain. "It's my head. Must've had steel tips on his shoes — the bastard."

Dolly gasped. So he had been beaten up. She didn't have to ask who was responsible. It must have been those thugs she'd just seen leaving the ward. Tom's hand grasped hers and, as if he'd guessed her thoughts, he said, "Don't worry about it. I'll sort things out when they let me out of here."

"How can I help worrying, Tom? Please tell me what's going on." She felt the tears rolling down her cheeks.

He squeezed her hand again and gasped with pain. "Don't cry, Dorothy. Everything will be all right. Just keep away from the shop for the time being, Ma will keep things ticking over."

The nurse rang the bell and the other visitors began to gather their coats and bags. But Dolly couldn't move. She clung to Tom's hand and tears dripped on to the stiff white counterpane.

Tom moved restlessly. "Please don't, Dorothy," he said. The nurse stood up, looking across at them and he whispered, "You'd better go. Look after yourself and don't forget — I love you."

Dolly leaned over and kissed him gently on his bruised cheek. "I'll come again tomorrow," she said, reluctantly moving away.

She was still crying as she paused at the door and looked back. The nurse smiled sympathetically. "It's always upsetting the first time you see them like that," she said. "But he is getting better, you know. He'll be out in a week or two."

CHAPTER
THIRTEEN

Tom moved painfully, trying to find a more comfortable position for his aching body. His head still hurt when he moved but at least now when he opened his eyes he only saw one of everything. Still, it was easier to keep them shut.

When a cold hand touched his arm, his eyes fluttered open. "Dorothy?" he whispered.

"It's Freda — your wife." The hard little voice brought him fully awake and he realized he must have drifted off after Dorothy left. The lights were on and it was evening visiting time.

He struggled to sit up. "What are you doing here? I said I didn't want to see you again."

"Where else do you think I'd be with my husband lying at death's door?"

"Where's Tony?"

"At Derek's. Don't worry, he's being properly looked after."

"I don't want him round there. And if you had any sense, you wouldn't either."

"Derek's my brother — he's family."

"Family." Tom made a disgusted noise and sank back on the pillows. "Who do you think put me in here then?"

"You got what you deserved, Derek says. If you'd looked after me properly like you promised, this wouldn't have happened. But you can't help yourself can you, Tom? A pretty girl's only got to smile at you and you're away."

"Freda, I swear to you, I've done nothing wrong." Tom salved his conscience with the thought that he hadn't actually done anything — yet. "I haven't been with another woman since we got wed. It's all in your mind, love."

"Maybe — but you'd like to, wouldn't you? And anyway, you walked out on me — that wasn't part of the bargain, was it?"

It wasn't. And that's why he'd ended up in here. He'd tried to make a go of things. But the marriage was doomed before he'd ever met Dorothy. He didn't care what the Rose brothers did to him, he wasn't going back. He tried to reason with her once more, knowing it would be futile. "Look, Freda — you know it's impossible, you and me living together. Rows and arguments all the time — it's not good for the boy. Besides, I'm still supporting you. You can't say you or Tony want for anything."

"That's not what marriage is about, Tom — you made your vows in church. You should stick to them."

Tom didn't answer. He'd believed that himself at one time. But that was before Derek and Arthur had frog-marched him up the aisle of Holy Trinity Church and stood over him till the deed was done. Surely vows made under duress didn't count? Besides, he wasn't a Catholic, didn't believe in all that mumbo jumbo.

Freda was still talking at him, snapping out short sentences in a low voice like the rattle of a machine-gun. "You can't say you haven't been warned. Derek told you, didn't he? And what about that snotty little cow? The one who works for you? Wanna see her looks spoilt, do you?"

"Leave Dorothy out of this. She's done nothing to you." He thought he was shouting. But it came out as a hoarse whisper and he closed his eyes. He felt her breath on his cheek as she leaned over him, smelt the thick musky scent of "Evening in Paris". At one time it had turned him on. Now he just felt sick.

"You're my husband, Tom. And you'd better start acting like it," she whispered. She straightened and said in a louder voice. "Must go now, darling. Take care of yourself."

Tom watched her go. As the ward door swung open he saw her brothers waiting outside. Arthur's right hand made a slashing movement across his throat and Derek pointed a finger, grinning through his broken teeth. The doors closed, leaving Tom to his despairing thoughts.

And lying there in his hospital bed, unable to move, he had plenty of time to think. One mistake he'd made — well two really — and it looked like he was going to pay for the rest of his life. Why had he ever let the Rose brothers talk him into driving the lorry all those years ago?

He'd been sixteen, fed up with working on his dad's stall for pocket money. He'd been game for a bit of a lark. When things started to go wrong, he realized too

130

late that this wasn't the sort of excitement he wanted. He'd parked the lorry in the narrow cobbled lane behind the warehouse and sat there in a cold sweat, knowing the Rose brothers and their mates were inside.

When the policeman focused his torch on Tom's face, he was terrified. "This your lorry, son?" he said.

"It's me dad's, I'm just on me way home," Tom stammered.

The man grinned in recognition. "You're Sam Marchant's lad from the market, ain't yer?" His voice hardened. "And this ain't his van."

Tom didn't know if the others had been caught but he could hear police whistles in the distance. He'd have to brazen it out. But would the copper believe him? All he knew was that if he grassed on the Roses he'd be in more trouble than just being done for stealing a lorry.

He held his hands up in surrender. "You're right, officer. But I only took it for a dare. I was boasting I'd learned to drive and one of me mates bet me I couldn't. We were in the pub . . ."

"Underage drinking, too," the policeman interrupted.

"Yeah, like I said — we were all showing off a bit. We came out the pub and saw the lorry parked round the corner. I jumped in and drove off. I was going to take it back, honest I was. But then you turned up." He'd grinned at the policeman, hoping his air of innocent mischief would convince him.

"I'm not sure I believe you, son. Sounds a bit too pat to me. You'll have to come down to the station."

That had been his first mistake. For years Tom had tried to live down the humiliation of being hand-cuffed, his dad called out in the middle of the night to vouch for him, and worst of all his mother's tears and recriminations. Now he was reaping the bitter harvest of his early association with the Roses.

Despite his vow not to get in any more trouble, they wouldn't leave him alone. Whenever they needed a lookout, he was roped in with threats.

It wasn't until he married Freda — his second mistake — that the brothers stopped involving him in their crimes, realizing it wouldn't do their sister much good if he was in jail. Since then both the brothers had done time, while Tom had worked hard, saved his money and started his own business.

If only he'd realized who Freda was when he chatted her up at the dance hall — just one in a long line of girls who were more than willing to succumb to his winning smile and twinkling dark eyes.

He hadn't been Freda's first and he was sure he wasn't the last. When she told him she was pregnant he was sure the kid couldn't be his.

But the Rose brothers thought otherwise. He'd do the right thing — marry Freda or suffer the consequences. Not only would they make sure he never walked again, but they'd also shop him for his involvement in the warehouse robbery all those years ago.

He couldn't bear the thought of Dad and Ma finding out. And, at nineteen, he certainly didn't want to get married. Now, he was stuck with Freda — her brothers would see to that. He sighed, knowing he'd have to finish with Dorothy — it was only fair to her — and the boy. He couldn't deny Tony was his son. The cheeky brown eyes and thick dark hair were exactly like his own. He was Tony's father and he must do his best for the boy.

Painfully, he pulled himself up in the bed and called hoarsely for the nurse. When she reached his bedside, he said, "That girl who came yesterday — I don't want her to see me like this. Can you keep her away if she comes again?"

"I'll do my best," she replied.

Tom nodded gratefully and asked her for a pen and some paper. This would be the most difficult letter he'd ever written in his life.

When Dolly returned to the hospital at visiting time and was told "No visitors," she was convinced Tom was really ill, dying even. She was frantic. He must have had a relapse. Being kicked in the head was serious.

She crossed the road and stood at the bus stop in murky drizzle watching the Christmas lights coming on in the shops. A car pulled up across the road and the two men she had come to hate got out, followed by the young blonde woman she'd spoken to yesterday.

Tom hadn't told Dolly much about his family, except to say that he didn't get on with them, apart from his widowed mother. His brother was in the army and he didn't see much of his married sister because he didn't like her husband. No wonder, if the husband was the hulking Derek with his broken teeth and sneering smile, Dolly thought.

She really didn't want a confrontation with Derek Rose. But she must find out how Tom was. As she hesitated, the bus pulled up at the stop and her nerve failed.

When she got home, it was to find her sister-in-law slumped in Fred's armchair in front of the range. The house struck chill as she came in, but Annie seemed oblivious to the temperature and the fact that Steven was sitting on the cold lino grizzling. In her own distress, Dolly couldn't feel any sympathy for the other girl.

"Whatever's the matter with you — letting the fire go out and poor Stevie shivering with cold too?" she snapped.

Annie looked round vaguely and Dolly could see she'd been crying. "It's Billy," she said, flapping her hand at the piece of paper on the kitchen table.

"What about him?" Dolly snatched up the letter with shaking hands. Was he ill, hurt? She really couldn't stand any more. As she read, her breathing steadied but relief made her snap at Annie. "It only says he won't be home for Christmas — it's not the end of the world."

Annie burst into tears. "It is for me," she sobbed.

It was just like last time Billy had let her down. Dolly shot her an exasperated look and set about building up the fire. But her annoyance was for her stepbrother who didn't seem to realize what they had to put up with while he was away. Annie couldn't help the way she

134

was. How many times had she defended her when people said she should pull herself together? But Fred would be home soon and he wouldn't be too pleased if his meal wasn't on the table. And he'd have no sympathy if Dolly told him she'd been hanging round the hospital all day trying to see Tom. So she bit her tongue and got on with it — just like she always did.

By the time Fred came in, potatoes were bubbling on the hob, sausages sizzled in the pan and the mouth-watering smell of frying onions filled the air. The kitchen had warmed up and Steven was clean and fed and crowing in his high chair.

Fred chucked him under the chin. "How's my boy today?" he asked, laughing as the little boy blew a bubble.

He took his wet coat off and hung it over the back of a chair, sniffing appreciatively as Dolly put his plate in front of him. She dished up for herself and Annie but neither of them ate. Fred was halfway through his sausages and mash before he noticed.

"What's up with you two then? You both look like a wet week in July." He put his knife and fork down. "Has something happened to our Billy?"

Dolly hastened to reassure him. "Billy's OK — but he won't be home for Christmas. Ship's got engine trouble — got to stay in New York till it's sorted out."

Relieved, Fred started eating again. Then he looked up at Dolly. "That don't account for your long face, though."

Dolly looked down at her plate. Fred didn't approve of Tom although he'd never met him so she wasn't about to confide her worries to him.

Annie turned to her. "Oh, Doll. I'm sorry — I've been so taken up with my own problems, I never asked about Tom. Everything's all right, isn't it?"

"What's all this then? What's he done?" Fred banged his knife and fork down on the plate. "He'd better be treating you right, my girl . . ."

"It's all right, Dad. He hasn't done anything. He's in hospital . . ." She shook her head as Annie started to speak. "He had an accident — got knocked down by a lorry."

"I'm sorry to hear that, girl. But wasting good food won't help him to get better." Fred cleared his plate. "What's for pudding?" he asked.

Dolly sighed and got up to see if the rice pudding was done.

When he'd finished, he got out his paper and settled down with a cup of tea and a cigarette, while Dolly cleared up around him. Annie had gone up to put Steven to bed and still hadn't come down by the time she'd finished.

She went upstairs, reluctant to face a long evening listening to Fred's comments on Hitler and the shortcomings of the British Government. Her heart cried out to return to the hospital for news of Tom but she knew it wouldn't do any good. She'd have to be patient.

Annie was crooning over Stevie's cot, stroking his hair as his eyes fluttered and closed. She turned as Dolly entered the room and whispered, "He's gone off — I hope." She gave her a funny look. "I thought you said Tom had been beaten up," she said.

136

"I don't want Dad to know. Don't say anything, please. You know how he rants on about Tom at the best of times."

"I won't tell. But he might hear from someone else." Annie put her hand on Dolly's arm. "Why? Was it a robbery — or has someone got a grudge against him?"

It was relief for Dolly to be able to tell someone. Annie listened sympathetically as all her worries and fears about Tom's past and his association with the Roses poured out. Tears were pouring down her face as she finished. "I don't know what to do, Annie. They won't let me see him and he could be dying . . ."

"You'll just have to go back to the hospital in the morning and refuse to leave till someone tells you something," Annie said with uncharacteristic vehemence. "That's what I'd do if it was Billy in trouble. I'd make them tell me." She put her arms round Dolly and patted her back.

At last Dolly stopped crying and squared her shoulders. "You're right, Annie. That's what I'll do," she said.

But the ward sister refused to let her in. And a few days later, when the letter arrived, she realized why.

Dolly would be glad when Christmas was over and they'd seen the New Year in. Surely 1939 couldn't be any worse? Those carefree months of the previous summer might never have been, the happy memories erased by the weeks of misery since she'd received Tom's letter.

Not since those grim childhood days in Mrs Jenkins' basement had Dolly spent such a miserable Christmas. For the family's sake, she made an effort, putting up paper chains and holly and mistletoe, filling Stevie's stocking and shopping in the market for a goose for Christmas Day, a ham and tin of salmon for Boxing Day when Ruby and John came to tea.

But no amount of festive trimmings could make up for the misery that seemed to have communicated itself to the rest of the family.

Even Ruby, the radiant bride of less than two years ago, seemed to have shrunk in on herself, brooding quietly by the fire whenever she wasn't snapping at John. Dolly almost preferred the old Ruby — throwing her weight about and breathing fire whenever anyone disagreed with her.

Dolly was in the kitchen making sandwiches while the rest of the family sat in the front room, listening to the wireless, which Fred, in an unaccustomed bout of extravagance, had bought so that he could keep up with the news. She wished he hadn't. It was bad enough him reading bits out of the paper — now they had to put up with his one-way arguments with the radio announcers.

She could hear him now, laying down the law about the war he was sure wasn't far off. "Well, why would they be digging shelters, if they didn't think old Hitler had his eye on us next?" Fred demanded. "Just 'cause Chamberlain came back with his bit of paper, d'you think that's gonna save us?"

And Ruby's sharp voice in reply. "Give over, do — it's Christmas, we're supposed to be enjoying ourselves if you don't mind."

Annie as usual was silent. She was missing Billy and Dolly sympathised, knowing how she felt. But at least Billy would be home soon. Dolly hadn't seen Tom since that brief visit to the hospital and the worst thing was that she didn't know if she ever would again.

Unwilling to believe what he'd said in his note, she'd haunted the hospital until a kindly porter took pity on her and told her Tom had been discharged. She went up to Shepherd's Bush market but the shop was empty, boarded up with a "To Let" sign in the window. Big Sid told her he'd moved away — to Kent or Sussex he thought.

Tears blinded her as she buttered the bread and she went over the letter in which Tom confessed to handling stolen goods for the Rose brothers. When he'd refused to continue, *for her sake*, he emphasized, they'd beaten him up and threatened to harm her. "*I love you too much to put you at risk, so I'm going away where they won't be able to get at me — and you will be safe,*" he'd written. "*Maybe, one day, when all the fuss has died down, I will get in touch again.*"

At least he'd said he loved her, Dolly thought, sniffing and putting the finished sandwiches on a tray, together with the cake and a plate of sausage rolls.

Fred had turned the wireless on again but the cheerful strains of Henry Hall's BBC Dance Orchestra did little to lighten the atmosphere. Dolly got down on the floor to play with Stevie and the wooden engine

139

Billy had sent him for Christmas, but it was a relief when Annie declared it was the little boy's bedtime and Ruby and John stood up to leave.

Dolly had never known such a long and depressing winter. The cold grey days matched her mood as she struggled to get over Tom. But however hard she tried she just couldn't believe it was all over between them. He'd been so sweet and tender that day at the hospital. If only he'd agreed to see her once more, she'd have convinced him that she wasn't frightened of the Rose brothers. Well, it was no use brooding about it. He knew where she lived if he changed his mind.

There were a few bright days in mid January when Billy finally got home on leave. Annie was a different person when he was around and her gaiety infected the whole household. She roused herself to cook a special meal and a cake and they'd left the decorations up so that it was like Christmas all over again. If only she was like this all the time, Dolly thought. Then she could go back to work and at least there'd be less time to brood.

But as soon as Billy returned to his ship, Annie sank into depression again. She refused to go out and didn't seem to notice when Stevie needed feeding or changing. As usual, it was left to Dolly.

"I try to be patient," she told Janet as they queued outside the Silver cinema for their weekly outing to the pictures — her only treat these days. "But she just drives me mad — sits there rocking in that chair, gazing into space."

140

"Didn't the doctor give her something last time?" Janet asked.

"She won't see him — but you're right, it is an illness. She's so thin, won't eat. It's a good job she moved in with us. Goodness knows what would happen to poor little Stevie otherwise."

Janet put a hand on her friend's arm. "Forget them. Try to enjoy yourself for a change."

Dolly smiled but, although she was looking forward to the film, she wasn't sure if even Gracie Fields' ebullience would be enough to cheer her up tonight. The title of the film, *The Show Goes On*, seemed to echo the way she felt. Me and Annie make a good pair, she thought as the queue started to move. But at least I'm making an effort.

The next morning, Dolly took Steven to St Nicholas's monthly children's service. It was bitterly cold, with icy patches on the pavement. But the sun shone and Dolly breathed deeply of the fresh air, holding tightly to Steven's hand, warmly encased in the woollen mittens she'd knitted him. He looked up at her and his solemn face creased in a smile, turning Dolly's heart over with love.

"Go in the park, on the swing?" he asked.

"Maybe later," she promised.

As she neared the church, the Vicar was greeting Pete and his mother. Dolly paused by the gate. She didn't want to talk to him.

When he took a step towards her, Mrs Crawford tugged his arm and they disappeared inside. She didn't turn round but Dolly knew the older woman had been aware of her.

She followed them in, leading Steven to the pews in the south aisle, where Jessie Spencer was shepherding the Sunday school children into their places. Between making sure the children were reasonably quiet and well-behaved and her own inner turmoil, Dolly didn't take in much of the service.

She scarcely realized the Vicar's sermon had droned to an end and it was only the children's shuffling as Jessie urged them to their feet for the final hymn that brought her down to earth. She lifted Steven up on the pew beside her, sharing her hymnbook with him as he pretended to read and sing. She smiled down at the fair head. Thanks to Annie's continued apathy, the result of her nervous illness, Dolly had almost sole care of her nephew, almost taking his mother's place — and she thanked God for it. The little boy was her reason for carrying on, for putting Tom Marchant in the past where he belonged, and for getting on with life, whatever it had to offer.

Outside, Stevie tugged at her arm. "Swings, promised," he said.

She took Stevie's hand and turned the corner into the recreation ground where she and Pete had spent so much of their childhood.

As if her thoughts had conjured him up, she looked round to see him watching. She lifted Stevie off the swing, ignoring his protests. "We've got to go home and see Mummy," she told him.

Pete caught them up. "Dolly, please talk to me," he pleaded.

"There's not much to say," Dolly replied as they began to walk towards Seaton Road.

Pete pushed his glasses up. "You do realize there's going to be a war," he said.

"Not you too. I'm fed up with hearing about it. Dad talks of nothing else."

"Well, he's right. You don't think Hitler's going to stop at just one country, do you? He'll gobble up the rest of Europe given half a chance and then start on us."

Dolly knew he was right. But she'd been too wrapped up in her own personal life to give a thought to the wider problems of the world. Besides, it was something she hadn't wanted to face up to with Billy at sea and all her energies taken up with reassuring Annie that nothing would happen to him. She nodded slowly as Pete said, "If he invades Czechoslovakia, we'll have to do something."

"Why are you talking like this?" she asked.

"I'm joining up — the RAF," he announced.

"But you can't. What about your studies?" she protested.

"Doesn't matter. I can finish later, if necessary. Lots of the chaps are leaving to join the forces."

"Will you learn to fly?"

"Probably not — chaps who wear glasses don't often become pilots. But I want to be air-crew, maybe a gunner, something like that." He smiled proudly. "You won't know me in my uniform."

"Oh, Pete — do you have to join? What about your mother?"

"I haven't told her yet. I won't — not till the deed's done and it's too late." He flushed. "Maybe they won't have me, and I don't want her upset unnecessarily."

They reached the corner of Seaton Road. "I'd better get home. Mum will have my dinner ready." He paused. "Dolly, will you write to me while I'm away? I know things haven't been the same between us lately, but you're not seeing that market chap now, are you? Maybe we can still be friends."

"All right, Pete — but just friends, eh? Don't go thinking anything else."

He grinned and turned the corner into Carlton Road.

A few weeks later Dolly received her first letter. True to his word, Pete had abandoned his studies and was now stationed at an RAF aerodrome in Norfolk.

His mother hadn't taken the news well, as Mabel Atkins had delighted in telling Dolly over the garden wall.

"You should've heard the language," Mabel said, eyes gleaming maliciously. "And her so high and mighty. The poor lad couldn't get a word in. Always was a mummy's boy. God knows where he got the guts to go and join up . . ."

Her voice ran on, and Dolly could only nod as she wrestled with the sheets against the brisk wind. It had taken guts to stand up against Mrs Crawford, especially for a young man who'd always followed his mother's wishes. But three years at University had given Pete confidence and maturity.

Now, as she read his letter, Dolly detected a new strength of character in his determination to cope with the challenges of his new life. It seemed that the rigours of basic training were making a man of him at last.

Her smile faded as she read, "Dearest Dolly, I have always loved you. I know I shouldn't say this, but you'll get over that other chap, and when you do, I'll be here. Please say I can hope. It would help me to cope with whatever lies ahead to know that you care for me and that one day we might be together."

Dolly screwed the letter up and sat at the table with clenched fists. He'd promised to just be friends. And she wasn't going to get over Tom; she loved him. Pete would only ever be second best and she wasn't prepared to settle for that.

A stab of guilt pierced her heart. Pete knew, as she was now prepared to admit, that war was bound to come. She could be kind and let him fly off with the false hope that she'd be waiting for him when it was all over — or she could tell the truth. Surely that would be kinder in the end.

She smoothed the crumpled letter out and read it again, got out pen and paper. Best to get it over with before she changed her mind, she thought.

CHAPTER
FOURTEEN

That summer the talk was all of war and Dolly was fed up with it — fed up with Annie too and her constant worrying about Billy. She had enough troubles of her own. She often cried herself to sleep when, despite her best intentions, thoughts of Tom overwhelmed her.

For weeks she'd tortured herself with the fear that he'd been so badly injured that he was in a convalescent home somewhere. Sometimes she even imagined he was dead. She refused to think about the note he'd sent — the note that said he didn't want to see her any more. Somehow she couldn't — wouldn't — believe he'd really meant it. Maybe when he'd settled in his new life, wherever that was, he'd contact her again.

Desperate for news, she swallowed her pride and went up to the market, sought out Big Sid Pearson on the fish stall and asked if he'd heard anything.

"Ain't got a clue, love. As I told you before, he's given up the shop and moved away."

"But did he get over the accident?" Dolly asked anxiously.

"Yeah, take more than a boot in the head to keep old Tom down." Sid Senior chuckled. "He's still got the scars though. And a bit of a limp. Saw him a coupla weeks back when he came to visit his ma."

So, he'd been back then. And made no attempt to see her. Maybe Janet was right and she should try to forget him.

But she couldn't and she haunted the market, hoping for a glimpse of him. When Big Sid told her about Ma Marchant's sudden death, she clutched his arm, demanding to know when and where the funeral was.

"You're not going, are you?" Janet asked, disapproval written all over her. "You just want an excuse to see *him*. Oh, Dolly, I thought you were over it. Can't you see, he was just using you."

"You're probably right. But I need to see him, clear the air. Otherwise I'll always be wondering . . ."

A thin drizzle cloaked the world in dismal grey as she came out of Baron's Court underground station and walked briskly towards the cemetery gates. She probably shouldn't be here. It was hardly the right occasion to tackle Tom. But she had to know if it really was all over between them or if Janet was right.

The drizzle increased to a downpour as she reached the group of figures huddled beside the open grave. There was a huge crowd, more than she'd anticipated. But Ma had been well known in the market and people were bound to come and pay their respects.

Dolly hesitated, screened by a large stone angel. She'd wait and catch Tom as he left. Snatches of the familiar prayers came to her on the wind as she stared at Tom, handsome in a dark suit, his head bowed, hands clasped in front of him. Beside him stood the fair girl she'd seen at the hospital and behind them, the Rose brothers. Of course, they were "family".

Dolly peered round the monument, recognizing some of the market traders. A dark-haired young woman sobbed quietly, her face buried against the broad chest of a tall man in army uniform.

The prayers finished, the mourners started to walk away. Tom stopped and shook hands with the Vicar, glancing back at the open grave. Dolly took an involuntary step forward and he looked up. Even from this distance the livid scar etched down the side of his face stood out. She gasped. Somehow, she always pictured him as he was before the beating.

He started to move towards her. But his brother turned and spoke to him. He shook his head and walked away deep in conversation with the other man. He didn't look back.

Dolly didn't know how long she stood there, her heels sinking into the mud, rain mingling with the tears pouring down her face. He *had* seen her — and he'd turned away. What had she done to be treated like that? Fallen in love with the wrong man, that's what, she told herself. Well, he wouldn't get another chance. But, as she brushed the tears away and walked purposefully out of the cemetery, Dolly asked herself, if he came to her now, would she be able to say no?

The rain had stopped at last and Tom stepped outside the back door of Ma's house, the house he'd grown up in. He took a deep drag from his cigarette, wishing everyone would leave — or that he could. But if he sloped off back to Borstall Green now, they'd see it as a sign of disrespect. He uttered a short laugh, wincing as pain shot through his temple. They were quick to point the finger but surely it wasn't any more disrespectful than going through her things like vultures. They wouldn't be doing it if his dad was still alive.

He leaned against the doorjamb, easing the weight off his bad leg, putting off the moment when he'd have to face them. Freda and her brothers were in the front room, eating his food and drinking his booze as if they had a perfect right to be there. He might have known they'd turn up.

His sister, Ethel, called him and he reluctantly went inside. "Dick's gone — he said goodbye." She held a bundle of papers. "Did you know about this?"

He took them from her, his eyes widening as he recognized the deeds to the house. "I thought it was rented," he said.

"So did I."

He looked up and saw Freda's gleam of interest. She'd stick to him like a leech if she thought there was something to gain. He made a quick calculation in his head — sell the house, if the others agreed, split the money three ways. He'd be able to put a bit by for Tony as well as get rid of a substantial chunk of the bank loan he'd taken out for the shop.

The brothers were staring too. Tom handed the papers back to Ethel. "We'll deal with it later. Talk to Dick first. I'm sure he had no idea either." He didn't

149

want to discuss their financial affairs in front of the Roses.

Ethel didn't argue. "We've got to be getting back soon anyway. Ron's mum's looking after the kids. You do what you think's best and let me know."

At last they'd all gone. As Freda left, he said, "I'll drop by tomorrow. We've got to talk," he said.

"We certainly have," Freda said, her lips set in a thin line.

"I want to see Tony," he said. No use letting her think there was any other reason.

At last the house was empty and he busied himself clearing up the plates and glasses and tidying the room. Typical of Freda not to offer to stay and help. He looked round at the drab room, which hadn't changed ever since he could remember. The same brown lino covered the floor, brightened by a rag rug Ma had made when he was a nipper. There was the cabinet in the corner full of knicknacks from days at the seaside or won at fairgrounds over the years. Ethel would like those, he thought.

A china figure caught his eye and he took it out of the cabinet, a girl on a swing, fair hair tumbling over her shoulders, head back laughing. He ran his fingers over the smooth porcelain and sank slowly on to the sofa, finally allowing the image of Dorothy to overwhelm him. It had been quite a shock to see her in the cemetery, a small defenceless figure huddled against the huge stone monument.

No one would ever know how hard it had been to ignore her. Only the presence of Freda's brothers had

150

stopped him rushing over, gathering her in his arms and pouring out his love for her in front of everyone. The brothers were quite capable of carrying out their threats if they had any idea how he felt about her. Better that they should think she was just another bird he'd fancied for a while. In their eyes he'd wronged their sister and he must pay for that. But that didn't mean Dorothy should be made to pay as well.

On a fine evening in August, Dolly's mind wasn't on the news. She didn't care about Poland, or all the other previously unheard of places that were occupying people's minds these days. It was three weeks since Ma Marchant's funeral and she was still trying to cope with Tom's rejection. He should at least have spoken to her. But to walk away without a word . . .

For days she'd lived in a state of nervous anticipation, starting at every knock on the door, afraid to go out in case he called. Surely, he'd make some effort to get in touch. She couldn't believe he now felt nothing for her.

She jumped when Fred turned the radio up. The prime minister was telling the nation that he wouldn't hesitate to go to Germany again if it would do any good.

Fred snorted. "Rubbish — the man's clutching at straws."

"You think there'll really be a war?"

Fred nodded. "Hitler's won't take any notice of us — we didn't do anything when he invaded Czechoslovakia. He'll just walk into Poland and then . . ."

Annie looked up with a worried frown. "What about Billy — what'll happen to him?"

"There won't be a war," Dolly said, with more conviction than she really felt. "Dad, you shouldn't frighten her like that."

"Best to face up to things," Fred said.

Dolly shot him a dirty look. Maybe, she thought, but not until you have to. What was the point of getting Annie all worked up when there was no need? She smiled and tried to reassure her sister-in-law, but deep down she knew Fred was right. He read the papers and took a keen interest in politics. And he'd been right before — about Spain, Abyssinia and Czechoslovakia.

In the days that followed, Dolly's mind was on her own problems and she closed her eyes to the war preparations all around her. The only bright spot on the horizon was Janet and Norman's wedding — and that had been brought forward because Norman might be called up.

Dolly turned her face up to the sky, hoping for the promise of a patch of blue sky. If only the sun would shine on her friend. But before the bus came along, she was soaked through. A typical English summer day, she thought. After the weeks of hot sunny weather it had to rain on Janet's wedding day. It had made her hair frizzy too and she was glad she'd had the sense to put her best shoes and the new dress in a bag, ready to change into at Janet's house.

Janet didn't care about the rain, smiling as she came downstairs in her long white dress and veil, with her

152

two bridesmaids — Dolly and her little cousin Rose. Mrs Carter handed over the bouquet of carnations and freesias and opened the front door. Outside, Mr Carter held the door of the big car he'd hired for the occasion. The church was only round the corner, but his daughter wasn't going to walk, especially in the rain.

In church, Dolly took Rose's hand and swallowed a lump in her throat as she followed her friend down the aisle to where Norman and his best man, Dennis, were waiting. Dennis turned and smiled at her. But she couldn't smile back. How she wished it were she and Tom standing there. Seeing him again so recently had made her realize once and for all that she'd never forget him. And while she still felt this pain in her heart, she'd never look at another man.

CHAPTER
FIFTEEN

Friday, the first of September and the house was in an uproar. Germany had invaded Poland, war now seemed inevitable, and Annie and Steven were being evacuated to the country.

Dolly could hardly hold back the tears at the thought of not knowing when she'd see her little nephew again.

Annie was in a worse state, still dithering about whether she ought to go.

"Suppose Billy comes home — his ship's due in next week. He won't know where we are," she wailed.

Dolly was tempted to snap that if Billy had any sense he'd stay in New York, but before she could say anything, Annie spoke again. "What's going to happen to him, Doll? Will he have to fight?"

"How do I know? I expect there'll be an announcement on the wireless. We'll just have to wait and see, won't we?" It was hard to keep calm and utter the soothing words. The truth was, she felt as churned up inside as her sister-in-law. She just didn't show it, that was all. Their lives would be forever changed by what was happening in the world far away from their cosy little terrace. But they had to put a brave face on things if only for Stevie's sake. The little boy looked from his mother to his aunt, his face creased in bewilderment.

Bending down, Dolly took him in her arms. "You're going on a big train with Mummy," she said. "You're going to see cows and chickens and horses — like in your picture book. Won't that be fun?"

"Dolly come too," Stevie said, putting his thumb in his mouth.

"No, lovie. Dolly's got to stay here and look after Grandad."

"Want Dolly," he wailed, clinging to her skirt as she stood up.

Annie pulled him away and slapped at his legs. "Dolly can't come and that's that," she snapped.

"No need for that," Dolly said quietly. "He's bound to be upset."

"He's not the only one," Annie said, bursting into tears.

Comforting her and soothing Stevie took all Dolly's energy and she was exhausted by the time they reached Paddington.

At the station, there was pandemonium, the noise echoing from the high girdered roof. Annie clutched Stevie's hand. "Where do I go, Dolly — which platform?"

Good job I came too, Dolly thought, going up to a woman in a tweed suit and red jumper, who seemed to be in charge. "Name?" the woman snapped, her eyes on the clipboard she was holding.

"My sister-in-law, Mrs Watson and her little boy."

The woman ticked the names on her list. "Somerton, platform three. Next."

Dolly nodded and went back to Annie. "Come on, this way." She lifted Steven in her arms, leaving Annie to carry the bags. Another WVS woman ticked Annie's name off on her list and looked questioningly at Dolly.

"I'm just seeing them off," she explained.

Stevie stopped crying when he saw the train belching out its clouds of steam and hissing gently as it waited for the carriages to fill up. "I gotta train," he said. "Where's my train?"

"It's in the suitcase," Dolly said hastily as his little face started to crumple.

"You did pack it, didn't you?" Annie said anxiously. "He won't go to sleep without it."

"Yes, I'm sure it's there."

"I wish we didn't have to go," Annie said as the WVS ladies started shepherding the children on to the train.

"You're lucky, Annie. At least you get to go with Stevie," Dolly said, her gaze on a pathetic group of children clutching paper parcels and wearing luggage labels on their collars. "Send us a post card as soon as you have an address. I'll send Billy's letters on . . ."

The guard's whistle pierced their eardrums, doors slammed and Annie held Stevie up to the window. Dolly kissed his cheek. "Be good for Mummy, love," she said, turning away before the tears spilled over.

The house was quiet when Dolly got back from the station — too quiet. Were they panicking over nothing — sending the children away like that? She picked up

156

Stevie's wooden engine which had fallen down behind the coal scuttle.

He'd be upset when he discovered it wasn't in the suitcase as they'd promised. She'd have to send it on — when she had an address. "Somerton," the lady had said. Where was that? The sudden realization that they'd really gone swept over her and she sat at the kitchen table, clutching the toy.

She was still sitting there when Fred came in.

"They've gone then," he said. "It'll be strange without the little fella." He took his coat off and hung it on the back door. "What's for tea then, Doll?"

Dolly covered her face with her hands. Every day, the same thing — "What's for tea, Doll?" Was that all he thought about? Didn't he realize her heart was breaking? She bit back an angry retort.

"I've been busy, Dad. Why don't we have fish and chips?"

"Suits me," he said, sitting down at the table and opening his evening paper.

"Well, give us the money then."

Fred sighed and dug in his pocket. If he says one more word I'm really going to snap, Dolly thought. No wonder Mum left. He's so insensitive at times. As she hurried down Seaton Road towards the fish and chip shop she calmed down a bit. It wasn't Fred's fault — he was no different to any other man, thinking he'd done his job just by going to work and putting food on the table.

She stood in the queue, breathing in the smell of frying and the sharp tang of vinegar, remembering the times as a child when they could only afford a bag of chips between them with a few scratchings sprinkled on top. She couldn't deny things were better now and Dolly knew she should be grateful. Fred had always treated her like one of his own, even after Mum had walked out. What would her life have been like if he hadn't come along and rescued them from their life of poverty?

Someone behind her in the queue nudged her and she realized with a start she was next. "Cod and a pennorth, twice, please," she said.

As she left the shop, a tall figure limped towards her out of the gathering dusk. Gasping, she looked into a face etched with a livid scar which ran from the left temple to below his eye. Her heart steadied as she recognized him. What was he doing here? And how dare he frighten her like that.

"Dorothy," Tom said, catching hold of her arm.

"What are you doing here? I thought you'd moved away." Her voice came out more sharply than she'd intended but his badly-scarred face had frightened her, looming out of the dark like that.

He waved his free hand vaguely. "Had a bit of business down this way. I was hoping to see you, wasn't sure it was you in the fish shop."

"You were waiting for me?"

"I just wanted to see how you were," Tom said.

"Well, as you see — I'm OK. And I've got the family's supper here — don't want it to get cold, so I'd better be off." Dolly pulled her arm away, amazed at how calm she sounded once she'd got over her fright. Now her heart was racing for a different reason.

"Please, Dorothy, don't rush off. I need to talk to you." He caught at her arm again.

"No, Tom — you're the one who wrote and said it was all over. I don't think there's any more to be said." She could hardly believe what she was saying when all she wanted was to fly into his arms. But she wasn't ready to make a fool of herself.

"I just want to explain —"

"There's nothing to explain. You said you didn't want to see me any more." Dolly walked away, hoping he wouldn't see the threatening tears, wouldn't realize how desperately she wanted to stay and listen. She pushed open the door of Number Thirty-Six, leaning against it as she fought to control herself.

"That you, Doll? Thought you'd gone to sea to catch the fish," Fred called.

"Sorry, Dad, there was a queue."

Dolly went into the kitchen and plonked the parcel down on the table, turned to get plates and cutlery off the dresser.

"Don't bother with that. We'll eat out of the paper. I'm too hungry to wait," Fred said, pulling the newspaper parcel towards him and unwrapping it.

The smell of the food, so appetising earlier, now made Dolly feel sick. She wouldn't be able to eat a thing. As she picked at the batter, Fred looked up. "You all right, love?"

Dolly summoned a smile. "Just thinking about Annie and Stevie, wondering how they're settling down." It wasn't really a lie. The meeting with Tom was still uppermost in her mind. But she couldn't help worrying about how her sister-in-law would cope among strangers.

"I must admit, the house seems empty without them," Fred said.

Dolly spoke without thinking. "I don't know what I'm going to do with myself all day now there's just the two of us. I think I ought to go back to work."

"Oh, no, Dolly. There's no need for that."

Fred's reaction was predictable but Dolly was determined. She cleared away the greasy newspapers and poured the tea. "Dad, they wouldn't have evacuated the kids if they thought old Hitler was going to give in. And when it starts, they'll need workers — women workers, like they did last time when all the men went off to fight."

"Well, you needn't think about that just yet." Fred pulled his cup and saucer towards him. "We'll talk about it later."

Dolly smiled, confident she'd sowed the seeds. Fred, after thinking things over, would come round eventually. She got her work-basket and sat down again. If she was going back to work, she'd have to look smart. Time she sewed those buttons on her blouse and mended the hem of her skirt, jobs she'd been putting off for ages. Besides, she needed to keep busy to take her mind off that unsettling encounter with Tom Marchant. Just seeing him had made her realize that, in spite of the way he'd treated her, she still loved him.

160

How terrified she'd been when that scarred figure had loomed out of the darkness like a monster in a Bela Lugosi film. But the scars didn't really matter. He was still her Tom. She wished now she'd listened to what he had to say. But maybe it was for the best. She'd only get hurt again.

She jumped when a voice from the wireless boomed out. Fred had turned it on for the news — none of it good. "Well, he's been warned what'll happen if he doesn't back down — we'll know for sure in a couple of days," he said.

Dolly tried to imagine what it would be like. War — the word had an ominous sound. They'd been hearing it for over a year now, but now it really meant something. Billy and Pete were already in the forces. But all the young men would be called up — people like young Sid who worked in the market, John and Norman too, even though they were married. And Tom. No — not Tom. Dolly felt a little flutter of relief, mingled with shame, as she realized Tom's injuries meant he was probably unfit for active service.

On Sunday morning when Fred switched on the wireless Dolly held her breath as Chamberlain's measured tones told them, "*this country is now at war with Germany.*" In a way it was a relief. Now the suspense was over and they could get on with doing whatever they had to do.

But the limbo existence seemed to go on for weeks. Nothing happened — or seemed to be happening, beyond endless announcements of various rules and regulations, including rationing of tea and sugar. Dolly was busy making black-out curtains for the windows and the town hall was surrounded by sandbags. Shelters were built in back gardens and on street corners. But the threatened bombers never came.

Although Annie had always been quiet and reserved, Dolly missed her and Stevie more than she'd thought possible. It was a relief when a letter came from Charlton Bruford near Somerton in Somerset.

"It's a huge house," *Annie wrote.* "The Vicar lives here all alone with his housekeeper — imagine, two people in this great place. I share with Stevie and there's two other women and seven kids. It's not too bad, though I'd rather be back in London with you and Fred. Stevie's fretting for his toy engine. And is there any news of Billy? I know you'll send his letters on but I can't help worrying."

Dolly parcelled up the toy with a letter reassuring Annie that everything was quiet here in London, although there'd been a panic when the air raid siren was tested and everyone thought the bombers were on their way. She managed to make it sound humorous, although at the time her heart had been in her mouth.

Billy wrote to say he was still in America and a lot of work was being done on the ship. Dolly wrote back straight away, telling him where his wife and child were, and posted his letter on to Annie.

As she addressed the envelope she said to Fred, "I don't know when he'll get this — if he ever will. I wonder if the big liners will be laid up until after the war?"

"I expect they'll be requisitioned. Last time they were used for troop carriers and hospital ships," Fred told her.

"Poor Annie."

"She's not the only woman with a husband in the forces — it'll be the same as if he was in the Royal Navy," Fred said. "She'll just have to get on with it — like everybody else."

Once the first flurry of activity was over Dolly got bored — the black-out curtains were made and attached to wooden rods which fitted closely over the windows, the forms filled in for their identity cards and ration books. With only herself and Fred to look after, there really wasn't enough to do and once more she mentioned going back to work.

"But I like you here when I get home. It's a bit grim coming home to a cold empty house when you've been working hard all day," Fred said.

"But, Dad, I read in the paper that women will be called up soon. I could be sent anywhere as I'm single. But if I'm already doing war work, they can't send me away."

Fred looked up from his paper and gave her his full attention. "What war work could you do?"

"I'll try and get my old job back at Cherry Blossom. Then I'd be able to stay home and look after you."

Fred got out his packet of Woodbines and stuck one in his mouth. Fiddling with the matches, he said, "Don't see how making polish counts as war work, though."

"Well, soldiers need polish for their boots, don't they?" She grinned and Fred smiled back.

"You'd better get up there then, hadn't you?"

"I'll go in the morning," she said and went back to her mending. She didn't tell him she and Janet had already arranged an interview. Norman had received his call-up papers already and Janet couldn't bear the thought of being alone. "I'll go mad with nothing to do," she'd said and Dolly agreed with her.

Dolly left the house early, neatly dressed in her navy blue skirt and jacket, a clean white blouse and the blue felt hat she usually wore to church. Janet was waiting for her outside the factory and they linked arms, strolling through the gates and feeling as if they'd been away ages. As they walked up the staircase towards the offices and saw Miss Potter waiting for them, they turned to each other with suppressed giggles, managing to stifle their laughter as they greeted their former supervisor.

There had been some changes to the factory since Dolly left nearly three years ago. When war had seemed inevitable, the Company's management decided to install underground air raid shelters. On their first day back, Miss Potter gave them a conducted tour, explaining that there was room for all employees, their families and the company's tenants.

"We're very fortunate to have such considerate employers," she told them. "The shelters aren't quite ready yet, but eventually there will be individual bunks, heating and cooking facilities."

Dolly shivered, looking round the dark underground rooms and passages. "Let's hope it won't be necessary," she said. Even with heat and light she didn't like the thought of being stuck down there when the bombers came.

Before long it was as if they had never been away, except that there was no Norman or Dennis to chat to in the dinner hour — not many young men at all in fact. The Cherry Blossom factory was now staffed by boys too young for call-up, older men called out of retirement, and — unheard of in former times — married women.

"No Ruby, though — thank God," Dolly said.

"What's she doing for the war effort then?" Janet asked.

"You know Ruby — won't lower herself to come back on the production line now her husband's been made head of sales. She's doing the Lady Bountiful bit."

Janet laughed. "Your Ruby — Lady Bountiful?"

"Lady Muck more like. She's joined the WVS — hobnobbing with the posh old dears from Kensington. Ever since she and John moved into that flat in Strathmore Mansions — pardon me, luxury apartment I should say — she's thought she was too good for us."

Janet giggled. "I can just imagine her — like the girl in that film, *Pygmalion*. Who was it?"

"Wendy Hiller with Leslie Howard," Dolly said.

Janet put on a posh voice. "Not *bloody* likely," she said and dissolved in giggles.

"Shhh. Don't let Old Potty hear you." They were on their way back from the canteen and as usual Miss Potter was standing at the top of the stairs looking at her watch.

They parted at the door to the typing pool and Dolly went on to the accounts department. As she worked through the columns of figures detailing the firm's exports, Dolly felt bad for laughing at Ruby. In truth she was pleased her stepsister had found a new interest even if, when she came to tea on Sundays, she had to listen to her going on about the "ladies" she worked with on the mobile canteen in Kensington Gardens. It was better than her usual griping and Dolly thought she seemed happy at last.

Dolly and Janet had fallen back into their old habit of spending Saturday afternoons together, shopping in the market and ending up at the pictures. It wasn't quite the same though. She couldn't bear to pass the boarded up sweet shop under the arches. Her throat closed up and her stomach tensed as she remembered those short months of happiness when she and Tom had worked together.

How naïve she'd been, reading so much into what, for Tom, had proved to be just a casual affair. Given his reputation, how could it have been anything else? She should have listened to Janet and not got involved in

166

the first place. Even his own mother had warned that he would break her heart.

"Have you got your Christmas food in yet?" Janet asked, breaking into her bleak thoughts.

"It won't be much of a Christmas this year with all the shortages. I'll do our shopping during the week at the Maypole. They stay open later now — with so many women working, I don't think they do much trade during the day."

"It's a wonder they do any trade at all, seeing they haven't got much to sell," Janet said. "It's a nightmare. I'm going round my mum's for Christmas."

"I don't want to think about it — there'll just be me and Dad. It won't be the same without Stevie."

Dolly walked on, hardly glancing at the stalls, gloomily contemplating the coming holiday, cooped up in the house with only Fred for company.

"Hang on a bit, Dolly. I want to get some winkles for tea tomorrow," Janet pulled her to a stop beside the fish stall and she waited while her friend was served.

"Hey, if it isn't young Doll," a voice said. It was Big Sid Pearson. "Haven't seen you around lately. What you bin up to?"

"I'm back at Chiswick Polish now."

"Pity — I was gonna offer you a job." He laughed as he dug the pewter mug into the heap of winkles and shot them expertly into a paper bag.

Dolly smiled, sure he wasn't serious.

"True. As soon as I saw you, I thought, we could do with a smiling face behind the stall."

"What about Sid, and your other boys?"

"Called up, every one of them. Sid went last week."

"I'm sorry, Mr Pearson — I've already got a job, otherwise I'd think about it." It wasn't true — she hated the smell of wet fish. But he'd always been kind to her. She wanted to ask if he had news of Tom, but couldn't bring herself to broach the subject. But as he handed Janet her change and they turned away, he said, "I didn't see you at Ma's funeral, love."

"I didn't want to intrude." Dolly hesitated. "How is Tom — do you see much of him these days?"

"Not lately."

Dolly didn't know what to say. She felt Janet's tug on her arm and, as they walked on to the next stall, Sid called out, "If I see him, shall I tell him you were asking?"

She tried to turn back, but Janet hung on to her arm and dragged her away. "What was that all about? I thought you'd got over Tom Marchant," she said.

"I never said I was over him." Dolly's eyes filled with tears.

"But it's been ages — you should have put it behind you. He threw you over, remember." Janet gave an exasperated shrug. "Come on, we'll miss the newsreel if we don't hurry," she said.

In the dark of the cinema, Dolly's attention wasn't on the screen. She was wishing she'd asked Sid if he had an address for Tom. Surely it wouldn't hurt to write. Yes, she'd ask him next time she saw him.

CHAPTER
SIXTEEN

Behind the counter of the village store in Borstall Green, Tom was writing out his order for the wholesaler — not that it took long these days; the shortages were already beginning to bite. God knows how much worse it would get if the war dragged on — as it now looked like doing.

It was early closing day and he was taking the opportunity to catch up with his paperwork. He picked up a sheet of paper and read it again — another batch of rules and regulations from the ministry. How did they expect anyone to run a business like this? He threw the paper down and ran his hands through his hair, his fingers touching the raised ridge of the scar. Would he always be reminded of that dreadful night when they'd almost killed him?

If only he could forget, put the past behind him. Still, Derek Rose, along with most of the young men he'd grown up with, was in France now and Arthur would probably be called up soon. No chance of them catching up with him in the near future. Not that anyone knew where he was — even Freda didn't know his exact address.

His face creased in a grimace as he thought of his wife and he clenched his fists, remembering their last encounter. Why wouldn't she listen to reason? You'd think she'd be glad to let Tony come here, away from the threat of the bombing. He'd even tried to persuade her to come too, to try to make a go of their marriage — for Tony's sake.

Tom wanted his son to grow up with fresh air and space, away from the grimy factories and the cramped terraces he'd known all his life. He was determined to build a business he could be proud of, something to hand on to his son. But Freda wouldn't leave London and she wouldn't let Tony go either.

Well, he'd done his best and now he was determined to make a go of things here. Maybe when Tony was old enough to make his own decisions, he'd come and live with him.

His thoughts turned to Dorothy as they always did sooner or later. Try as he might, he couldn't get her out of his head — or his heart. She'd be a proper wife to him as well as a partner in the business. She'd be able to make sense of this bloody paperwork too. The untidy pile of forms fell to the floor as he pushed them aside with a groan.

Maureen, the post office clerk, looked up from her cage in the corner of the shop. "Everything all right, Mr Marchant?" she asked.

"These forms give me a headache." He attempted a smile and picked up the scattered papers.

He knew Maureen would willingly help but she had enough to keep her busy with the post office and telephone exchange. Tom had bought the stores from the Lees, Maureen's parents, who had retired to nearby Chichester. It was a thriving business, the post office bringing people in from the surrounding villages.

At first, he had his doubts about managing it on his own. Fortunately, Maureen agreed to stay on and run the post office, coming in by bus every day. Tom would have to learn how to operate the telephone system in case of emergencies and, if things got too busy, there were always people looking for part-time work.

"I really wanted to do war work but I can't leave my parents, not with Dad so ill," Maureen had told him. "But they say the post office and operating the telephone is just as important."

At first, Tom had been wary of working with someone else but he soon realized he'd never have managed without her. She was a plain girl, quiet and mousy but with a lovely warm smile. In the old days he would have flirted with her, tried to make her blush. But he didn't have the heart for such carryings on now.

As he thought of Dorothy, his fingers closed over the dark blue ledger, the one she'd bought when she first came to work for him. Just the sight of her neat handwriting brought her vividly to his mind. He could see her now, bent over the table, one hand holding her hair back from her face as she carefully added and subtracted, making sense of his haphazard book-keeping.

With another groan he admitted to himself that it wasn't just her expertise with paperwork that he missed. He hadn't been able to stop himself trying to see her again when he was last in London. Now that he'd made the final break with Freda, he'd decided to see if she would give him another chance. Surely if he wanted to re-marry, Freda would see sense and agree to a divorce.

But Dorothy had rejected him. He could hear again her cold little voice, the echo of her heels on the pavement as she walked away. She hadn't accused him, but maybe someone had told her about Freda. He couldn't blame her for turning away.

The house was quiet, and for the first time in weeks, Dolly had time to herself. Her ARP duties, on top of the long hours at the factory and queuing for food, were tiring. But it was a mental exhaustion born of boredom and the tension of waiting for the raids that never came.

While Fred was out all night on warden's duty, she kept herself busy with meaningless tasks, Now there were no toys to pick up, no small items of clothing hanging over the fireguard to dry and, with a sob, she remembered how once she'd longed to have the house to herself. She'd give anything to have Annie sitting opposite her in the rocking chair, little Stevie playing at their feet.

Letters just weren't the same. She had screwed up several sheets of paper and thrown them in the coal bucket when a loud knock at the front door made her leap up in alarm. Was it the warden? Surely she wasn't showing a light.

She walked down the dark passage, taking a deep breath before easing the front door open. For a moment she couldn't make out the features of the tall man standing there.

Her heart began to hammer. "Tom?" It came out as a whisper.

"Yes, Dorothy — it's really me. Can I come in?"

He stepped quickly inside, brushing against her in the narrow passage. She closed the door and went through to the kitchen, turning to face him as he followed her into the room.

"What are you doing here? I said I didn't want to see you again." Her voice was sharp. Why, when all she wanted to do was melt into his arms?

Tom leaned against the doorframe, smiling down at her. "I don't really know what I'm doing here, Dorothy," he said, his face serious. "I just had to find out if you really meant it."

She looked closely, saw the lines around his eyes that hadn't been there before, the flecks of silver in his dark hair. But the livid scar had faded a little, was now a thickened line snaking across his temple to the corner of his left eye and down his cheekbone.

"Sit down, Tom," she said, more gently now. "Tell me how you are, if you've recovered now . . ."

"I'm well enough. Still limping a bit and I get these headaches sometimes. But the doctors say they'll pass." He came towards her and pulled out a chair while she busied herself stoking the fire under the kettle.

"I expect you'd like a drink," she said.

"No, Dorothy. I won't stay. I shouldn't have come but . . ." His voice trailed away and he looked round the room. "Where is everybody?"

"Annie and Stevie have been evacuated and Dad's at the ARP station on duty."

"What are you up to — keeping busy if I know you." Tom laughed. He seemed nervous.

Dolly put out cups and saucers, trying to act normally. "I'm back at Cherry Blossom — working with Janet again. Just like old times. I thought of joining up — all the forces want women now. But Old Potty, my supervisor, says we're doing war work just by keeping the factory going."

Tom raised his eyebrows. "Making polish?"

"Yes, for the Army — and we've started making stuff to clean their other equipment too."

"So, you wouldn't consider giving it up to work for me then?"

Dolly paused as she lifted the kettle to make the tea. "Do you mean it?"

He was smiling but his eyes were serious. "I've got a shop down in Sussex. And, yes — I really mean it." He stood up and took the kettle away from her. "Leave that — I told you I didn't want tea." His arms came round her and he pulled her towards him. "It's you I want. Dorothy, my sweet, I've missed you so. I just couldn't keep away any longer. Tell me you feel the same way . . ."

Dolly turned her face up to his, her eyes misting over. But she could see her need of him mirrored in his eyes. He groaned and bent to kiss her and she returned

174

the kiss in full measure. This was what she had wanted all these months of lying awake, thinking about him, telling herself it was all over, but secretly hoping that one day he would come back. And now he was really here, she was in his arms and she wanted nothing else.

His hands were eagerly exploring her body, undoing the buttons of her blouse, his lips on her neck, the curve of her breast. She didn't want him to stop, but with a moan he pushed her away. "Your Dad — what if he comes in," he said hoarsely.

Dolly smiled and took hold of his hand, replacing it exactly where it had been a moment ago. "He's on night duty," she said. "We've got plenty of time."

They kissed again and this time it was Dolly pulling at his clothes, wanting to get closer to him. Almost without realizing, they were in the passage, stumbling up the stairs. At the door to her bedroom, Tom paused. "Are you sure, my love?"

"Yes, I'm very sure." She led him into the room and closed the door.

Their lovemaking was everything she had dreamed it would be. Even the stab of pain she expected was as nothing, gone in seconds as she crested a wave of pure bliss. It was as if they had always meant to be like this. Now the words of the marriage service made sense to her — "one flesh".

But they weren't married, were they, she thought as she lay beside him, her fingers trailing over his chest and tangling in the thick hair. And, to her surprise, she realized it didn't matter. If it was someone you truly loved, it was all right.

She snuggled up to Tom, revelling in the feel of his body next to hers and he put his arm round her, pulling her closer. "No regrets, love?" he asked.

"Of course not. I love you."

"And I love you, Dorothy, more than I realized. But this won't do, you know — suppose your dad comes in?"

"I told you. He's not due home till morning — we've got all night."

He propped himself up on his elbow and looked down at her laughing. "You mean you want to do it again — you shameless hussy."

Dolly felt herself blushing, then realized he was teasing. He leaned over and kissed her. "We've got some serious talking to do first. I want us to get married," he said. "But there's a problem."

She looked alarmed.

"It's all right, nothing I can't deal with. But you know why I moved away."

"To start afresh, get away from those criminals you've been associating with."

"That's right, love. I made sure they couldn't track me down. But if they get wind I'm back in London, God knows what they'll do."

"Do they really still have a hold over you?" Dolly asked, frowning.

"They think so. And they threatened to hurt you if I didn't do what they wanted. That's why I didn't contact you. I wanted them to think you meant nothing to me."

"Oh, Tom," Dolly murmured.

176

"I know — stupid of me. I knew I wouldn't be able to keep away."

"So what are we going to do?"

"You have to promise me you won't tell a soul. Just pack up and leave, join me down in Sussex. I'll get a special licence."

Dolly's mind was in a whirl. It sounded exciting — running away to get married. And hadn't she been saying for ages she was fed up skivvying for Fred? With Annie and Stevie safe in the country, she needn't feel guilty about going.

She leaned towards him, offering her lips, her body. "Whatever you say, Tom."

Tom's arm had gone numb and he eased it gently from under Dorothy's body, trying not to disturb her. He brushed the hair back from her cheek and smiled. She looked so innocent in sleep. Who'd have guessed at the passion hidden behind those childlike blue eyes? He knew he should get up, leave before Fred Watson came home. In the past that's exactly what he would have done, couldn't bear to hang around for the talking and cuddling that women seemed to want. Once his needs had been satisfied, he'd be up and on his way.

Not now though. Dorothy was the one he wanted, not just for a fling, or for sex. She made him feel different, the way he'd never dreamed he could feel. He wanted to be with her forever, to hold her, to smile at her when she opened her eyes. And he wanted to share his life with her too, pictured her working alongside him, building the business, bringing up their children.

He'd never felt like that with Freda — even after Tony was born and he'd stayed from a sense of duty.

He'd been to see her yesterday — one last try at getting his freedom but he hadn't told her he wanted to re-marry. Derek might be overseas in the Army but his brother was still around. He and his minions were already taking advantage of the shortage of goods, using his contacts in the underworld to build up his black market business. Freda only had to say the word and Arthur and his mates would be on to him.

Dorothy stirred and smiled in her sleep and Tom felt as if his heart was being squeezed. He shouldn't have mentioned marriage — not till he was free. He'd promised himself he'd be honest with her. But Dorothy wasn't the sort of girl to agree to living in sin. He'd have to put a ring on her finger. Besides, deep down he knew he'd never be free of Freda. Why shouldn't he take his happiness where he could?

Since the war started he'd realized how precarious their existence was. His wounds were healing and it was possible he'd be called up once he was fully fit again. Then who knew what would happen? As Dorothy slept beside him, he stifled his pangs of conscience, knowing that if she ever discovered his deception it would be the end of them. But she wouldn't find out — he'd make sure of that.

Dolly yawned and stretched, glancing at the clock on the bedside table. Quarter to six. Fred would be home soon and she ought to be cooking his breakfast. She sat up abruptly as memory flooded back and a flush crept

178

over her body. Had she really done that last night, behaved in such a wanton, abandoned way?

Panic caught in her throat as she realized Tom had gone. Mum was right then. A typical man, he'd got what he wanted and left. But he'd explained all that, the need for secrecy. And he couldn't be here when Fred got home — her stepfather would kill him — and her.

Dolly pushed the sheet back and swung her legs to the floor, sighing. He might have woken her and said goodbye, she thought.

She started as footsteps sounded on the stairs. Oh no, Fred was back and she was sitting here naked. Surely he'd guess what she'd been up to. She reached for her nightdress as a low chuckle came from the open door.

Tom stood there, bare-chested, carrying a tray with two cups and saucers on it. "Tea is served, my lady," he said, giving a small bow.

"Why didn't you wake me? Dad'll be home soon. You'll have to go." But even as she babbled, she was acutely aware of his muscular chest, the dark hairs curling in the centre. She saw again the scars that the steel tips of the Rose brothers' shoes had left. But they, like the scar on his face, did not detract from his handsomeness in her eyes.

"We've got a few minutes, love." He put the tray down and sat beside her on the edge of the bed, reaching up to push a strand of hair out of her eyes. "No regrets?" he asked.

She shook her head and leaned against him, wanting him all over again. But he poured the tea and handed her a cup.

"Did you mean it — about us getting married?" she asked.

"Of course I did. But you have to keep quiet about it — I explained why."

Dolly nodded. It wasn't how she'd pictured things, but if she could be with Tom, she didn't care.

"You mustn't even tell Janet. Her husband's in the same regiment as Derek Rose. I don't want him or his brother causing trouble." He took a swig of his tea and set the cup down. "Better go before Fred gets home. Besides, I can't leave Maureen to manage on her own for too long."

Dolly watched as he put his shirt on, knotted his tie, bent to put on his shoes and socks. As she stood to pick up the tray, Tom caught her eye and grinned.

"Better put something on before you go downstairs," he said.

She laughed, a carefree, happy laugh, tossing her hair back over her shoulder. She slipped her nightdress over her head and put an old cardigan over it, buttoning it up to the neck.

"Just in time," Tom said. "I nearly grabbed you then."

She stuck her tongue out, picked up the tray and ran lightly downstairs, gasping as she saw the hands of the kitchen clock were nearly on the six. Tom followed her gaze and pulled her towards him, kissing her hungrily.

Then he broke away abruptly and hurried down the hallway.

"This time next week," he said. "I'll meet you at Chichester station, then it's off to the register office and back to our new home in Borstall Green."

"I can't wait," Dolly said, opening the front door and looking up and down the road. It was almost light now but to her relief there was no one in sight. Tom kissed her cheek. "You sure you'll be all right getting the train on your own?"

"Of course."

"I'll be at the station to meet you next Thursday then," he said, kissing her again, At the corner he paused to wave. Then he was gone. A whole week. Could she wait that long?

As she got dressed, she wondered how she'd be able to act as if nothing had happened. It wasn't difficult to hide things from her stepfather. He only noticed if things went wrong, like no clean shirt or dinner not on the table. But could she keep the secret from Janet?

CHAPTER
SEVENTEEN

"Today's the day", Dolly sang as she hastily washed and dressed. Her case was already packed and the letters written — to Fred, Annie and to Janet. She propped the note to her stepfather on the mantelpiece. She'd pop the others in the box at the end of the road on the way to the station. Several times during the past week she'd been on the verge of spilling it all out to Janet. But fear of her friend's reaction kept her quiet. She didn't want another lecture on Tom's unsuitability as a husband.

Besides, Janet was sure to tell Norman, who was in the same regiment as Derek Rose. Dolly couldn't risk him finding out that Tom had moved to Sussex. But, after saying goodbye to Janet the day before, she was filled with remorse for not confiding in her. The thought of cutting herself off from her old friend was unbearable. So she'd written a long letter of explanation, swearing her to secrecy.

She just hoped Janet would forgive her, she thought, glancing at the clock. She'd have to hurry if she was going to catch that train. As she tidied her hair in the mirror over the sink, hurriedly smearing on a dab of lipstick, a knock came at the front door.

Muttering a curse, she opened the front door, trying to look welcoming as she saw who was there. Why did they have to turn up just as she was leaving? But then she was smiling and hugging Annie, bending down to pick up young Stevie. "Well, young man, did you miss your Auntie Doll then?" She turned to Annie. "Back for a visit are you? How long are you staying?"

"I'm not going back." Annie sniffed and glared as Dolly made to protest. "You've no idea what it was like. I hated it — and Stevie was unhappy. I couldn't stay there."

Dolly took Stevie's hand. "Let's talk indoors. You must be exhausted."

Annie followed Dolly and Stevie into the kitchen. "You were just on your way out — don't let me keep you," she said. "And what's with the case? Where are you off to?"

"I'm being sent away — war work," she said, hoping Annie didn't notice her flushed face as she poked the range into life and swung the kettle over the hob. "Have you had breakfast?" she asked.

"We had some biscuits on the train. I thought we'd get here last night but we were stuck in the middle of nowhere for hours."

"Whatever possessed you, Annie? Coming back without letting us know?"

Without waiting for a reply, she got the bread out of the enamel bin on the dresser and started to slice it. "I haven't got much. Bread and jam will have to do. You'll have to go shopping later on. And if you're going to stay, you'll have to register your ration books with the Maypole and with Mr George, the butcher."

While she bustled around, Annie slumped at the kitchen table, Stevie clutching her skirt and gazing at Dolly with his thumb stuck in his mouth. He was nearly four now and he'd grown, his face had filled out and he looked a different child from the peaky toddler he'd been six months ago. He may have been unhappy down in Somerset, but the country air seemed to have done him good.

Dolly slapped the plate of bread and jam on the table and poured the tea. "I'm sorry, Annie — you'll have to manage now. I don't want to miss my train."

"Must you go? I was looking forward to seeing you."

"Yes, I must. They don't give you much choice these days." Dolly hated lying but she couldn't tell Annie the truth. The other girl would only beg her to stay and make her feel guilty for putting her own happiness first. As if she didn't feel guilty enough already.

Dolly's eyes went to the envelope behind the clock. When Annie bent to lift Stevie on to a chair, she took the letter to her sister-in-law out of her bag and put it with the one for Fred.

Buttoning her jacket she grabbed her handbag and said. "Right, I'm off." She gave Stevie a hug, patted Annie's shoulder and rushed out of the house before she could change her mind.

At the end of Seaton Road she jumped on the bus, not looking back as it swung round the corner. She hated leaving Annie and her little boy and wondered how they'd manage. But the thought that by the end of the day she and Tom would be man and wife, pushed all other thoughts out of her head.

When she reached the station, hundreds of soldiers, some on crutches, some wearing blood-stained bandages, were pouring off the train and she had to fight her way through the crowds. It brought home to her the reality of the war and, although the threatened bombs hadn't come, she prayed that Annie hadn't made a mistake by returning to London.

Tom stood on the station platform and gazed up the line. He'd been standing here for over an hour and, despite frequent announcements over the tannoy system, he was beginning to think Dorothy's train would never arrive.

She'd be getting worried, especially if the train was shunted off to a siding to allow the troop trains to pass. He glanced at his watch. He'd booked the Registrar for two o'clock and he didn't want to be late. Besides, he had to get back to the shop before closing time. Maureen had been very good about holding the fort and he didn't want to take advantage of her good nature.

The signal clanged down and Tom stepped forward impatiently as a plume of smoke crept round the bend, resolving itself into a huge green engine pulling at least twelve coaches. As he craned his neck for a glimpse of her, he felt a pang of guilt. Was it too late to change his mind? Could he persuade Dorothy to wait till he was free?

But the welcome he got as she leapt off the train and hurled herself into his arms drove such thoughts away. How could he shatter her illusions? No, he would have to keep up the deception.

"Sorry I'm late," she said, kissing him fervently, careless of the grinning porters.

He returned her kiss in full measure. "You're here now, that's all that matters," he said, taking her case. Holding her hand, he hurried through the barrier and over the level crossing.

Dolly scarcely had time to look about her, to take in the ancient medieval market cross in the town centre, the spire of the Cathedral towering over the row of quaint old shops. Soon they reached the registry office, where the registrar stood in the doorway looking at his watch.

He gabbled through the ceremony, and Dolly made her responses in a daze. Then the witnesses, strangers brought in from the street, were shaking hands, they had signed the register and Tom was ushering her into the battered old van which was parked outside.

"It should be a Rolls Royce really," Tom said, apologizing for the lack of comfort.

Dolly laughed, her eyes shining with happiness. "I don't care. So long as it gets us home as soon as possible." She twisted the ring on her finger. "Home," she murmured, gazing out of the window as they left the town behind.

The van struggled up a steep hill and down an even steeper one into a valley bisected by a meandering river. Up another hill and down a winding lane and

186

they came to the village — a narrow street of cottages with a pub at one end and the village stores at the other.

"Here we are," Tom said, helping her out of the van.

Dolly's first glimpse of the shop left her speechless. She had imagined something like the little lock-up under the arches in Shepherd's Bush — well, maybe not, since Tom had told her it was three cottages knocked into one, two of the front rooms containing the shop, the other the post office. There were storerooms and a kitchen at the back and bedrooms and bathroom above. But she hadn't been prepared for the size of it.

The shop windows contained a display of tins and groceries — dummy packets, Tom said, because the shop got the full sun during the middle of the day and the goods would be spoiled. There were cardboard placards on stands advertising "Lyons Tea", "Sunlight Soap" and "Tate and Lyle" golden syrup — not that there were many of these actually in the shop these days.

"How could you afford a place like this?" Dolly asked.

"I'd saved a bit — and Ma left some money. But it's on a mortgage of course."

"Groceries and provisions — and a post office," Dolly said. "Is it really all yours?"

"Ours," Tom said, throwing open the door with a flourish. "Would you like me to carry you over the threshold, Mrs Marchant?" he said.

187

He put down her case and lifted her into his arms. Inside the shop, he put her down, keeping his arms round her and crushing her lips against his. "Oh, Dorothy, I can't wait," he breathed.

She kissed him back with matching urgency, then pulled away. "Tom, behave," she said with a breathless little giggle.

He let her go, laughing. "Good job there's no customers. But I'd better introduce you to Maureen."

Dolly blushed as Maureen came from behind the post office partition and said a shy hello.

"Everything been all right?" Tom asked her.

"Yes, Mr Marchant. We were quite busy earlier but it's slowed down a bit now."

"Thanks for holding the fort. Do you mind carrying on while I show my wife round?"

Tom picked up the suitcase, grabbing Dolly's hand and leading her through to the storeroom. He pushed the door shut with his foot as he reached for her again. "I think I should show you the bedroom first," he said.

It was quite some time before Dolly, dressed and hair neatly combed once more, got a proper glimpse of her new home.

Tom buttoned his shirt, watching her as she smoothed her skirt over her hips. "I feel bad about you not having a proper wedding — and no honeymoon," he said.

"All I care about is that we're married, Tom. I'm just so happy . . ."

"Your Ruby went to Paris though, didn't she?"

"Tom, it doesn't matter — I've never been jealous of Ruby, whatever she might tell people. We'll go to Paris one day — when the war's over maybe. Meanwhile we'll work together to make a success of this business — something to pass on to our children." She blushed and smiled.

"Yeah — Marchant and Son. Has a nice ring to it, don't you think?"

Dolly thought it sounded wonderful. Well, if she wasn't pregnant already, she soon would be if they kept on like this, she thought, as Tom reached for her again.

It was hard to push him away, but they had all the time in the world now. She laughed. "Later," she said. "I want to see my new home properly. And what will Maureen think?"

"She'll probably be jealous," Tom replied, the twinkle back in his eye again.

CHAPTER
EIGHTEEN

Dolly was pregnant. She'd been hopeful for a couple of weeks. Now she was sure. She stood in the tiny bathroom, her hands on her stomach, smiling at herself in the mirror over the washbasin.

Wouldn't Tom be pleased. In the months they'd been in Borstall Green they'd often pictured the sign above the shop in years to come — "Marchant and Son". Surely it would be a boy — not that it mattered of course. But a boy would be nice — for Tom.

For a brief moment she doubted her right to be happy, questioned the wisdom of bringing a new life into a world fraught with danger and uncertainty. But life had to go on. Reminders of the war were never far away — the threat of invasion had gone since the Battle of Britain but even in this sleepy Sussex village, they were aware of the devastating blitz on London, leaving Dolly consumed with worry about Annie and Stevie. And now, night after night, the bombers roared overhead, seeking out the docks and factories in Portsmouth and Southampton, as well as the RAF aerodrome just down the road.

Last night they had lain awake for hours, listening to the drone of airplanes, the sporadic stutter of anti-aircraft guns up on the Downs.

But the terrors of the night had faded when Dolly checked the dates and realized that her dream was about to come true. Was it so wrong to feel happy?

It was Sunday, her favourite day of the week. Once, she would never have dreamed of lying in bed half the morning, would have been up and off to early Communion. But, she realized guiltily, she hadn't been near a church for months, hadn't even thought about it. She told herself she hadn't had time, what with sorting the house out, helping Tom in the shop and getting the books in order. Then there were all the new forms and paperwork from the ministry, the ration coupons to be counted and accounted for against the stock. But she really ought to make the effort, if only to give thanks for her present happiness.

Dolly gave a final pat to her hair and went downstairs. Even after all these weeks she still felt a little jolt of pleasure whenever she opened the door to the big room with its scrubbed wooden table in the centre, the deep sink under the window and the gas water heater on the wall beside it. Best of all was the shiny gas stove against the other wall. The kitchen didn't get much sun but the buttercup yellow walls and white and yellow gingham curtains at the window made it look bright and welcoming.

It was getting late and Dolly quickly lit the gas under the frying pan, got bacon and eggs out of the larder. Then she put the eggs back — there were only two left. Tom would have to make do with bacon and fried tomatoes today. Sometimes Dolly found it hard to remember the rationing, surrounded by food as they

191

were. But it wouldn't do for them to be caught breaking the rules.

She laid the table and cut slices of bread, glancing at the clock again. She hoped Tom would be up soon. She didn't mind him having a lie in — he worked hard enough all week. But she didn't want to go and fetch him. He would try to coax her back into bed and, much as she enjoyed their Sunday morning romps, today she had other things on her mind. She touched her stomach again and a secret smile played about her lips.

She jumped as Tom's arms came round her from behind and his lips nuzzled her ear. "What are you grinning at? You look like the cat that got the cream," he said, pulling her round to face him.

"Tom," she said sternly, waving the spatula at him, "I'm in the middle of cooking — be careful." Then she relaxed into his arms. "I'm just happy, that's all." She wouldn't tell him just yet — she'd wait till they went out later on.

Running a grocer's was hard work, especially in wartime. Sometimes, when his back was aching from unloading sacks of sugar and flour, or his eyes were swimming from poring over ledgers and ministry directives, Tom almost regretted giving up his little shop under the arches, even thought back nostalgically to the market stall. But he only had to look at Dolly, to glance round at his little empire, to know it was all worthwhile.

He missed the bustle of the market, but his determination to get away from the darker aspects of life in Shepherd's Bush had paid off. He no longer went to sleep at night dreading a knock on the door, no longer woke sweating after nightmares of lying curled defencelessly under Arthur Rose's vicious steel toecaps.

And it was all due to Dorothy, his wife — his true wife as he thought of her. She was sweet and loving, passionate in bed, and never complained at the long hours she worked alongside him, serving in the shop, cleaning and cooking, and most of all sorting out the hated paperwork. He knew he'd never have made a success of things without her.

He stole a look at her as she sat beside him on the bench on the village green. She was leaning back on her hands, eyes closed, her face turned up to the sun, smiling. His chest tightened at the thought of how he had so nearly lost her. Fear of what the Roses would do to him — and to her — had almost driven him back to Freda, a woman who hated him even as she clung on to him. His only regret was that he'd never know his son, would miss seeing Tony grow to manhood and maybe one day become the "Son" of "Marchant and Son".

He reached out and touched Dorothy's hand and she turned to him, her eyes full of love.

"Remember what you said this morning, Tom?" she said.

"What?"

"The cat that got the cream — that's what I feel like. I've got everything I ever wanted — or I soon will have."

He gazed at her, not understanding at first. Then a big grin broke out on his face and he laughed aloud. "You mean you're . . .? You're sure? When?"

"End of January, maybe the beginning of February, I think."

"Why didn't you tell me?"

"I just did." Dorothy's cheeks were tinged with pink.

She always did blush easily, Tom thought, pulling her to her feet. He kissed her, his earlier darks thoughts banished as he realized that the past no longer mattered. His future was with this woman, soon to be the mother of his child.

As they walked towards the shop, they scarcely noticed the sandbags round the anti-aircraft gun emplacement and other signs of war all around them, even in this remote little village.

Tom laughed. "I never thought I'd be happy away from the market," he said.

"But you were always ambitious. And you do like it here?" Dorothy asked.

"I love it — especially now I've got you."

They walked on slowly, enjoying the warmth of the late summer afternoon. It was true, Tom had been apprehensive about moving away from his familiar surroundings, the place he'd lived all his life. But he was beginning to settle down now. He had everything he'd ever wanted — his own business, a loving wife, and now a baby on the way. What more could a man ask for, he thought, refusing to dwell on what would happen if Dorothy ever discovered her baby would be illegitimate. How could anyone find out, tucked away as they were in this quiet little backwater?

Dolly might have given up her earlier ambitions — to be independent, to get on in her career — but she was still determined to be respectable, and, as Mrs Marchant, wife of a man with his own business, she was becoming a respected member of the community. She worked hard and would not allow her pregnancy to slow her down, despite Tom's protests. The shop was always clean and tidy, and the shelves, if sometimes sparsely stocked, arranged attractively.

Deliveries were becoming haphazard, what with the shortages of supplies as well as the bombing of the London docks and warehouses, but as a businessman Tom was allowed a small ration of petrol and once a week he made the trip to the wholesaler's to stock up on whatever he could get hold of.

Dolly had every reason to be proud of her step up in the world and she thanked God in her prayers every night that Tom had come back into her life.

So she was worried, as well as a little annoyed, when Tom came back late one Thursday afternoon and started unloading boxes from the back of the van. She came downstairs to help him, gasping at the sight of the boxes full of tins.

"Peaches! How on earth did you manage to get so many?" she asked.

Tom didn't answer, hefted another box into his arms and went through to the storeroom. Dolly followed, counting the boxes, multiplying them by the number of tins in each box — there must be enough here for every household in the village.

"Tom, you must have far more than your allowance here. What's going on?" she demanded.

"Nothing's going on — they just wanted to get rid of them, that's all. First come, first served. I just happened to be there at the right time," Tom said. But he didn't look her in the eye.

Dolly thought she'd successfully forgotten Tom's past association with the Rose brothers. But now suspicion flooded in. With the very first rationing a flourishing black market had sprung up and most people saw little harm in getting hold of a few "extras" to supplement the adequate but rather boring wartime diet. But it was against the law and Dolly had a horror of anything even remotely shady. Besides, Tom had promised he'd put all that behind him and she desperately wanted to trust him.

She attempted a little laugh. "Well, better not let our customers know how many we've got — we'll have a riot on our hands," she said.

Tom turned from stacking the tins at the back of the storeroom. "Look, Dorothy, it's not what you think. They aren't stolen, honestly."

"I didn't suggest they were," she said. But that's what she'd been thinking.

"There was a big raid last night and the warehouse was on fire and they wanted to save the stock. Like I said, I was in the right place . . ." His voice trailed off and Dolly put her hand on his arm.

196

"I believe you, Tom, really I do." And she did, she told herself.

But she couldn't help brooding about it as she prepared their evening meal.

Later, as they sat at the table in the kitchen, she toyed with her food, although she'd been too busy to eat all day and should have been hungry. She put down her knife and fork and picked up her plate. As she took it over to the draining board, Tom said, "What's up with you then?"

"Nothing, I'm just a bit tired."

"Come on, Dorothy. I know when you're upset about something. It's those bloody peaches isn't it? I swear to you . . ."

She turned from the sink and said sharply, "I said I believed you." She came over to the table and put her hand on his shoulder. "I know you wouldn't do anything wrong," she said in a gentler voice. "It's just that I worry about you getting into trouble. What with all these rules and regulations and inspectors from the ministry coming round. They might think . . ."

"Let them think what they bloody well like. Besides, I did it for us, Dorothy."

Dolly's eyes widened. "Oh, Tom . . ."

"I mean, well — I just grabbed the opportunity, that's all. I didn't think." Tom stood up and starting pacing the room. "It was all legit, I swear but . . . All right, I did have a couple of extra cases."

Dolly started to protest but he went on. "I can't help thinking about what that old cow, Mrs Smythe said when she was in here last week." He put on a high voice. "Oh, Mr Marchant, are you sure you don't have any little extras hidden behind the counter? My neighbour, who shops at Green's in town, says he always keeps a little something by for his best customers." He ran his fingers through his hair and sighed. "You know what she was implying don't you? If I don't find her a few 'little extras' she'll take her custom elsewhere, and all her cronies will follow her. Then where will we be?"

Dolly sank into a chair and gave a little laugh. "Tell me, do you ever read all that stuff from the Ministry?"

"Only if it seems important — why?"

"Tom, you silly. She can't take her custom elsewhere. She's registered with us and she can only change grocers if she has a good reason."

"You sure?"

"Yes. So what's she going to do then? Go to the Food Office and tell them her grocer won't supply black market goods? No — we're stuck with Mrs Smythe and her cronies at least until the war's over." She started to laugh and Tom came over and hugged her.

"I'm really sorry. I didn't realize you had such strong opinions about this sort of thing." He shook her gently. "I don't know why you're laughing."

"I was just picturing the old bag's face if she knew we had hundreds of tins of peaches stashed away."

It was the first time they'd come anywhere near quarrelling and Dolly was determined to put the incident behind them. She was sure Tom wouldn't do anything like it again. It was never openly mentioned again but occasionally Tom would put half a dozen tins under the counter and sell them to whoever could produce the requisite number of points. It took months to get rid of them and Dolly breathed a sigh of relief when the last one was sold a few days before Christmas.

But by then she had other things to worry about. As she grew heavier, her feet and ankles swelled up and Tom insisted she saw the doctor, who told her that long hours behind the shop counter were not a good idea for someone in the seventh month of pregnancy. She should rest as much as possible otherwise he couldn't answer for the consequences for her or the baby.

Maureen helped as much as possible but she too was busy with the extra post office administration that the war had brought. Tom tried to get a temporary assistant for the shop but all the young men and women were in the forces or doing war work. Even the married women were already doing their bit. They'd just have to manage.

For a couple of weeks, Dolly did as she was told, pottering around in the mornings and spending the afternoons with her feet up, sewing and knitting things for the baby. But she'd never been able to sit idly while someone else did the work and, as the swelling in her ankles had subsided, she didn't think it would hurt to help in the shop when they were busy.

Tom gave in when he saw she was determined. He placed a chair in a corner behind the counter, insisting that she sat down at every opportunity.

★ ★ ★

Tom had joined the Home Guard and Dolly hated it when he was on night duty. Listening to the drone of the bombers overhead, she shivered, thinking of her family in London, riven with guilt for not contacting them. In the excitement of her runaway marriage she hadn't really given them a thought or if she had, it was to tell herself she didn't care — they weren't her real family after all.

But since the bombing started, she'd written to Fred, trying to explain once more and asking him to forgive her. He'd never replied and she hadn't heard from Annie either. She only hoped she'd been sensible and taken Stevie back to the country when the raids began. Janet hadn't answered her letter either and she wasn't sure whether to try writing again. She feared her friend would never forgive her for keeping her marriage secret.

During the day when she was busy and at night, safe in Tom's arms, it was easy for Dolly to dismiss them from her mind. But when she was alone, she prayed for their safety and made up her mind that after the baby was born she'd go and visit them, just to set her mind at rest.

Emerging from yet another night of broken sleep, Dolly stretched and yawned, gasping, as she felt the first stab of pain. She tried to sit up, but fell back against the pillows, just as Tom appeared in the doorway with a tray of tea and toast.

"Thank goodness you're home," she said, biting her lip.

Tom was at her side in a flash. "What is it, Dorothy? Not the baby already?"

"I think it must be. I've been having these twinges all night. Thought it was indigestion." She gave a little laugh that ended in a gasp.

"You should have called someone," he said.

"What was I supposed to do — run outside in my nightie? I told you, I didn't think it was anything . . ." She broke off and gripped his hand. "I think you'd better fetch the midwife."

If the next contraction hadn't come so soon and so painfully, Dolly might have laughed as Tom ran his fingers through his hair and dashed towards the door, muttering to himself.

But as the pains increased their intensity and Tom didn't come back she couldn't stop herself calling out. Surely Maureen would be here by now.

Maureen wasn't much use either and the baby was almost there when the midwife arrived and hustled her out of the room. With brisk efficiency, she finished the job, gently easing the baby girl into the world.

Dolly was so thrilled she felt like leaping out of bed and telling the world that she was a mother. But as Tom sat at her side, holding her hand and gazing down at his daughter, her eyes closed and exhaustion claimed her.

When she woke he was still there, a foolish grin on his face as he watched her feeding the baby, marvelling at how naturally it came to her. The child gave a little hiccup and Dolly cradled her in her arms, gazing at the soft fuzz of dark hair, the tiny dimples in cheeks and hands.

Tom reached out and stroked the baby's head, curling her hand around his finger. As she gripped it tightly, he laughed. "She's lovely. What shall we call her?"

They had only thought of boy's names. Dolly looked at Tom. "You don't mind it being a girl?"

"How could I? She's beautiful." He laughed. "We can always put "Marchant and Daughter" over the shop."

Dolly laughed too. What did it matter? They were a real family now. "I thought of a name, but only if you agree — Rowena."

"Where did you dig that one up?"

"Don't you like it? It was in a book I read once."

"I thought we'd have my mum's or yours. But I like Rowena." He reached over and stroked the baby's cheek again. "A pretty name for a pretty girl," he said.

After a couple of days Dolly tired of lying in bed, cut off from the bustle of the shop. Ignoring Tom's protests she got up and, leaving the baby in her cot, she went down to the kitchen. It wasn't in too much of a state considering, but there was a lot to do.

As she lit the gas under the enamel bucket on the stove ready to boil the accumulated nappies, she reflected that it was at times like this she really missed Annie. Back in Seaton Road there'd have been no shortage of neighbours popping in to whisk a duster round, see to the washing and help with the baby. But she didn't really miss her old home. She couldn't imagine living anywhere else now, she thought as she pegged the washing on the line stretched between two

202

apple trees. She loved to see the snowy nappies dancing in the warm breeze.

She brought Rowena down and put her outside in her pram, her cheeks flushed with the spring sunshine. Dolly was thankful that her child would grow up away from the dangers of the city. She also said a daily prayer of thanks that she hadn't suffered from the "baby blues" like Annie and that Rowena wasn't giving them sleepless nights as poor little Stevie had.

"It'll be a different story when she starts teething," Mrs Smythe said when another customer commented on the baby's happy disposition.

Dolly just smiled. "I'll worry about that when the time comes." Even snooty Mrs Smythe couldn't ruffle her feathers these days. Sometimes she felt guilty for being so happy when there was so much suffering in the world. But she only had to pick the baby up, rub her cheek against the soft skin, feel the tight grip of the little fingers round her own and happiness would engulf her again.

Her contentment was shattered the day she received a letter from Janet and she and Tom had their first real quarrel. The argument over the stolen peaches paled in comparison.

CHAPTER
NINETEEN

Dolly hadn't told Tom she'd written to Janet. He was so touchy about her friends and relations, insisting that she cut herself off from her old life. She told herself she understood. He'd made a new life for himself and he didn't want the past intruding and spoiling things. But surely that didn't mean she must never see or hear from anyone again.

She couldn't understand his anger when the letter from Janet came. He hadn't seemed to mind when she confessed to writing to Fred and her family, but he was obviously relieved when she didn't receive a reply. And she'd been so hurt that she'd told herself she didn't care and hadn't bothered to let them know when Rowena was born.

But, despite never hearing from Janet either, she'd sent a long letter telling her all about the shop, her new life — and the wonderful addition to her family.

Dolly had fed and changed Rowena and put her in her pram under the window. She'd finished cleaning up and the baby was still sleeping when the door slammed open. "Careful, you'll wake the baby," she said.

Tom held a bundle of letters and she reached out for them. "More bills, I suppose," she said, laughing.

Her expression changed as she noticed how pale he was, the scar on his temple livid against the pallor. "What's the matter, Tom?" She gripped the edge of the kitchen table. Something must have happened to Billy, Annie . . .

Struggling to control her voice, she whispered, "Tell me . . ."

Tom leaned over the table and she flinched as he shouted in her face. "I thought you weren't having anything more to do with that woman."

He threw the bundle of letters down and the hand-writing leaped out at her. "It's from Janet. What's wrong, Tom?"

"Why's she writing to you?" Tom's face was red now and he thumped his fist on the table.

"I expect she's congratulating us on the birth of our daughter," Dolly said, marvelling at the evenness of her tone. "That's what friends do, Tom. I wrote and told her about our marvellous little baby because I thought it would be nice to share our good news."

"I told you I didn't want you keeping in touch with anyone back there."

"She's my friend, Tom. And I don't think it's got anything to do with you who I write to."

"It's got everything to do with me. You're my wife, you do as I say." Tom thumped the table again.

The baby started to wail and Dolly said, "I'm not going to discuss it while you're in this mood. I'm going to see to our daughter. And you've probably got customers waiting." She crossed the room, her shoulders tense.

She picked the baby up and sank into the chair by the fire, automatically stroking and soothing until

Rowena settled back to sleep. She was still shaking, trying to come to terms with this new Tom. She'd seen him angry before — when the deliveries didn't turn up, when more forms arrived from the ministry, but these were minor things. He'd bluster and shout, maybe slam a door, then it was all over and he was back to his happy-go-lucky self once more, laughing at the world — and himself.

This was different. She'd even thought he was going to hit her and that wasn't like Tom at all. Maybe he was jealous of the close friendship she'd had with Janet. Then she remembered his fear of the Rose brothers, his insistence that they must never find out where he was. And, of course, Janet's husband was in the army with Derek Rose. But surely after all this time it didn't matter. As if Janet would give Norman their address anyway. It didn't make sense.

The shrill whistle of the kettle made Dolly jump and the baby stirred in her arms. She put her in her pram, tucking the blanket securely round her, and switched off the gas.

The letters were still on the table and she picked up the white envelope and tore it open. She didn't care what Tom said, she had to read Janet's news.

After congratulating her on the birth of her daughter, Janet went on to say that Norman was convalescing from a wound received in the Dunkirk evacuation. *He's going to be all right and, with any luck won't have to go back for a while.*

"Thank God," Dolly murmured as she turned the paper over. Then a lump rose in her throat as she read.

"Sadly, his friend Dennis didn't make it. He was killed in the same shell burst that injured Norman."

She read the rest of the letter through a mist of tears. There were others she'd known at the Cherry Blossom factory, killed and injured. Neighbours had been bombed out of their homes. It was a catalogue of woe that brought home to Dolly how close the war really was. So far, she'd escaped, with nothing to grumble about but a few sleepless nights and the petty rules and regulations that governed all their lives.

She dashed her hand across her eyes. She must make her peace with Tom — there was enough trouble in the world already. Of course she'd eventually forgive him for his outburst. She even understood — a little. He still sometimes had nightmares over the beating he'd received.

As she went through to the shop Tom was meticulously cutting the coupons out of a customer's ration book. He didn't look at her.

"Here's your tea," she said, putting the cup on the ledge under the counter.

"Thanks," he said. But he didn't smile and she couldn't say anything in front of a shop full of people.

They were busy for a while and Dolly worked alongside Tom, hoping he would turn and smile or make one of his little jokes. But he avoided her eye, although he seemed his old self when serving the long queue of housewives, making jokes and winking at the older women.

At last the shop emptied and Dolly put her hand on Tom's arm. "I want to talk to you," she said.

"There's nothing to say. You disobeyed me." His voice was cold. He got a cloth and started to wipe the marble counter where they cut the cheese.

Dolly was about to protest when Rowena let out a wail.

"Better see to her. You shouldn't have left her on her own," Tom snapped.

Dolly stalked out of the shop without a word.

She picked the baby up and soothed her, changed her nappy and laid her down again, began to prepare a bottle. She was still annoyed with Tom but, as she sat down to feed the baby, she tried to understand. She couldn't blame him for still worrying about the brothers tracking him down. No one lightly crossed them, as Tom's scars testified. But that was all in the past. They were probably in the Army by now. What could they do? And how could her writing to Janet have any bearing on Tom's quarrel with them?

Tom polished the bacon slicer till it shone, his stomach churning as he wondered what Dorothy wanted to talk to him about. Had Janet found out about Freda and passed the news on? What a fool he'd been — he should have come clean right from the start or at least destroyed the letter like all the others. But Maureen had picked up the post and commented on the one addressed to Dorothy.

He put down the cloth and sighed, looking round at his little empire. Was he about to lose it all? He consoled himself that she hadn't flown at him with accusations. Just that quiet statement. "I want to talk to you." Did that mean she hadn't found out, or was she saving the row for later?

The shop emptied and Tom knew he could not put off the inevitable confrontation.

Well, he'd have to face up to it. If she still hadn't found out about Freda he'd have to give some explanation for his behaviour. But how to explain the sick dread every time the post arrived, every time a stranger walked into the shop? He wasn't a coward, but for a long time after the Rose brothers' beating he'd been nervous, jumping at shadows.

Now, there was the added fear that Dorothy would discover what he'd done. Dorothy's strict code of morality would never condone their living in sin and the fact that their child was illegitimate. Hadn't she told him many times how she'd suffered from the label "bastard" when she was a child?

He'd thought them safe from discovery so far away from his old home, using wholesalers in another part of London. But the bombing hadn't helped. He'd had to scout around wherever he could to get supplies, and there was always the risk of bumping into someone from his past. And he'd been a fool over those peaches. Word soon got round, a story told in a pub, a connection made. He kept his ear to the ground himself and knew that Arthur Rose was now running a black market gang who'd stop at nothing to make a hefty profit from the war. Suppose his criminal activities spread outside London?

Tom looked up and down the narrow village street, deserted now in the spring sunshine. As usual,

Maureen took her sandwiches and her book through to the storeroom and he turned the sign to "closed", pulling down the blind on the door.

As he opened the kitchen door Dorothy was mashing potatoes. "It's nearly ready," she said quietly.

Tom let his breath out. So it wasn't to be a screaming match then, full of accusations and recriminations. That wasn't her way though. She would cut him with words rather than thrown crockery.

Silently, she plonked a dollop of potato on the plate alongside a meagre slice of liver and plenty of fried onions. A generous helping of gravy followed and she pushed the plate towards him as he sat down.

"This smells delicious, love," he said.

The look she gave him would have frozen boiling lava. Tom shifted uncomfortably in his chair, forced himself to pick up the knife and fork and to start eating. He tried again. "Rowena all right, is she?"

Used to Freda's fishwife tactics, her silence unnerved him. If she was angry she should say so, have it out, clear the air. He'd rather have a good row and get it over with.

She sat down and started to pick at her dinner, making patterns in the potato. She wasn't angry, just upset, he realized. How he wished he could confess everything. Surely, if she really loved him, she'd forgive him? He bit back the impulse. He couldn't risk losing her. But he'd have to say something. Start by apologising, he told himself.

He dropped his knife and fork and pushed his chair back, put his arms round her. "I'm sorry," he murmured. Their lips met and he tasted the salt of her tears. He pushed the hair back from her face. "Dorothy, love, I shouldn't have got so angry. It's just . . ."

"I understand. And I should have said I'd written to Janet." She wiped her hand across her face and gently pushed him away. "No more secrets, eh?"

"No more secrets," he repeated. He swallowed and got slowly to his feet. "I should have told you . . ."

"I understand, Tom. If it had happened to me I'd want to get as far away as possible from those thugs. But Janet's not going to tell anyone where we are." She smiled at him. "Now, get on with your dinner before it gets cold. We've got to open in a few minutes."

He'd meant to tell her. If she hadn't interrupted he would have, he told himself. But the moment had passed. He forced himself to eat, to ask if there was any pudding.

"Semolina," she said.

He pulled a face.

"It's all right with jam on it. And I've still got some of that homemade from the blackberries we bottled last autumn."

She took the plates to the sink and took the saucepan off the stove. As she ladled the pudding into the bowls she suddenly paused. "What were you going to tell me?"

"What?"

"You said you should have told me something."

He thought furiously, unwilling to face up to things. "Oh, it's about those peaches. If we're not keeping secrets, I should own up — I did steal them."

"Oh, Tom."

He felt himself colouring at the look on her face. "I'm sorry. I know I shouldn't have — but I couldn't resist when everyone was grabbing what they could from the fire." He put his spoon down and pushed the bowl away. "I was a fool, especially as I promised you I'd never do anything like that again."

"Suppose you'd been caught? Didn't you think about me, about our baby?"

"Yes — I did. And I'm sorry, even more so now." He stood up and began to pace the room. "You see, that's why I got so mad about you writing to Janet. I heard that the Rose gang were looting that warehouse at the same time. If they found out I was involved too, they'd have something else to hold over me. Another reason why I don't want anyone to know where we are."

"You should have thought of that before," Dorothy said.

"I know — it was stupid. I wasn't thinking straight." He walked back to where she sat at the table, laid a hand on her arm. "Please forgive me. I promise I'll never do anything like that again. I hate it when we row."

She put her hand over his, lifted it to her lips and kissed his knuckles. "I love you, Tom, and I've already forgiven you. But please, in future, don't lie to me."

He pulled her to her feet and held her close, hiding his face in her hair. His whole life was a lie — but if he spoke up, he'd lose her. How could he tell her the truth now?

CHAPTER
TWENTY

Rowena had started to crawl and pull herself up on the furniture. Dolly was proud of the little girl's progress, but she couldn't keep an eye on her all the time, especially as she was always busy in the shop and Tom was often out, looking for supplies now their deliveries were so erratic.

Tom broke up some crates and nailed the pieces together to form a playpen. He carefully sanded the rough edges of the wood, making sure there were no protruding nails.

"She'll be right as rain in there, see?" he said, proudly displaying his handiwork. "Put a blanket on the floor and then pop her in there with her toys. If we leave the door open, one of us can keep an eye on her all the time."

Life was so much easier after that and Rowena seemed perfectly content in her wooden cage as long as she could see what was going on.

Dolly, despite the sleepless nights and the worry when Tom was on Home Guard duty, knew she had a lot to be thankful for. At least her husband came home each day. So many women were struggling to bring children up on their own while coping with the stress of not knowing when their men would return — if they ever did. Now, she understood what Annie went through, sometimes not hearing from Billy for months, not even knowing where he was.

She tried not to think about her family these days. Fred had never answered her letter and she couldn't really blame him. She deserved it — running away to get married and not letting them know where she was. But she'd hoped Annie would forgive her and keep in touch. They weren't her real family, but they were all she had and sometimes she missed them. With a sigh she put them out of her mind. She had Tom and Rowena now — she didn't need anyone else.

Tom's decision to move away from his childhood home and start afresh had been a good one, especially after his marriage to Dorothy and the birth of his daughter. Sometimes he even managed to forget that their visit to the registry office had been illegal. Besides, he thought of Dorothy as his true wife.

These past eighteen months had been the best of his life, despite the sick dread in the pit of his stomach every time a letter arrived from Janet. Would this be the one that blew his happiness apart, wrecking everything he'd worked for?

At first, he'd been tempted to intercept the letters as he had in the past, to let Dorothy think her friend had forgotten her. But he'd promised — no more secrets or lies. The big lie was buried deep in his subconscious. Freda belonged to another life, she no longer existed for him. But he couldn't forget his son and he longed to be able to do something for the boy — so long as it didn't jeopardise his new life. To salve his conscience he paid a sum of money regularly into a bank account so that at least Tony would never want for anything. He tried not to think about the danger his son was in since Freda had refused to send him to the country.

As he walked back from a night on Home Guard duty he knew he'd have to find out if Tony was all right. From his post at the top of the Downs he'd seen fires raging over Portsmouth way, could imagine the scenes of devastation. It was probably even worse in London.

At breakfast he was still trying to think of an excuse to go to London when the post arrived. There was another letter from Janet and he shoved his hands in his trouser pockets, clenching his fists as he waited for Dorothy to open it. He watched intently as she quickly scanned the one sheet of paper, letting out a breath as a huge grin spread over her face.

"Janet's expecting a baby," she said. "She's thrilled to bits — Norman doesn't know yet. He's been sent overseas again — Africa she thinks but she hasn't heard from him."

"Are you going to write back?" Tom asked.

"Of course. Why?"

Tom wanted to ask her not to, to say she didn't need friends when she had him and their baby. But he'd never make her understand. "I thought you could ask if she had any news of your dad," he said lamely.

"I'm not bothered about them — they obviously don't want to know me now," she replied shrugging her shoulders. She seemed indifferent but Tom wasn't deceived.

She stood up. "Better open up. There's a queue outside," she said.

He unbolted the door and Dolly shoved the letter into her apron pocket, turning to smile brightly at their first customer of the day.

Tom started the tedious task of weighing out minute amounts of cheese and butter. His heart had returned to normal but he still felt a bit shaky as he always did when Dorothy got a letter. One day Janet would find out and she'd lose no time communicating the news to her friend. She had never trusted him and Dorothy had laughingly told him that Janet had warned her not to get involved with him. It was no good, he'd have to try to intercept any future letters from Janet.

Dolly tried to keep her mind on serving as the queue got longer, stretching along the narrow village street. The shoppers were in sombre mood today after the terrible raid on Portsmouth the previous night. There were none of the usual grumbles about the lack of goods and most of them waited patiently as Dolly clipped the coupons from the ration books and apologized for the dearth of stuff on points.

"You're looking cheerful today, in spite of everything," old Mrs Brown said sourly.

"Had some good news today — my friend's expecting a baby."

216

"Don't know what's good about that — bringing an innocent child into the world as it is nowadays," the old woman said.

There were murmurs of agreement. But Dolly couldn't be depressed today.

The last customer left and Dolly went through to the kitchen, leaving Tom to lock up. She heated soup and cut slices of bread. There was no time to cook a proper meal.

As they sat down to eat, Tom said. "Can you manage on your own this afternoon? I was going to Portsmouth to stock up but after the raid it's not a good idea. I thought of going up to the Bush — might strike lucky up there."

"I thought you'd decided to keep away from London," Dolly said.

"Can't let the Roses frighten me out of business."

He was right, Dolly thought. But she wasn't happy about it. She wiped Rowena's face and spooned more soup into the baby's eager mouth. Besides, if he went to London he could check up on her family. Despite telling herself she didn't care, she'd feel better if she knew they were safe.

"You're too soft-hearted, love. They've proved they don't care about you," Tom said. But he promised to call at Seaton Road.

When he'd gone Dolly managed to keep busy and put the nagging anxiety about her family to the back of her mind. She had a lot to be grateful for. Thanks to Tom she'd been able to leave her past behind — to shake off the stigma of being the unwanted illegitimate daughter of a woman with a dubious past. Thanks to Tom she was now a respectable woman. She should be happy. But deep down there was always the sadness that she had no real family, and that the only family she'd ever known had rejected her.

Tom slowly drove the old van towards Putney Bridge, negotiating bomb craters and making detours where roads had been sealed off. He didn't care how long it took him to get home, dreading the moment when he'd have to tell Dorothy the news. He wasn't deceived by her seeming indifference to being cut off from her family. Now he was awash with guilt at the part he'd played in her estrangement from them.

The day had started well, despite the difficulties of driving through the devastated streets. It was business as usual at his old supplier and he'd filled the van with a reasonable load. He was about to start for home when he remembered his promise to seek news of the Watsons. What he found there sickened him more than all the other devastation he'd seen that day; he hated the thought of telling Dorothy. Guilt overwhelmed him as a selfish part of him hinted that now he wouldn't have to worry about her contacting her family and revealing their whereabouts.

Dolly's eyes were red and swollen from crying. It was a week since Tom had returned from Chiswick with the news that Fred, Annie and Steven had been killed, every time she thought about it the tears welled up again, threatening to choke her. The fact that it had

218

happened almost a year ago seemed to make it worse somehow. How could she have enjoyed such happiness? While she'd been enjoying her Sunday walks with Tom on the village green, delighting in her coming baby, they'd already been dead.

In her imagination she pictured how it must have been for Annie and her little boy, cowering under the stairs, cringing as the bombs rained down.

Her hysterical outbursts upset Rowena and she had become fretful, her sobs adding to the discord. Dolly knew she should try to pull herself together for the sake of the family she still had. Tom was fast losing patience with her, although he tried hard to be sympathetic. But for days, she couldn't even bring herself to help him in the shop. She just sat at the kitchen table, her head in her hands, sometimes cuddling Rowena and refusing to let her go even when the little girl protested and wriggled to get down. Now, she understood how Annie had felt.

Tom tried to comfort her but it was no good and in the end he threw up his hands in despair and left her to it. How he wished he'd never gone near Seaton Road. And why hadn't he kept quiet about what had happened? He should have told her all was well, but she was bound to find out some time. He'd expected her to be upset, despite her constantly assuring him she cared nothing for the Watsons. But this guilt-ridden hysteria was more than he could cope with.

Fred Watson had been killed in one of the first raids on Fulham. A delayed action bomb had gone off while he was helping ARP wardens to rescue a trapped family. Ironically, Fred had been on his way home and had escaped the bombing of the power station where he worked. A few days later, Annie and Steven had been killed when most of the houses in Seaton Road had been flattened. September 1940 had been the beginning of six months of horror for the people of that part of London.

Hearing it on the news was one thing, witnessing it at first hand quite different, and Tom, after seeing the great piles of rubble, the craters in the ground, had been reluctant to venture up to Shepherd's Bush. He'd steeled himself, knowing he must make sure Tony was all right. He'd sat in the van outside the school, heaving a sigh of relief when his son came running out with a group of his friends. He'd driven away without trying to speak to him.

Now, he didn't want to talk about it. The horror of what he'd witnessed compounded his own guilt at the part he'd played in cutting Dorothy off from her family. He had enough to cope with back here, what with running a shop which had very little to sell and worrying about Dorothy and the baby.

Despite her grief, Dorothy pestered him for details. Was he sure they'd been killed? Had they suffered? Who had he spoken to?

"I just can't believe they're all gone," she said, over and over again. "And what about Billy — do you think he knows?" She started to cry again. "I don't even know where he is," she sobbed.

Trying to comfort her, he made the mistake of saying that at least Ruby and her husband were still all right.

"I don't care — Ruby hates me. But Annie was my friend, and little Stevie . . ." And she burst into tears again.

He was fed up with it all. She wasn't the only one who'd lost family in this bloody war. Still, he tried to be patient — he knew how he'd feel if it had been Tony.

He said goodnight to Maureen and closed the shop, wondering if Dorothy would be any better today. To his relief he saw that at least she'd made an effort at preparing a meal. A fire burned cheerfully in the grate and she'd even combed her hair and put some lipstick on. Rowena was bathed and in her sleeping suit, lying on the rug in front of the fire and crowing contentedly.

He kissed Dorothy's cheek. "I'm glad to see you're looking better, love."

He knelt down on the rug and tickled Rowena's tummy, making animal noises and laughing. Dorothy dished up the meal. She was pale and her eyes were still puffy. But she managed a glimmer of a smile as they sat down at the table.

"I'm sorry I've been such a wet week," she said. "I don't know why you put up with me."

"I love you, that's why, Dorothy. I'm just worried about you, that's all."

"I've been thinking — I'd like to go back." She toyed with her mashed potato, looking down at her plate.

Tom almost choked on his mouthful of tinned peas. "Are you mad?"

"I want to see where Dad and the others are buried. And I'd like to visit Janet — make sure she's all right. And I could see Ruby, find out if there's any news of Billy."

"Why not write? I don't think it's a good idea to visit," Tom said, trying to keep his voice even. "It'll only upset you — I've been there and I know what it's like." He didn't want her nosing round Shepherd's Bush, gossiping with Janet and her old friends at Chiswick Polish. He didn't care about himself, though he knew what he'd done was illegal. It was the effect on Dorothy if she ever found out that their daughter was illegitimate. It would crucify her and he couldn't bear the thought of how badly she'd be hurt. But she wouldn't find out. There was no way he'd let her go.

"I suppose I could write to Cunard about Billy. But I need to see Janet. It's hard to explain — letters aren't the same. If I could see her, I'd know she was OK."

"Why not invite her here?" The words were out before he could stop them.

"Really, Tom? You wouldn't mind? I know you don't really like her, but she is my dearest friend. And I'm sure she'd love to see Rowena." Dorothy got up from her chair and put her arm round his shoulders, kissing him enthusiastically.

Tom smiled. He didn't want the woman here, prying into his business. But it would be worth it to see Dorothy happy. Already her eyes were sparkling and he was pleased to see signs once more of the girl he'd fallen in love with.

"Anything for you, my love," he said.

222

Dorothy cleared the plates and stacked them on the draining board. "I've just had an idea, Tom. You realize we haven't had Rowena christened yet and she's nearly ten months old. Why don't we ask Janet to be godmother?"

Tom sighed. He'd been hoping the subject wouldn't come up. Knowing how religious Dorothy had been when he first met her, he was surprised it hadn't been mentioned before. But of course, they'd had other things on their minds lately.

"We can't have a big do," he said cautiously, "what with the rationing and all."

"That's not what it's about, Tom. It's the service that's important. We could just have Janet and Norman as godparents, and Maureen of course."

"I suppose so, though I don't expect Norman will get leave."

"I'll go and see the vicar later on," Dolly said, getting her writing paper out of the dresser drawer.

As Tom went through to re-open the shop, he thought about having to go to church and being polite to the vicar. He wasn't looking forward to it. He'd had enough of all that church nonsense with Freda, having to get special permission to be married in St Mary's because he wasn't a catholic, being dragged along there again for Tony's first communion. He wasn't sure if he even believed in God in any shape or form. But, for Dorothy, he'd put up with it. And having something to look forward to had certainly put the smile back on her face.

On their next early closing afternoon, Dolly went to see the Reverend Taylor to arrange a date for Rowena's christening. She'd been to All Saints a few times since coming to the village and enjoyed the services, and she'd got to know his wife quite well when she came in the shop.

The vicar opened the door, looked at her vaguely, then his face cleared. "Mrs Marchant — do come in. I can guess why you're here — that lovely little daughter of yours, isn't it?" he said, showing her into his untidy study. He invited her to sit down and then looked sternly at her over the top of his glasses. "I normally only perform baptism for my regular parishioners," he said.

Dolly started to interrupt. But he held up a hand and smiled. "I understand that these are not normal times and I have seen you at matins on the odd occasion. My wife tells me you work very hard."

"I wish I had more time for church," Dolly said. "Before my marriage, I was a Sunday School teacher at St Nicholas's in Chiswick." She stifled a smile, imagining his reaction if he knew she'd not only been married in a register office, but had slept with Tom before they were married. She bit her lip and managed to say briskly, "I'd like to get it done as soon as possible — say, the Sunday after next."

The vicar consulted his desk diary. "That should be fine." He made a note. "You've chosen the godparents?"

"Maureen Lee and an old friend, Mrs Huish from Chiswick."

He nodded. "Well then, I'll see you on the fifteenth at three o'clock," he said, standing up and holding out his hand.

Rowena had behaved perfectly and Tom had only fidgeted a couple of times during the service. Now they were back home tucking into the high tea that Dolly had managed to scrape together.

Janet was enchanted with the baby, picking her up at the slightest provocation. Her pregnancy was obvious and Dolly wondered how she'd managed the tedious train journey. But she was glad to see her.

"You must let me know the minute your baby arrives and I'll come up and visit," she said. "And if there's anything I can do . . ."

"You've done enough already," Janet said, indicating the bag of baby clothes Dolly had given her. "I was beginning to think the poor child would go naked. They give you extra coupons for nappies and things — but it's getting hold of them that's the problem."

"Well, as Rowena grows, I'll be able to pass on more things to you."

"Are you sure you shouldn't keep them for later?" Janet asked with a twinkle. "Surely, you're not going to stop at one."

"One's enough for the moment."

She got up and went into the kitchen, returning with a bowl of tinned peaches, the last of the "forbidden fruit" as she called it. She was glad to see the back of them, fed up with the assaults on her conscience every time she saw the tins lurking in the back of the pantry.

"Peaches," Janet exclaimed. "Haven't had them for ages. How did you manage to get hold of those?"

"I've been saving them for a special occasion."

"Well, I suppose, having a food shop, it's a bit easier for you to have a few luxuries," Janet said.

"It most certainly isn't. We have to be even more careful. There're the inspectors from the ministry, not to mention the customers getting funny."

"All right, sorry I spoke." Janet laughed. "I couldn't imagine you having anything to do with the black market anyway — you always were a bit straitlaced."

Dolly blushed and hoped Maureen wouldn't notice. She ate her dinner in the storeroom but always had her nose stuck in a book so she hadn't appeared to notice the boxes cluttering up the storeroom earlier in the year.

Tom switched the wireless on and Janet said, "I hate listening to the news. I don't want to know what's going on in the desert. Poor Norman." She gave a little sob. "Oh, Dolly, I just want him to see our baby. I can't bear to think of it growing up without a father."

Dolly hugged her friend, not knowing what to say. Once more it struck her how lucky she was, having her husband at home and she felt a cold pang, suddenly realizing that now he was fit again, he could very well be called up if the war went on much longer.

Next morning Dolly went on the bus to Chichester with Janet. As usual the train was delayed. "Will old Potty be angry if you're late?" Dolly asked, remembering how in awe they'd been of the supervisor when they first started work.

226

"She can't say anything — not with me in my condition." Janet stroked her bulge and laughed. "She's had to put up with a lot of changes lately. Not only married women working — pregnant married women too. Still, I'll be leaving soon."

The train came round the bend and slowed to a halt. Dolly hugged her friend, wiping a tear from her eye. "Take care, I'll be thinking of you. And let me know as soon as . . ."

"I will. And don't worry."

Dolly waved until the train was out of sight. Seeing Janet had made her realize how much she missed her. Much as she loved Tom and enjoyed his company, there was no substitute for a good old gossip with another woman. Men just didn't understand.

CHAPTER
TWENTY-ONE

At the end of the first week in December two items of news dominated Dolly's thoughts: the main one of course was the bombing of Pearl Harbor and the entry of America into the war.

The other news was from Janet saying she now had a baby daughter called Pearl in honour of the Americans. She'd had a bad time, giving birth in their Anderson shelter at the height of a raid.

"Poor Janet — I must go and see her," Dolly declared, white-faced after reading the letter. "I'll go up on Sunday when we're closed."

Tom made a gesture of annoyance. "Do you have to? We don't get to spend much time together these days." He crumpled his newspaper and threw it down.

Dolly picked it up and began smoothing the pages automatically. Newspaper was too valuable these days to be thrown away. "It's not just anybody's baby — it's my best friend's," she said. "Besides, Mrs Carter said Janet's not well — I'd really like to see her." She sighed. It was always the same when it was anything to do with her friend. "Never mind, I'll go another day."

"I know she's your best friend — but she's got her mum and dad there. It's not like she's on her own."

228

Why didn't he like Janet, Dolly wondered. Well, he couldn't stop her seeing her friend. And Sunday was their only full day off. With the trains so erratic, she'd need a whole day to get up there and back. She was about to say so when Tom spoke again. "If you're so determined to see her, why don't you go today? It's early closing and I'm sure Maureen and me can manage on our own for one morning."

She put her arms round him and gave him a hug, her irritation forgotten. "Do you really mean it? It's not just Janet — you know I've been wanting to go back. I still haven't heard anything about Billy. Maybe I'll call in and see Ruby too — see if she's got any news." She did so want Tom to understand.

"Whoa there," he said. "You're only going for a day." He looked at her earnestly. "It's going to be quite a shock for you, love. It's really dreadful — the devastation. But you've made up your mind. So what can I do?"

"I'm not going for fun, Tom." She started to clear away the breakfast things. There was a lot to do. "Do you think they'll let me take Rowena's pram on the train?"

"You're not taking the baby," Tom said. "It'll be hard enough as it is getting across London, without having to worry about her. Don't worry, Maureen will help me look after her."

Dolly could see the sense of it. Travelling in wartime was hard enough. And it wasn't as if the shop was busy on early closing day. Rowena was a contented child, happy enough in her makeshift playpen so long as she had a few wooden bricks and her beloved teddy bear to play with. And she always had a long sleep in the afternoons. Dolly shuffled off her feelings of guilt and determined to make the most of this unexpected day off.

As she waited for the bus outside Victoria station, listening to the chirpy London voices, she saw that everyone was going about their daily business seemingly without a care in the world. Their clothes were shabby, their faces grey and careworn, but they smiled and cracked jokes. They were "taking it". Unconsciously, Dolly pulled her shoulders back and stuck her chin out.

After several detours due to the craters in the road and burst gas mains, Dolly finally turned into Seaton Road. The row of terraced houses was now an ugly heap of rubble, roughly fenced off and already overgrown with rank weeds. Only two houses in the row remained, boarded up and deserted now.

She turned away, tears welling up at the thought of Annie and little Stevie. They had made life bearable for her, filling the gap left when her mother had run off with her fancy man.

A voice behind her made her jump. "Dolly Dixon — I thought it was you coming up the street."

It was Mabel Atkins, their old next door neighbour. "Where have you been then? I heard you got married — run off without a word to anyone."

Dolly wiped her face with the back of her hand. "Yes — we moved away, down to Sussex." Normally, she wouldn't have given the nosy old woman the time of day. But she had to ask about the air raid.

"My husband told me . . . but I didn't realize . . ." She waved a hand towards the bomb site as tears threatened to choke her again.

"It must have been a dreadful shock, dear," Mabel said, taking Dolly's arm.

"Tell me what happened," she pleaded.

Mabel said that when the siren had gone she tried to get Annie to accompany her to the public shelter in the recreation ground. "But she said she'd wait for Fred to finish his shift. Well, he never got home, did he? And when the all clear went and I walked back up the road — well, you saw what it was like."

Dolly couldn't answer. It was just as Tom had told her. She swallowed a lump in her throat, overcome with guilt. She should have been here. She'd have forced Annie to take Stevie to the shelter. She turned away. "I've got to go."

Mabel looked disappointed. "I'm staying at my sister's round the corner. I hoped you'd come and have a cuppa. You haven't told me where you're living or anything about your husband. And why did you have to run away to get married?" The woman's eyes narrowed suspiciously. "You weren't expecting, were you?"

Dolly felt her face flushing. "No, I wasn't. I really have got to go."

As she hurried away to catch the bus to Janet's, she wished she hadn't come. Mabel's description of the raid, as well as the sight of the crater where the house had been, had brought the reality home to her. Until the moment she'd walked round the corner, she'd still nurtured the faint hope that Tom had got it wrong.

By the time she reached Janet's parents' house she'd recovered a little. It was no use crying. She'd have to bear the guilt of abandoning her family.

Janet welcomed her with open arms and after cooing over baby Pearl and handing over the bag of Rowena's cast-off baby clothes, Dolly sat down at the dining table. Mrs Carter was happy to share their rations and set out a plate of cold meat and a huge bowl of mashed potatoes with a selection of pickles.

It was more than three years since Dolly had seen the Carters at Janet's wedding, yet they treated her like one of the family. She warmed to them as they plied her with food and asked her about her life in Sussex.

"Janet tells us you have a nice little business," Mr Carter said.

She smiled, telling them about the shop and village life.

After the meal, Janet brushed away her offer to help with the washing-up. "If you're going to see Ruby, we could put Pearl in her pram and walk over there."

"I don't really want to," Dolly confessed. "But I'm worried about Billy."

"Well, let's go and find out, shall we?"

It was quite a walk to Ruby's posh block of flats just off Holland Park Avenue. When she saw the place, Dolly had to admit that her stepsister had done well for herself.

But even Strathmore Mansions bore the scars of two years of war. The spacious lobby was darkened by the sandbags heaped in front of the doors and halfway up the windows. The lift was out of order too and Janet said she'd wait in the little park across the road, rather than try to drag the pram upstairs.

As Dolly rang the bell, butterflies hovered in her stomach. It was a long time since she'd seen her stepsister.

The woman who answered the door was pale and drawn, wearing a cotton housecoat, her hair hidden by a turban. But the lips were painted a vibrant red matching the fingernails which curved round her cigarette.

Ruby's eyes flashed with anger at the sight of her visitor. "What are you doing here?" she demanded. And before Dolly could reply, her lips drew back in a snarl. "Get out. How you've got the nerve . . ."

Dolly put her hand on the door. "Please, Ruby. I only came to say I was sorry . . ."

"It's a bit late for that. My dad's been dead a year and you turn up out of the blue saying you're sorry." Ruby's face almost crumpled as if she was about to cry. But anger won. "You went off without a word. Worried sick, he was. But you didn't give a thought to the family that took in a bastard brat and her whore of a mother."

"I did write . . ." Dolly protested.

But Ruby was in full flow now. "Selfish little cow, just like your mother. Only thinking of yourself and your fancy man . . ."

233

"He's not my fancy man. We got married." Dolly interrupted.

Ruby screeched with laughter. "You expect me to believe that?" She gave Dolly a little push. "Go on, get out, before my neighbours find out I'm related to a whore."

Ruby's vindictive words hardly registered and Dolly stood firm. "I'm not going till you tell me if Billy's all right."

"I see — not content with getting your claws into one bloke, now you're after my brother. You always did smarm round him when you were a kid. Well, the last I heard he was on his way to America so he's safe — from your clutches at least." Ruby pushed Dolly again and slammed the door in her face.

She leaned against the wall, trying to steady her breathing, blinking back tears. From the moment she'd rung the bell she'd realized it was a mistake.

Well, painful as the encounter had been, at least now she knew Billy was all right — for the time being. She'd write to him, care of the Cunard shipping office, and hope that he wouldn't turn from her as Ruby had. She caught her breath at the memory of her stepsister's vindictive snarl, the hatred in her eyes.

Then she remembered her first sight of Ruby when she'd opened the door — the drawn face, the haunted eyes. Poor Ruby wasn't happy. And she'd always been jealous. That's all it was — jealousy, and anger that her family had been wiped out while Dolly was still safe.

By the time she rejoined Janet she'd resolved to put Ruby out of her mind. She wouldn't write to Billy either. He'd probably blame her for the death of his family too. Though what she could have done to prevent the bombs falling on Seaton Road she hadn't a clue.

To her relief Janet didn't question her and Dolly didn't want to talk about it. She just said Billy was all right.

Janet touched her arm. "I don't know what Ruby said to you, but you mustn't blame yourself, Dolly. The only one to blame is that maniac Hitler." Her voice broke and she bent over the pram, straightening the blanket over baby Pearl. "I sometimes wonder what I've done, bringing a child into the world . . ."

"You mustn't think that. Our children are the future, we've got to cling on to that. Besides, now the Americans are in, it can't go on much longer — can it?"

Her friend's words had pulled her up short. You just had to get on with your life. Suddenly, she longed to be back with Tom and Rowena — they were her family now. As far as she was concerned the Watsons no longer existed. She had offered the hand of friendship to Ruby for the last time.

CHAPTER
TWENTY-TWO

Dolly sometimes felt as if she'd always lived in Borstall Green. It had taken a while for the villagers to accept them but she smiled when she realized they were no longer referred to as the new people.

Her friendship with Maureen helped. And with her still running the post office, the villagers, slow to accept change, were reassured that their shop would continue as it had done for years — a meeting place for gossip and, more recently, exchange of views on the progress of the war.

The news from the Far East was bad but there'd been a surge of optimism when the Eighth Army had entered Tripoli in January. Dolly was more worried about Billy and his ship's frequent crossings of the Atlantic. March had been the worst month of the war for the sinking of allied shipping by German U-boats. Despite her resolution not to have anything more to do with the Watsons, she always remembered her stepbrother nightly in her prayers as well as Janet and her family.

After her visit to London and their promises to keep in touch, Janet hadn't answered Dolly's last two letters. She couldn't believe they'd both gone astray. But there was no time to dwell on her friend's defection. Her life was too full. As well as working almost full-time in the shop, she'd learned to operate the tiny telephone exchange and deal with the official forms in the post office so that she could take over from Maureen when necessary.

Rowena was growing into a lively toddler now, full of mischief, inquisitive. She'd outgrown the makeshift playpen and Dolly was always having to chase after her to stop her putting herself in danger led by her prying fingers.

Maybe she should tie her to a chairleg with a long red ribbon like the little girl in *Silas Marner*, Dolly thought as once more she had to leave a customer standing while she extricated her daughter from a heap of tins she'd knocked over.

But she wouldn't change her life for anything. She loved being part of the small community — the centre of it really. For the village shop was where everyone came, some of them every day. Every household in the village and surrounding area was registered with Marchants' for their groceries and it hadn't taken long for Dolly to remember all their names — with a little help from Maureen.

Tom seemed to have settled too. But he was still ambitious and talked of having a chain of grocer's shops after the war although he seldom mentioned it these days. He was too busy with the Home Guard and with turning the garden behind the house into a vegetable plot. He'd shown a surprising aptitude for growing things, so much so that last summer they'd had a surplus which they'd sold in the shop.

He was out there now, digging over the ground to put in seed potatoes while she chopped carrots for a stew. It could simmer on the stove for hours while she was busy in the shop. Rowena played quietly at her feet with a box of wooden blocks and old cotton reels that Tom had painted in bright colours.

Dolly gave a sigh of pure contentment. Despite the war, the loss of her friends and family, she'd never been happier and sometimes she felt a pang of guilt. Did she deserve to be so happy when all around her people were suffering the effects of the war? The bell over the door jangled and she shook the thought away as she threw the rest of the vegetables into the pan.

Her first customer of the day was the vicar's wife. Mrs Taylor always looked harassed but today she seemed even more so. Trailing behind her were two shabbily dressed but clean little boys. Most of the evacuees had returned to London now that the threat of bombing had diminished. But these two, who'd come with their mothers at the beginning of the war, had been left in her care when the women had gone to work in the munitions factory in Woolwich.

They stood quietly to one side while Mrs Taylor took out her reading glasses and consulted her list. "Oh dear, I don't think you'll have all the things I need. I might have to go into town," she said. She took her glasses off and smiled nervously. "I'm so sorry, Mrs Marchant. I didn't mean . . . Oh, dear."

"Just tell me what you want and I'll see what I can do," Dolly said, smiling.

"It's just — well, it's Easter coming up and the Rural Dean's coming to do the service and I have to ask him and his wife to lunch and I just don't know what to give them."

Dolly gestured at the almost empty shelves. "I'm afraid I can't help much," she said. "As you can see . . ."

"I've got some points saved up, though goodness knows it's hard with these two — always hungry as they are."

Dolly smiled sympathetically. "I've got a few cooking apples out the back, from our own tree. I could let you have some for a pie — but you'll need sugar."

"Oh, that's wonderful. Sugar's no problem. I've finally managed to persuade the vicar that tea without tastes just as good so we manage to save our ration for puddings and so on — for the children."

Dolly collected the items on Mrs Taylor's list and piled them on the counter, then clipped the coupons from the ration book before taking the money. She went out to the storeroom and selected several of the biggest and best apples from the box.

The vicar's wife thanked her. "I hope we'll see you at the service, Mrs Marchant," she said as she left the shop.

Dolly nodded and smiled. She'd managed to attend more often since Rowena's christening and had come to love the little church with its carved wooden screen and stained glass windows. She wished she could

239

persuade Tom to come too but, although he didn't mind her going, he usually made some excuse. He hadn't been brought up to go to church and she knew he found it hard to understand why it was so important to her.

Her next customers were a couple of land girls who'd cycled into the village from a farm three miles away. They were giggling together and Dolly smiled as she realized their attention was more on what was going on outside than on their purchases. A large truck had pulled up in the narrow village street, full of American airmen in their smart uniforms. They were from the nearby fighter base which acted as escort to the bombers on their raids over Germany.

Dolly often heard their noisy vehicles roaring through the village but the men seldom came into the shop. They had no need — they had their own store on the base which supplied all their needs. Rationing did not feature in their lives and Dolly couldn't really blame the girls for hanging round in the hopes of a bit of extra chocolate or a pair of nylons.

The older villagers disapproved of course, the women primly condemning what they saw as loose morals, the men angry that foreigners were taking over "their women". As the girls left the shop, still giggling, Dolly saw Maureen staring after them, lips pursed.

"They ought to be ashamed, throwing themselves at those men," Maureen said.

"They're only having a bit of a laugh," Dolly said. "They're miles from home and so are those young lads. Why shouldn't they enjoy themselves while they can?"

240

Maureen smiled grudgingly. "I suppose you're right. But — Americans. Why can't they stick to their own?"

The bell tinkled and someone else came in. While Dolly served, her mind was on their conversation. She remembered how she and Janet had giggled together over the boys in the factory. She could just imagine what they'd have been like, surrounded by good-looking young men in smart uniforms. But since she'd met Tom she'd had eyes for nobody else.

A few weeks later Mrs Taylor came into the shop as she did every week to collect her rations. The little boys were at school this time and she lingered for a chat, confiding to Dolly that the Rural Dean's visit had been very pleasant and the lunch, thanks to Dolly's cooking apples, had been a great success.

"And now, I'm afraid I'm after something else," she said.

"How can I help?" Dolly was used to contributing items for church functions.

"It's the Sunday school outing. Since the war, we haven't been able to take them to the seaside. We're going to have a picnic this year, with games and races. It would be for all the village children — not just the churchgoers."

Mrs Taylor paused for breath and Dolly took the opportunity to say, "If it's food for the picnic . . ."

"The parents will provide that — everyone will bring something. No, I wondered if you . . ." She paused, then said, "I know you were once a Sunday School teacher and we wondered if you'd help with the children — organize some games perhaps."

"Well, I don't know. With the shop and everything. If it's a Saturday, we're usually quite busy."

"If you could help, I'd be so grateful. It's not for a few weeks — why not think about it and let me know."

The post office was usually closed on a Saturday and Maureen had the day off. But she offered to come in and mind the shop. Dolly wouldn't hear of it. She was sure Tom could manage on his own. Maureen's parents relied on her being there at weekends.

But Maureen insisted. "Mum and Dad can manage for one day. After all, they cope during the week."

Dolly suspected Maureen wanted an excuse to get away. She didn't have much time to herself. And when Tom agreed to mind the shop, Dolly asked Maureen to join her on the picnic.

The sun shone and the war news was better than it had been for ages. No allied shipping had been sunk since May and the Allies had invaded Sicily. It looked as if things were starting to go right at last. But Dolly couldn't stop worrying about Billy as well as her friends in London. Not that she had time to think about that today, surrounded as she was by hordes of screaming children.

The Taylors had enlisted the help of the land girls and a group of Americans from the nearby base, as well as several RAF airmen. The picnic was held in the grounds of a large house on the edge of the airfield where the RAF officers were billeted.

The children rode from the village on two hay wagons, pulled by tractors driven by the land girls. When they reached the paddock, they jumped down, screaming with excitement and started chasing each other round the field.

Dolly clutched Rowena's hand, wondering how she was ever going to organize them. "Stay close to me, Rowena," she said.

"Don't worry about her," Mrs Taylor said, coming up to Dolly with a list in her hand. "They're all quite safe here. The paddock is fenced off so the little ones can't stray. And we have plenty of people to keep an eye on them." She waved a hand to where the trestle tables had been set up.

Despite running the shop, Dolly was sure she hadn't seen so much food for years. "What a spread," she said.

"Thanks to the generosity of our American friends," the vicar's wife said. She introduced them to some of the officers who were unloading even more food from the back of a jeep — sides of ham, huge tins of fruit and, wonder of wonders — ice cream.

Some of the mothers set to opening the tins and pouring the contents into large bowls. One of them sliced the ham while another buttered a mound of bread — real butter and plenty of it. Several small boys eyed the food with ravenous eyes.

The vicar came over and said, "I think we'd better start organizing the games, otherwise we won't be able to keep them away from the food." He laughed. "I can hardly take my eyes off it myself."

He turned and blew a shrill blast on the whistle which hung round his neck. There was instant silence and he took the opportunity to divide the children into groups. The older boys were split into teams and the American officers started to initiate them into the mysteries of baseball. Another group were in the charge of the vicar and some of the fathers, running races and playing ball games.

Dolly and Maureen were left with the toddlers. They took them to a corner of the field and sat them on blankets in the shade of a huge spreading oak tree. Nursery rhymes and singing games kept them occupied for an hour until the heat of the day and the excitement tired them out and they settled for a nap.

The two women leaned against the trunk of the tree chatting quietly. "What a treat to spend an afternoon in the fresh air," Maureen said.

Dolly agreed. She sighed and looked up into the branches of the tree. It was so peaceful, who could believe the war was still raging? She tried not to think about it.

She heard the crack of the bat against the hard ball and the shouts of the boys egging each other on. Several RAF men had joined in the game, their crisp English voices contrasting strangely with the drawl of the Americans and the slow country burr of the village people. She closed her eyes and let the feeling of contentment take over.

Almost on the verge of sleep, she felt a nudge in her ribs. "I think that bloke's eying you up," Maureen said, laughing.

"Don't be silly," Dolly said, blinking against the strong sun. She sat up straighter and looked again. There was something familiar about the thin figure staring at her through thick glasses. "Oh, my goodness, it's Pete," she murmured.

"Who's Pete?" Maureen asked as Dolly pulled herself to her feet.

He came towards her, a big grin splitting his face. "Dolly, it is you. I wasn't sure at first. What are you doing here? Did you join up? Are you a land girl?" The questions tumbled over themselves and Dolly laid a hand on his arm.

"Yes, Pete, it's really me. I live here — well in Borstall Green just up the road. And you — you must be stationed here."

"I don't understand. Were you evacuated?"

The vicar appeared behind them. "Ah, I see you've met Flight Lieutenant Crawford," he said.

"We knew each other in London — went to school together," Dolly said, blushing, remembering the ten year old who'd vowed to marry him when she grew up.

"Fancy that," said Mr Taylor. "Well, Flight Lieutenant, it was a good day for us when Mr and Mrs Marchant took over our village shop. They've become a real part of our little community."

"Mrs Marchant? So you married him then?"

Dolly nodded. After the first surge of pleasure at seeing her old friend, she felt a bit awkward. She'd successfully put her old life behind her — so she thought. Pete was bound to ask how she'd come to leave London.

245

Maureen was getting the little ones to their feet and tidying them ready for tea. She seized the excuse of needing to help her and returned to the group. But Pete followed her.

"So — you really got married. It's that bloke from the market, isn't it?" he asked.

Before she could reply, Rowena came toddling towards her on her little fat legs. "Mummy, you left me," she pouted.

"No, I didn't, darling. I was just across the field there talking to the vicar. Anyway Auntie Maureen was there." Dolly picked the little girl up and settled her on her hip. "Pete, say hello to my daughter. This is Rowena."

"She's beautiful."

Dolly introduced Pete to her friend and the three of them shepherded the little ones to the table where they sat them on benches under an awning. The older children helped themselves from the other table and sat with their plates on the grass. When one or two of them hesitantly approached with their now empty plates, the American officer laughed. "It's OK, boys. Eat as much as you like. There's plenty more where that came from."

The vicar looked disapproving. There would be a lot of upset tummies tonight. But he couldn't say anything in the face of their allies' generosity. He shrugged and bit into his own ham sandwich.

Dolly was kept busy making sure the little ones got their share of the food and that it went into their mouths and not down their clothes. But every time she

246

looked up, Pete was gazing at her. She began to feel a little uncomfortable and thought she shouldn't have greeted him so enthusiastically. She didn't want him getting the wrong idea.

The long afternoon drew to a close as the vicar led the children in hymn singing, while the officers — British and American — dismantled the tables and cleared away the debris. The dirty crockery, which had been loaned from the air force canteen, was piled into a couple of tin baths to be taken back and washed up by the mess orderlies.

Mrs Taylor smiled at the thought. "Washing up is one of the worst chores of these events," she said, helping the ladies parcel up the left-over food, so that each child had some to take home.

When the hay wagons arrived for the ride home, Dolly turned to Pete, determined to make her goodbyes short. With luck they wouldn't bump into each other again. He was talking to Maureen and she smiled with relief. He'd probably forgotten that last intense letter he'd written — it had been several years after all. Now, he certainly seemed to be getting on well with her friend.

She climbed into the wagon, leaning down to offer her hand to Maureen. But Pete had already lifted her up. "It was nice to meet you, Miss Lee. And lovely to see you again, Dolly," he said. "Maybe I'll pop into your shop next time I'm off duty."

The wagons pulled away, bumping over the grass and making the children squeal. Dolly laughed. It had been a lovely day and it had ended happily too. She was convinced that Pete liked Maureen and, when her friend mentioned his name she went rather pink.

Dolly didn't tell Tom about the meeting with Pete. She didn't know why. After all, she had nothing to hide. But, despite more than three years of marriage, Tom still seemed uneasy when confronted with anyone from her early life. It was as if he thought their happiness might be threatened in some way. But hadn't she willingly left friends and family to follow him? Surely he must realize that no one could come between them — not even her childhood sweetheart.

But something stopped her from mentioning that Pete was stationed just up the road at the RAF fighter base and that they'd met at the picnic. She might have known she hadn't seen the last of him though.

He came into the shop on a pouring wet day towards the end of August. Dolly was busy with a customer when the bell over the door jangled. She finished serving and looked up. An airman was talking to Maureen through the grille which separated the post office from the main shop.

She smiled when she noticed the other woman had taken her glasses off and her cheeks had flushed a delicate pink. It wasn't until the man took his cap off and ran his hands through his ginger hair that Dolly realized it was Pete.

She slipped through the connecting door into the living room where Rowena was playing with her bricks in her playpen. Tom had just come in and was standing by the sink, towelling his hair. He'd been outside, repairing the lean-to which housed their store of winter logs.

"What a day," he said. "Not too busy in the shop then?"

"I think the rain's keeping them away."

"I've put the kettle on. Maybe we can sit down and enjoy a cuppa together for a change."

"Maureen's got a customer but I'll take her tea through when it's made," Dolly said. She still didn't tell him who the customer was and afterwards she wished she had.

Tom lifted Rowena out of the playpen and sat at the kitchen table with her on his knee. He kissed her and she chuckled. Dolly smiled watching them. She was so like Tom, with her dark curls and brown eyes, her ready smile and sunny nature.

The kettle began to whistle and Dolly made the tea, re-using the tea leaves from breakfast with the addition of one fresh spoonful. It didn't taste too bad and they were used to it by now.

Pete was still there when Dolly took Maureen's cup through and put it on the shelf under the counter. His face lit up when he saw her. "Dolly, I thought I was going to miss you. How are you?"

"Fine thanks, Pete. What brings you to Borstall Green then?" It was five miles from the base, a long way to come in this weather.

"I borrowed a motorbike. Had to go into town so I thought I'd drop by on my way back — say hello, you know. Didn't have much chance to talk at the picnic."

It seemed quite a feeble story to Dolly. "Well, nice as it is to see you, Pete, I am rather busy." She didn't want to talk to him, especially with Tom liable to come in at any minute. She smiled. "Anyway, I got the impression you came to see Maureen, not me."

Pete blushed and Maureen began furiously stamping a pile of forms.

"I'll leave you to it then," Dolly said and retreated to the back room.

Pete turned up at the shop whenever he could get away and Dolly was pleased that he seemed to be getting on so well with Maureen. They went to the cinema in Chichester, Maureen on the pillion of the motorcycle, clinging on with grim determination, and after that he often came by to give her a lift home. He'd even been invited to tea at the Lees' bungalow.

Tom commented on how Maureen had blossomed since getting a boyfriend. But still Dolly didn't confess she'd known Pete in London.

She and Maureen were sitting at the kitchen table sorting out the ration coupons and ministry forms while Rowena played quietly on the floor beside them. Tom was minding the shop. Dolly looked up as the one o'clock news came on. Italy had capitulated at last and there was speculation that they would declare war on Germany and come in on the side of the Allies.

"Does that mean the war might soon be over, do you think?" Maureen asked.

"I don't think so, but it can only help. One less front for our boys to fight on," Dolly replied.

They both tensed at the sound of aircraft overhead, the heavy drone of American bombers on yet another daylight raid. It was a sound they never got used to.

Maureen sighed. "Thank goodness Pete doesn't fly," she said.

"He wanted to, but he knew when he joined up his eyesight would let him down."

"You knew him well, didn't you? He often talks about his childhood, how you were his only friend at primary school."

"Well, he was my only friend too. He was bullied a lot because of his glasses and being brainy. As for me — I didn't fit in either." Dolly couldn't tell Maureen the names they'd called her — just because she didn't have a father and her mother hadn't been married when she was born. She couldn't tell her either that one of her chief tormenters had been her stepsister, Ruby. "We stood up to the bullies together. But things changed when he went to the grammar school and then to university. We grew apart." She stacked a pile of forms together then glanced up at Maureen. "You like him, don't you?"

"Yes, very much."

"I'm glad you two met. I hope things work out for you both." Dolly went back to her work. She was pleased. They both deserved to be happy. She hid a little smile, thinking of Mrs Crawford and her ambitions for her only son. Surely she'd be more accepting of Maureen Lee than the illegitimate Dolly Dixon.

251

CHAPTER
TWENTY-THREE

Tom leaned on the bar of the Plough, sipping his half pint of weak beer and listening to the murmur of conversation around him. As usual they were talking about the war. Since Italy's declaration of war on Germany there was a feeling that the Allies would invade Europe soon and that would be an end to it. Tom hoped they were right.

After years of coping with shortages and rationing he was beginning to think he was in the wrong business. Still, he didn't regret the move to the village. It had turned out better than he'd hoped and at last he was beginning to relax a little too, no longer constantly looking over his shoulder. There was little danger of someone from his past turning up here and, now he dealt with wholesalers nearer home, there was no need to go to London where he'd risk bumping into Arthur Rose and his cronies.

"Want another?" Bill Rogers, the Home Guard platoon sergeant, gestured at Tom's almost empty glass.

"No thanks."

Bill drained his glass and put it on the bar. "I'd better not either. The missus gets a bit fidgety if I'm late."

252

The two men left the pub and stood outside looking up into the clear frosty sky. It was eerily quiet, but later Tom knew he would hear the drone of the big bombers returning from their nightly raids over Hamburg.

"Beautiful, in't it," Bill said. "Hard to imagine what's going on over there." He jerked his head towards the Downs and the sea behind them.

Tom nodded agreement and started up the lane towards the shop.

Bill fell into step beside him. "Don't suppose there'll be many more of these exercises," he said.

"They'll be disbanding the unit. Not much call for Home Guard nowadays."

"Pity," Bill said with a laugh. "Good excuse to get away from the missus for a couple of hours."

Tom laughed too. But he couldn't imagine wanting to get away from Dorothy. He enjoyed her company, working alongside her in the shop, their rare moments of relaxation in front of the fire with Rowena tucked up in bed. It was all so different from his life with Freda — the constant griping and rows.

Tom's contentment lasted until the next day when he came through to the shop and said his usual cheerful "good morning" to Maureen, who'd just removed the grille from the post office and was settling down behind her counter. Dorothy was still in the kitchen clearing their breakfast things and getting Rowena settled with her toys.

"Good morning, Mr Marchant." Maureen's voice was more subdued than usual.

"What's up — boyfriend trouble?"

Maureen gave him a stricken look and burst into tears. Tom wished he'd kept his big mouth shut.

"Oh, Gawd, I'm sorry, love. What have I said?" He patted her arm awkwardly.

Maureen fumbled for a handkerchief and sniffed into it. "I'm sorry, it's just . . ." The sobs increased in volume and Tom, not knowing what else to do, called for Dorothy.

She came in wiping her hands on her apron, took one look at Maureen and roughly shoved Tom out of the way. "Come on, love. I'll make you a nice cup of tea." She guided her friend towards the door leading to the kitchen. "You'll have to mind the shop for a bit, Tom. I'll come back and give you a hand when I've sorted her out."

The bell over the door signalled the arrival of a customer and for the next half hour Tom was kept busy between selling stamps and postal orders and weighing out minute portions of cheese and bacon.

While he served the flow of customers, keeping up his usual flow of cheeky banter as he did so, Tom kept one ear cocked towards the kitchen door. He hoped they weren't going to have trouble with Maureen. It was hard getting staff these days.

The last customer left and Tom decided to hurry them up. Surely Maureen had calmed down by now. He'd probably open the door to find them sitting at the table drinking tea and gossiping or playing with Rowena.

254

He had his hand on the doorknob when Maureen's voice came, loud, hysterical. "He doesn't love me at all, he never did." He withdrew his hand. Better leave them a bit longer, she'd feel better once she got it out of her system. But her next words kept him fixed to the spot. "It's you he loves, Dolly. He never stops talking about you. Why didn't you tell me he felt that way about you?"

Tom held his breath, waiting for Dorothy's reply. "Don't be silly, Maureen. All that was years ago. Anyway, there was never anything — you know, like that — between us."

"Well, he seems to think there was."

"Nonsense, I hadn't even thought about him since I left London." Dorothy sighed and Tom waited tensely for her next words. "It was such a shock when I saw him at the picnic. But, Maureen, I was never in love with him — I don't care what he told you."

Tom clenched his fists. His first impulse was to barge in there and demand to know what she meant. She'd obviously known this bloke before and now that he came to think of it, she'd mentioned someone called Pete when he first knew her — an old school friend.

Maureen's voice again, husky with crying. "Well, all I know is, he's still in love with you. He as much as admitted that he only comes to the shop in hopes of seeing you."

"So why did he ask you out then?"

"He said he needed a friend, someone to talk to. I might have known he wasn't interested in me." Maureen's voice trailed off.

Unable to bear any more, Tom pushed the kitchen door open. Forcing his voice to remain steady he said, "Been a bit busy out there. Any chance of you two doing any work today?"

Maureen pushed her chair back and dabbed at her eyes. "I'm sorry, Mr Marchant." She shoved past him, letting the door swing shut behind her.

"What was that all about?" He waited tensely for Dorothy to tell him, to confess that she'd known Pete before. Surely, if she had nothing to hide, she'd speak up. But she looked at him steadily through those clear blue eyes.

"Poor Maureen, I think she read too much into this friendship. She's fallen in love, but he's not ready to commit himself."

"Maybe he's already got a girlfriend, maybe he's in love with someone else," Tom said, challenging her. This was her chance to tell him. He thought she coloured slightly but she turned her head away, got up and went to the sink, emptying the tea leaves into the drainer.

He couldn't stand it. He strode towards her, grabbing her wrist. "Tell me what's going on."

"I don't know what you're talking about." Her voice shook. "Leave go of me, Tom. You're hurting. Besides, you're frightening Rowena."

He dropped her wrist and she rubbed at the red mark he'd left. He thought she was going to cry. Conscious of the child, he tried to keep the anger out of his voice. "I heard what Maureen said. There is

256

something going on — otherwise you would have told me you knew that bloke back in London."

"I didn't tell you precisely because I knew how you'd react. You don't even like me having women friends — let alone a man. And that's all he is Tom — a friend."

"But she said he was in love with you . . ."

"Maybe he is. But that doesn't mean I return the feeling." She put a hand out, an imploring gesture. "Tom, it's you I love. You must know that."

"But you encouraged him, Dorothy. You must have told him where you lived when you met him at the picnic. And why else would he turn up here unless he hoped to see you and take up where he left off?"

Dorothy glared at him. "You don't trust me — that's it, isn't it. Well, if that's how you feel, there's no more to be said." She picked up the teapot and banged it down hard on the draining board. "It's time for Rowena's nap. And you'd better go and help Maureen — as you said, it's busy out there."

She snatched the toddler up and disappeared up the narrow twisting staircase.

Tom went back into the shop where Maureen was trying to do two people's work. He sent her back behind the post office grille and took over the grocery counter. For the rest of the morning as he weighed cheese, apologized for the small amount of butter available and juggled points for tins of spam and sardines, he hoped no one noticed that he wasn't quite his usual self. But he couldn't get the thought of Dorothy and the ginger-haired RAF officer out of his mind.

Pete Crawford wasn't much to look at, but he was a cut above the rough and ready market trader that Tom still was at heart. He'd been to university, would probably get a swank job after the war. He had so much more to offer than Tom — and he was free to marry. The last thought niggled at Tom like a hollow tooth. Deep down he trusted Dorothy. And he knew she loved him and trusted him, but he didn't deserve that trust.

He didn't blame her when she served his dinner in silence. He'd give her a bit of time, then try to make amends. But when they crawled exhausted into bed that night, for the first time in their life together she turned away from him when he reached for her. He lay listening to her even breathing, knowing she wasn't really asleep, unsure how to begin to heal the breach between them.

As he fell asleep he resolved to go to London again. As soon as he could find an excuse to get away, he'd go and see Freda, try to get her to see sense. If she'd divorce him, he could at least come clean with Dorothy. And once they were really man and wife, no one would be able to come between them.

Tom had gone off to a Home Guard lecture after eating his tea in silence and Dolly sighed with relief. It had been weeks since the row over her friendship with Pete and she couldn't stand much more of this cold atmosphere. Still, it was partly her fault. When he'd tried to apologize, she'd shrugged it off and he hadn't tried again. The longer the silence went on, the harder it was to break it.

Well, she wouldn't give in. She hadn't done anything wrong and she wasn't going to forgive his lack of trust just like that. Still, she wished he'd say something, even if it provoked another row. At least it would clear the air.

She crashed the crockery into the sink and poured hot water from the kettle.

"Mummy cross?"

Dolly turned, ashamed of her bad mood, and lifted Rowena from her high chair, hugging her tightly. "No, lovie, I'm not cross, just a bit tired."

She left the washing-up and carried Rowena over to the armchair in front of the blazing log fire. She leaned back, closing her eyes and stroking Rowena's dark curls, feeling the child relax and settle into a doze. The tension drained out of her. She was tired. It wasn't just running the shop and bringing up a child. It was the constant broken nights, the never being able to relax. Every night the drone of the bombers on their way across the Channel kept her awake.

Now, there was another worry. More men were being called up and Tom had been for a medical last week. He was still waiting to hear if he'd be passed fit. He was certainly in better shape than when they got married. The scar had faded and these days she scarcely noticed it. But occasionally he still suffered from violent headaches and, although he no longer walked with a pronounced limp, there were days when she knew he was in pain.

He tried not to let anyone see it, holding his own with his fellow Home Guards on their route marches and exercises. As rumours grew that the invasion of Europe wasn't far off, Dolly knew it was quite possible Tom would be called up. She shivered at the thought. But she'd have to cope, like thousands of other women. And she knew she could too. She'd keep the shop running, feed the chickens, dig the garden — anything if it meant that the war would end and Tom would come back to her and they could go back to how things had been.

Rowena stirred in her arms and Dolly gave a little laugh. Silly me, she thought, picturing him already marching off and leaving me when the chances are everything will be all right. As she got up and began to get Rowena ready for bed, she made a resolution. She'd never forgive herself if Tom had to go off and fight before things had been straightened out between them. As soon as he got home she would sit down and have a long talk with him. It didn't matter who was in the wrong — someone had to make the first move.

Dolly woke suddenly, shivering, squinting at the clock on the bedside table. She sat up abruptly. It was after eight o'clock. Why hadn't Tom woken her?

She got out of bed and went over to lift the edge of the blackout curtain. A misty drizzle obscured the view of the garden. A figure loomed out of the mist — Tom was feeding the chickens. She shivered and pulled an old cardigan on over her nightdress, went into Rowena's room. The little girl was sitting up in bed talking to her rag doll.

260

Dolly took her downstairs and put her in her high chair, filled the kettle and put it on the stove. The door opened, wafting in damp air and a hint of autumn. Tom put the basket of eggs on the table, tickled Rowena under her chin.

"Here's a nice egg for your breakfast, lovie," he said, ignoring Dolly.

She sighed, wishing he hadn't come in so late last night. She'd struggled to stay awake, determined to have a heart to heart with him before things went beyond repair. She'd woken once in the night and for a long time listened to him snoring, smelling the beer on his breath. He wasn't a drinking man and she knew he must be really fed up to be spending so much time in the Plough with his Home Guard cronies.

She put his breakfast in front of him and sat down opposite. "Tom, there's something I want to say."

"Aren't you having any breakfast?" he asked.

"Not hungry, too much on my mind. Look, we have to clear the air."

"Don't worry — the air's cleared."

"What do you mean?"

"What I mean is — that RAF chap's not going to be bothering you any more."

"What do you mean — Tom, what have you done?"

"Put a flea in his ear, that's what." Tom took a slurp of his tea and put the cup down with a bang. "Saw him in the pub last night — I told him, no more coming round here to see his *friend*. She's my wife, keep away from her, I said."

"Oh, Tom, you didn't have to do that. I told you — there's nothing going on. Why won't you trust me?" Dolly leaned towards him, tears in her eyes. "I've never done anything to be ashamed of."

An odd expression passed over his face. "I know you haven't, Dorothy." He pushed his plate away and stood up. "It's just — I can't help being jealous. I hate the thought of another bloke even looking at you."

Dolly managed a small smile. She wiped Rowena's chin and helped her take another spoonful of porridge. "I don't see that many looking," she said, trying to make a joke.

"They'd better not," Tom snarled, and went through to the shop.

She listened to him slamming the bolts back on the shop door, crashing around, making a noise as he always did when he was upset about something. Anger replaced the tears. Why should she try to placate him when it was all in his mind? The way he was carrying on you'd think he was the one with something to hide. A cold finger touched her heart. Was that it? Was he accusing her to cover up his own guilt?

When he came back into the kitchen and announced that he was off to London, she couldn't help wondering who he was going to see. Did he have a fancy woman up there? Accusing her of having an affair could have given him an excuse to look up one of his old flames. She wanted to beg him not to go.

But she said nothing. When she entered the shop Tom was sorting through the mail — more forms from the ministry, though there weren't as many these days thanks to the paper shortage. As she did every morning she wondered if there might be a letter from Janet. She'd hadn't heard from her, despite writing several times herself. She couldn't bear to think that her friend had forgotten her but that was better than imagining something far worse. She shuddered, picturing the crater in Seaton Road where her own home had once stood. If Tom was in a better mood she might have asked him to call and make sure her friend was all right.

"Any letters for me?" she asked.

"Just a lot of business stuff — your department," Tom said passing her a bundle of brown envelopes. He kept one back and shoved it in his jacket pocket.

"What's that?"

"Home Guard stuff."

"Aren't you going to read it?"

"No time. I'd better get on the road if I want to be back before dark." Tom left the shop, returning a few minutes later with his cap and scarf on. He bent and kissed Dolly's cheek — a brief peck, not the passionate breath-taking kisses that she'd been used to. She held on to the lapels of his jacket, wanting to say something, desperate for them to be back on their old footing. But the words wouldn't come. "Take care," she whispered past the lump in her throat.

He pulled away and seconds later she heard the van start up. She listened until the sound died away then forced her mind to the pile of bills and forms waiting for her.

Business was slow this morning and Dolly decided to leave Maureen to cope and try to get some household chores done. Normally, on a quiet morning like this, she'd have enjoyed a chat with Maureen. But since the row over Pete, things hadn't been the same. They no longer exchanged confidences, or giggled and gossiped over tea in the room behind the shop.

Dolly had tried, but her efforts at friendliness met with a rebuff. Maureen had even reverted to calling her Mrs Marchant. Dolly was sorry the romance with Pete hadn't worked out, but it wasn't her fault. If only I'd never gone on that blasted picnic, she thought for the hundredth time. As if the rationing, the sleepless nights, the constant draining fatigue weren't enough to cope with.

Still, it wouldn't hurt to take Maureen a cup of tea and make one more effort. The poor girl was obviously still unhappy.

The shop was empty. Despite the sunshine it was bitterly cold and there wasn't a soul about in the village street.

"Why don't you come through to the kitchen and drink your tea?" Dolly said.

"I don't think I should leave the post office counter unattended," Maureen said.

"Nonsense, we'll hear the bell if anyone comes in. Come and get warm — you look frozen."

Maureen got down from her stool reluctantly and followed Dolly into the kitchen.

"Are you all right, Maureen? You look a bit pale."

Maureen's reply was to burst into tears. She hadn't been her usual self since she'd broken up with Pete, but Dolly thought she'd got over it.

She patted the other woman's shoulder awkwardly. "Is it Pete?"

Maureen blew her nose. "Not really. I'm still upset about the way he treated me, letting me think it was me he was interested in. But . . ." She paused. "I don't know how to tell you . . ."

"What is it?"

"I've given in my notice to the post office and I'm going into the WAAF's."

"The WAAF's?" For a minute Dolly could hardly take it in. How would she cope with the post office and telephone exchange as well as everything else?

"I had to do something, Dolly. I was so miserable and I blamed you — I know I shouldn't but I did. I just wanted to get away. When I went into town and signed up, I wasn't thinking clearly."

"And now? Do you still want to leave?"

"I'm not sure," Maureen confessed. "I just felt so awful having to face you every day, knowing if I hadn't opened my big mouth, everything would still be all right between you and Mr Marchant."

"That's not your fault — he's just being pigheaded. If he used his common sense, he'd realize . . ." Dolly sighed and pushed her cup away. "Look, that's between me and him. We'll sort ourselves out; it's you I'm worried about." It was true, she realized. Her initial reaction had been selfish. "If you've changed your mind, I'm sure we could do something about it. After all, you were exempt from call-up because of your work here. If I said I couldn't manage without you, I'm sure —"

"No," Maureen interrupted. "I don't want to leave you in the lurch, but I was only upset because I didn't know how to tell you. Truthfully, though, I'm a bit excited."

"Have you told your parents yet?"

Maureen nodded. "They're not happy about it, but it's my life and now that I've told you, I can't wait. I just didn't know how to break it to you."

"When do you go?"

"Next week." Maureen's eyes glowed and her cheeks were pink. She was a different girl to the one who'd mooched around so miserably in the past weeks.

Dolly — now that she'd got over the initial shock — was pleased. There was something to be said for this war, she supposed. It had given women like Maureen the chance of an independent life.

It wasn't until she'd closed the shop and settled Rowena down for her afternoon nap, that she had time to sit down and tackle the paperwork that had piled up, including the letters that had come that morning. As she tore open the envelopes, she remembered the one Tom had shoved in his pocket.

CHAPTER
TWENTY-FOUR

As Tom turned the van into the main road, a convoy of lorries and tanks passed. There had been a lot of activity in the area recently and he wondered if rumours of the invasion were true.

The thought reminded him of the letter in his pocket which he guessed contained his call-up papers. He'd been expecting it since his medical a week or two back and in a way it was a relief. At least he'd be shot of Dorothy and her reproachful looks. Who was he kidding? Truthfully, he dreaded leaving her. For, although things hadn't been right between them for weeks, Tom loved her — and he knew she loved him. He'd been wrong to accuse her; his jealousy in the heat of the moment had got the better of him, that's all. And they'd both said things they regretted. Let's hope he could make amends before he had to leave.

But first he had to see Freda.

By the time he reached the outskirts of London, he was feeling depressed. More than four years of war had taken its toll. Boarded up shops, gaping windows, and piles of rubble made him appreciate he had nothing to complain of. They'd had their share of sleepless nights; the odd incendiary on the outskirts of the village; a stray bomb which had fallen behind the pub, killing a herd of cows, but somehow things didn't seem so bad in the country.

As he drove slowly towards Shepherd's Bush, he realized how stupid he'd been to let this business with Pete Crawford fester inside him like that. He should be thanking his stars for the good life he enjoyed, despite the war, the rationing, and the constant worry.

He pulled up at the door of what had once been his home, dreading the confrontation to come, but he had to see Freda, sort things out once and for all. There was no shirking it.

He walked up the short front path, knocked firmly at the front door, looking around at the once familiar street. The paint on the houses was peeling and the railings had gone, leaving the low walls scarred and pitted. The net curtains of his former home drooped, grey and heavy with dust. He saw a movement behind the dirty glass and a second later the door opened.

"So, you've turned up like a bad penny." Freda didn't remove the cigarette from her mouth as she spoke. She was wearing a dark blue boiler suit, tightly belted to reveal her curvy figure. Her hair was rolled into a turban, a few blonde wisps escaping and curling round her face.

Despite the rather masculine clothes, she looked as pretty as ever, her face carefully made up as usual, and Tom stared at her, remembering why he'd been attracted to her in the first place. She still wasn't a patch on his Dorothy though.

She raised a plucked eyebrow. "Are you going to stand on the doorstep all day so the neighbours can get an eyeful?" She opened the door wider.

Tom stepped into the narrow passage and she leaned towards him, brushing her lips against his cheek. The familiar smell of "Evening in Paris" enveloped him and he wondered how she'd managed to get hold of her favourite perfume. Of course, her brother was king of the black market, wasn't he? Or maybe she had another source of supply. He couldn't imagine Freda going without a man all this time.

He followed her into the back room. Nothing had changed. The chairs were still draped with clothes, the tablecloth stained and littered with crumbs. Piles of dirty crockery adorned the sink under the window.

She saw him looking and laughed. "Don't have time for housework now I'm a working girl." She took a drag of her cigarette and twirled round. "Like the outfit? Sexy isn't it — at least the blokes in the factory think so." She came close to him, took another drag and blew smoke in his face, laughing again. "Don't try to pretend, Tom. I know you still fancy me."

"You must be joking."

Before he could say anything else her hand came out and slapped his face. "What you doing 'ere then? And don't tell me you came to see the brat. You haven't been for nigh on years so you needn't think you can just walk in here and start playing the loving father."

The temptation to slap her in return was almost too great, but Tom clenched his fists in his pockets. His fingers closed round the unopened letter. That would shut her up, him having to join the Army, he thought, remembering the last time he'd seen her. She hadn't missed the opportunity to taunt him, especially as her brother Derek hadn't wriggled out of his call-up.

He wouldn't tell her yet though. "I don't deny it would be nice to see Tony," he said mildly.

"He's forgotten he ever had a father," Freda snapped, stubbing her cigarette out.

"I don't blame him — I haven't been a very good father, have I?" That shocked her and for a moment she was silent. Tom seized his opportunity. "Look, Freda, I know we parted on bad terms but I need to straighten things out."

Her eyes softened and she leaned towards him again. Oh, God, this was turning out all wrong. Why couldn't he just say the words "*I want a divorce*"? It couldn't be that hard. But he'd tried before and she either went all soppy and talked about the Church or else screamed at him like a fishwife.

Her lips parted and her eyes were moist. "I've missed you, Tom. I know I behaved badly, but . . ."

He gripped her arms just above the elbows and held her firmly away from him. "Listen to me, Freda. I don't care any more. It's all in the past. I just want . . ."

Her fingers fumbled with his tie, the buttons on his shirt. "I know what you want, Tom."

"You've got it all wrong, Freda." He pushed her away and pulled the envelope from his pocket, waving it under her nose. "I came to tell you I've been called up, and I want to straighten things out between us — but not the way you thought."

Her face changed, eyes narrowing, mouth pinched. "I might have known — goes off for years not even letting his own son know where he is and then comes waltzing back here to 'straighten things out'. Well, let me straighten out one or two things for you, Tom Marchant. I'm still Mrs Marchant and I shall expect an Army allowance from you. It's *my* name going on your paybook as next of kin, not some floozy you've been shacking up with." She snatched the envelope, but he grabbed it back, shoving it in his pocket.

He spoke quietly, firmly. "There's no floozy in my life, Freda. You're the only floozy I ever got involved with and I rue the day I ever laid eyes on you."

She flew at him then, scarlet nails reaching for his face, but he held her off. "That makes two of us," she screeched. "But don't think I'll divorce you. You're stuck with me, Tom Marchant, and you'll support me and my son whether you like it or not."

"I always intended to support Tony, there's money going in the bank for him every month as it is. But he'll have to wait for it till he's older. I don't want you spending it on booze and fags." He pushed her away and walked into the passage.

She ran after him, pulling at his arm. "Don't go, Tom. I didn't mean it. I just seem to say the wrong thing when you're around," she sobbed.

He ignored her and pulled the front door open. Her sobs turned to shrieks of fury and she pounded his back and shoulders with clenched fists. "Go then — and don't come back. But don't think you're getting away with anything. I'll find out where you live and by

271

the time my brothers've finished with you, you'll wish they'd done the job properly last time."

Tom strode down the path and got into the van, fixing his eyes on the dashboard as she stood in the doorway screaming insults. When he'd stopped shaking he took a deep breath and switched the engine on, praying it would start first time. If he had to get out and use the starting handle he wasn't sure he'd be able to resist bashing her with it.

The engine coughed and spluttered, then fired into life. He pulled away and drove round the corner. He couldn't wait to get back to Borstall Green and Dorothy.

Slowing down at the next junction he spotted a small scruffy boy mooching along, hands in pockets, head down, kicking at a piece of rubble from one of the bomb sites. The shock of black wavy hair was unmistakable. It was Tony. He stopped the van and wound the window down.

"Hello, son. Just finished school?" Trite, banal words, but he couldn't think what to say, wasn't even sure if the boy would recognize him. And why should he after all this time?

"My mum says I mustn't talk to strange men," the boy said, eyeing him suspiciously.

"Well, I'm not a strange man."

"Yes, you are. Least I ain't seen you round 'ere before."

Tom tried to smile but his heart was breaking. Tony didn't know him but he couldn't upset him by trying to

272

explain. "I used to live round here myself. I know you — Tony Marchant isn't it?"

The boy scuffed his shoe against the pavement and shrugged. "Might be. Who are you then?"

It was tempting, but Tom held back. "I'm an old friend of the family. Know your mum quite well, actually." That was true at least.

Tony's lip curled. "Oh, one of mum's fancy blokes, eh?" He ran off down the road, turning to stick his thumb to his nose and shout an obscenity, before disappearing round the corner.

Tom swore and cursed his way through the streets of London, sighing with relief when he finally found himself on the Guildford road. What a fool he'd been to imagine that Freda would see reason. And that encounter with Tony had really shaken him up. Freda didn't deserve a son. He should have grabbed the boy, told him who he was and that he was going to live with his dad from now on. Now he laughed at himself, a cynical laugh. Imagine Dorothy's face if he walked in with a strange lad, the explaining he'd have to do.

He pounded the steering wheel in frustration, seeking an answer to his dilemma. Maybe he'd have done better to see a solicitor. He surely had enough grounds to divorce Freda, if she wouldn't divorce him. And maybe he'd get custody of Tony, seeing the way his mother lived. But then Dorothy would have to know. There was no way he could keep that secret.

The thought frightened him. If she ever discovered what he'd done, he'd lose her for sure. He started shaking again and stopped the van. Good job he was being called up — at least he'd be away from it all and maybe a jerry bullet would solve the problem for him. That wouldn't solve the problem of who got his marriage allowance though.

Well, it would be Dorothy, of course. She was his true wife, despite the false marriage certificate. How would anyone know? And Freda didn't know where he lived, he'd covered his tracks pretty well, she wouldn't be able to find him.

Reassured by this last thought, Tom wiped a hand over his face and squared his shoulders. He'd just try to put this whole episode out of his mind. First thing when he got home, he'd apologize to Dorothy for being such a fool over that Pete bloke, try to get things sorted out with her. Then he'd have to break it to her that he was leaving for the Army. But when? It suddenly struck him that he hadn't even opened the letter, didn't know where or when he was supposed to report for duty.

He tore the envelope open, squinting in the faint light from the dashboard. "*Regret to inform you that you have not been passed as fit for active service.*" He blinked and read it again, his heart pounding. All his actions today had been based on the idea that he'd be joining the Army, that he ought to get his affairs in order just in case . . .

Tom started to laugh, hoarse hysterical laughter. He hardly realized when it turned to tears, great racking sobs that shook his body. At last he shuddered and sighed, wiped his face again and started the van.

He drove faster than he should have through the dark Sussex lanes, anxious to get home to Dorothy; to tell her he loved her; tell her again that he'd never doubted her, and that all he needed to make him happy was her and their little girl.

The shop and house were in darkness when he got home. He went round to the back door, closing it behind him quickly, anxious not to let the light spill out.

Dorothy was dozing in the armchair in front of the fire, Rowena on her lap, pink and rosy from her bath. He stood for a moment, watching, thinking he'd never seen a more beautiful sight.

She opened her eyes and smiled. "Tom, you're home. I've been worried."

He knelt in front of the armchair, kissing the top of Rowena's head and enfolding his wife in a hug.

"I've been behaving like an idiot. Can you forgive me?" he asked.

"I love you, Tom — of course I forgive you."

He kissed her, the sort of kiss he'd been missing lately. Rowena squealed, squashed between them as he and Dorothy clung together. He gave a shaky laugh. "Better put her to bed, you and I have some catching up to do."

Much later, curled up on his lap in the big armchair, her arms twined round his neck, she gave a throaty little laugh. "What brought all that on?" she murmured.

"I had time to think while I was out today — and I realized that you and Ro are the most important things in my life." He reached for his jacket and pulled the letter out of the pocket.

"I got this today. Didn't bother to open it 'cause I thought I knew what it was. I was terrified at the thought of leaving you, didn't know how to tell you. When I found out I didn't have to go, I realized how lucky I am."

Dorothy kissed him. "Tom, dearest, I've always known how lucky *I* am." She reached out and plucked the letter from his hand, wrinkling her nose as she did so. "The secretary who typed this must use a strong perfume. If I didn't know better I'd think you'd been with another woman."

The words were said lightly, with a smile, but Tom's stomach heaved. *Evening in bloody Paris.* He managed a laugh. "You're the only woman in my life." It was true. As far as he was concerned Freda no longer existed.

He screwed the letter up and threw it in the fire. He never wanted to smell *Evening in Paris* again. His arms went round Dorothy, his lips sought hers, ready to make love again. She responded eagerly, just as she used to before he'd made a fool of himself with his jealousy.

The fire crackled and flames licked at the envelope, illuminating part of the address — ". . . ll Green, Chichester". Freda had snatched at it before he pushed her away. Had she seen the address? His body responded to Dorothy's lips and hands, but his mind was in turmoil again. Would he ever be free of this nagging fear of discovery?

276

CHAPTER
TWENTY-FIVE

Dolly wasn't feeling well. She looked in the mirror, horrified at the pallor of her face, the dark shadows under her eyes, the way her hair hung in lank strands. She'd lost weight too. What was wrong with her?

She brushed her hair vigorously, applied a smudge of lipstick but it wasn't much of an improvement. Well, she didn't have time to spend prettying herself up. Since Maureen had left she hadn't had a minute to herself. They hadn't found anyone to replace her and Dolly now did all the post office and telephone work, as well as the books while Tom looked after the grocery side of things.

She put on her flowered overall and went downstairs, relieved that Tom had already seen to the chickens and brought the eggs in, lit the fire and put the kettle on.

Rowena was toddling round getting under their feet. She was getting to be quite a handful, curious about everything, always grabbing at things and asking questions. If only she weren't so tired all the time, Dolly would have been pleased her daughter was so bright.

She sighed impatiently, picked the child up and put her in the high chair where she immediately began to protest, wriggling to get down.

"Sit still. You can get down when we've had breakfast," Dolly said sharply.

Tom turned to her, surprised. "What's got into you — snapping at the kid like that."

"She's got to learn she can't have her own way all the time." She cut off a crust and gave it to Rowena, hoping that would keep her quiet for a few minutes.

Tom put his hand on her arm. "It's not like you to be so tetchy. Is there something wrong?"

Dolly softened at the anxious look in his eyes. She leaned against him and he put his arms round her. "I'm just so tired." She shouldn't complain. It was no worse for her than for everyone else. She shuddered. Last night what sounded like hundreds of bombers had gone over on their way to Germany and she'd lain awake until the last of them droned away overhead. Would it never end?

Tom kissed her cheek. "Sit down, love. I'll do breakfast. Plenty of time before we open up."

She smiled gratefully, sinking into a chair at the table. She leaned across and stroked Rowena's cheek. "Sorry I got cross, lovie. Mummy's just tired."

Rowena responded with a smile and a chuckle. At least she didn't grizzle for long.

Tom put the plates, piled high with scrambled egg on toast, on the table. "I bet there're not many sitting down to a breakfast like this," he said, tucking in straight away.

Dolly nodded, trying to smile, thinking once more how lucky they were able to keep chickens. But today she just couldn't face the thought of food. She pushed the plate away. "I'm sorry, Tom, I just can't eat it."

"Never mind — all the more for me," he chuckled, then glanced at her. "Just have a bit of toast then. You've got to eat something, love."

"No, I don't want anything."

He pushed his chair back. "What's up, Dorothy?"

She shook her head.

"You're going to the doctor's my girl — and no buts."

"I'll be all right — just tired." She went and sat in the armchair and leaned back, closing her eyes. It only seemed a few moments later that she felt Rowena pulling at her skirt.

"Mummy — play."

She sat up and rubbed her eyes, glanced at the clock over the mantelpiece, shook her head in disbelief. The door opened and Tom came through from the shop.

"Feeling better?" he asked. "I thought you ought to go back to bed but I didn't have the heart to disturb you."

"Tom, you should have woken me. What about the post office?" She stood up and stretched, rubbing the back of her neck. Despite dozing in such an awkward position she felt refreshed by her sleep — and, she now realized, ravenously hungry. That's all she'd needed — to catch up on her sleep.

"I'm managing perfectly well. You just rest," Tom said.

"I'm fine now. I'll just wash my face and I'll be with you."

"No, you won't. You're having the rest of the day off. You're not setting foot in that shop till tomorrow — and only then if I think you're well enough."

Dolly smiled and made no further protest. There were times when it didn't hurt to let the man think he was the boss. There were plenty of jobs she could do around the house and she could also spend some time with Rowena.

For the next week or so Tom insisted on Dolly taking it easy. She refused to go to the doctor, insisting that all she'd needed was more rest. They still hadn't managed to find a replacement for Maureen and Dolly had showed Tom how to operate the telephone exchange. The shop itself wasn't so busy these days, except when rumours swept the village that they'd had a delivery. Then the queues stretched down the street past the Plough. They'd also started opening later and closing earlier in compliance with government regulations to save electricity where possible, although the evenings were getting longer now.

With the coming of spring Dolly started to feel better. She told herself she'd just had a touch of the winter blues.

The bombers were still passing overhead every night — only last week the RAF had dropped 3,000 tons of bombs on Hamburg. Dolly didn't try to imagine the damage that number of bombs could do. She shuddered when she heard the news on the wireless and told herself they were only getting what they deserved. She only had to think of poor Annie and Stevie and the thousands of other Londoners who'd died to convince herself of that.

Although she hadn't been to church for ages, she still prayed for her family — even Ruby. Despite their last acrimonious meeting, she didn't wish her ill. And Janet too — the friend who seemed to have abandoned her, never once answering her letters over the past three years.

Since Tom had returned from that last trip to London just before Christmas, things had been wonderful. They were like newlyweds all over again. He showed his love in all sorts of little ways, from helping her in the house when she wasn't well to bringing her a bunch of the first snowdrops and leaving them in a glass on her bedside table. If only she felt fitter, Dolly couldn't have been happier.

It looked as if the war couldn't go on much longer. Everyone was speculating about the invasion of Europe, as convoys of Army lorries rumbled through the village. Up on the Downs behind the village, camouflaged tents sprung up overnight.

"Getting ready for the big push," Tom said from the doorway of the shop. He shaded his eyes against the spring sunshine and looked up the hill. He came back into the shop and leaned on the counter. "Not much doing today. Think I'll go out the back and turn over that patch of ground. Those seedlings will soon be ready to plant out."

"Would you take Rowena with you? She needs a bit of fresh air and you know how she loves to help in the garden."

Tom laughed. "Hinder you mean. All right, I'll keep an eye on her."

Dolly stood for a moment after he'd gone, savouring the peace and quiet. But she couldn't stay still for long. The lorries made such a dust. She got a damp cloth and busied herself wiping down the shelves and rearranging things so it looked as if they had something to sell.

She was so engrossed she was unaware of the lorry pulling up outside. She jumped when the shop bell jangled and a couple of soldiers entered.

"Sorry — no cigarettes," she said automatically, smiling to show her regret.

"That's not what we're after, lady." One of them held up a canvas bucket. "We need some water. The old girl's boiled over and we can't get her going." He gestured at the lorry, its hood up, the radiator steaming gently. "Hope it's not too much trouble."

"No trouble at all," Dolly reached out for the bucket, glancing curiously at the other soldier who had his back to her, puffing on his cigarette and looking out of the window.

She filled the bucket and carried it through to the shop. The soldier reached over the counter, lifting it easily. "Come on, Del," he said to his mate.

The other one shrugged. "Won't be a mo." He turned and grinned at Dolly through a mouthful of broken teeth. She stepped back, her hand on the kitchen door, heart racing as she recognized him.

Before she could speak, he gestured with his cigarette. "Marchant — that's what it says over the door. Knew a Marchant once, back in London. Wouldn't be the same geezer would it?"

282

She was sure he hadn't recognized her, but she knew him — Derek Rose, the man who was married to Tom's sister. He'd not only beaten Tom up, but had led him into trouble in his teens, mocked his efforts to go straight, and tried to involve him in his shady deals.

She gripped the doorjamb and forced a smile. "Marchant's not an uncommon name. What makes you think this is the same one?"

"Well now. He moved out to the country to open a shop — that much I do know. And I knew it was round this way. I only had to ask around the villages."

"What do you want with him?"

Derek Rose grinned evilly. "So it is the right Marchant — Tom Marchant who used to run the veg stall down Shepherd's Bush."

Dolly shook her head and Derek wagged a nicotine-stained finger under her nose. "No use pretending — I know it's the same bloke and I want a few words with him."

"He's not here." Dolly prayed Tom wouldn't come in before she got rid of him. "Look, I know you're his brother-in-law and you don't get on. He doesn't want anything to do with you. So why don't you just leave?"

"Because I want to know why he's treating my sister so bad — that's why. He should be supporting her. He's got a nice little business here so he can afford to make 'er an allowance."

"And why should he do that?" Dolly's knees were shaking but she spoke aggressively. She wasn't going to let this bully see how frightened and confused she was.

"Because a husband should support his wife — that's why." Derek leaned over and thumped the counter, making the bacon slicer rattle. "Now where is he — I'm really gonna lose my temper if you don't tell me."

"Leave my wife alone — go on, get out of here, now." Tom had come in through the storeroom. His face was white, the scar standing out lividly on his temple. He stabbed a finger at his face. "You got away with giving me this, but you're not going to intimidate me any more. It's over, Derek. Get out."

Derek smirked. "Your *wife* did you say? I did hear right, didn't I? Well, well. I wonder what Freda will have to say about it."

Outside, the lorry's horn sounded impatiently and the other soldier came in. "Come on, Del. We've got her going. Best be off or we'll 'ave the Sarge after us."

Derek's fist crashed down on the counter again. "Don't think I've finished with you, Marchant — not by a long way. We'll be off across the Channel soon but don't go getting your hopes up. I'll be gettin' in touch with Arthur before I go. So, even if a jerry bullet gets me, you'll still 'ave 'im to answer to."

He followed his mate out of the shop, slamming the door so that the windows rattled. Dolly, her knuckles white on the doorframe, breathed deeply, willing the trembling in her stomach to ease. She wouldn't faint. She looked at Tom, noticed the beads of sweat on his pale face, saw that his knuckles were tense too.

He took a step towards her. "Dorothy . . . Let me explain."

284

Why didn't he laugh and tell her it was all a mistake? She put a hand up, warding him off, struggling to make sense of what she'd heard. Derek Rose hadn't denied he was Tom's brother-in-law but it seemed she'd got it wrong. He wasn't married to Tom's sister at all. He'd mentioned someone called Freda — his sister. Was she Tom's wife? Did that mean he'd been married before? No wonder he hadn't wanted to marry in church if he was divorced. Why hadn't he told her? She'd have tried to understand. She stared at Tom. "Why?" The one word came out in a strangled whisper.

Tom didn't answer straight away. He walked round the end of the counter and pulled down the blind on the shop, turned the sign round to *closed*. "Come and sit down, Dorothy. You've had a shock."

She stumbled into the kitchen and sat down, her fingers clasped on the table in an effort to stop them trembling. He pulled out a chair and sat opposite, reaching across to take her hand. She snatched it away. The trembling stopped, replaced by a cold anger. "Well go on then — explain."

"I don't know how to begin. It's all so complicated." He ran his hand through his hair, touched the scar at the side of his head.

It was a gesture Dolly usually found endearing. Now, she steeled herself for what was to come. It wasn't so much the fact of a former wife, but that he'd never so much as mentioned her name. She remembered all the times Janet had tried to warn her, his mother too. But she'd thought that was because of his reputation as a womaniser. And since they'd been together, she'd stake her life he'd never looked at anyone else.

He was talking, gabbling now. Trying to reassure her that she was the only woman he wanted. "Ever since I laid eyes on you, there's never been anyone else. You must believe me."

Why should she? He'd lied to her — by omission at least. "Were you still married to her when we started going out together?" she asked.

He nodded, opened his mouth to speak. But she forestalled him. "That's why you moved away, isn't it? It wasn't to protect me from the Rose brothers. You wanted to get the divorce settled before you came back to Chiswick to ask me to marry you?"

He nodded again, his face crumpled as if he were about to cry.

Her heart melted. "Oh, Tom. Why didn't you trust me? I would have waited for you." She got up and tried to put her arms round him. This time, he held her off.

"Sit down, Dorothy. I haven't told you everything. It's time I owned up. You'll probably say it's because I've been found out. But I've been finding it harder and harder to keep it from you." He hesitated, breathed deeply and rushed on. "I'm not divorced. I'm still legally married to Freda."

Dolly felt sick. No, he wouldn't do this to her. Respectable Dolly Marchant — Dixon, she amended. Church-goer, pillar of the local community — not really married at all? She thought of Rowena, still playing contentedly in the garden, her beloved daughter

286

— a bastard. Just like you, Dolly, she told herself, beginning to laugh hysterically.

She woke in her bed, realized the sun was shining through the drawn curtains. What was she doing here in the middle of the day? Was she ill? Her head felt muzzy, pain throbbed at her temples and when she tried to sit up, nausea overcame her and she sank back on to the pillows.

Memory slowly returned and she relived the horror of that morning — from the moment she'd recognized Derek Rose to Tom's final, devastating revelation, her hysterical laughter, the roaring in her ears. She must have fainted.

She sat up slowly and swung her legs over the side of the bed, reached for her blouse and skirt. She ought to go down and help in the shop. Hysterical laughter threatened again. How would she ever show her face in the village again? But no one knows, a little voice said.

Could she act as if nothing had happened, pretend she was a happily married woman, while all the time knowing she was living with a bigamist? Her heart said that, despite everything, she loved Tom, couldn't bear the thought of losing him. But the part of her that had so yearned for acceptance and respectability, told her that she'd never be able to live with the fear of someone finding out.

There was only one thing to do. She'd go back to London. She and Rowena could stay with Janet for a while, till she sorted herself out. She had no doubt that her old friend, despite not being in contact for so long, would stand by her.

She stood up, finished dressing and reached up for the suitcase on top of the wardrobe. It wouldn't take long to pack — she didn't have many decent clothes after more than four years of make do and mend.

She packed the pearl-handled brush and mirror that the girls at Cherry Blossom had bought her when she left the factory and took her Bible and Prayer Book from the drawer in the bedside cabinet. She clutched them to her. What would the Reverend Taylor and his wife say if they knew her dreadful secret?

Well, it was hardly her fault, was it? She was the innocent party — she and Rowena. But she should have sensed something wrong — Tom's insistence on keeping their marriage secret, his aversion to Janet — all made sense now. But why hadn't he divorced Freda first? Why risk being exposed as a bigamist? A furious surge of anger quelled the small flicker of joy she couldn't help feeling — that he had loved her so much he was willing to risk everything to be with her. She didn't think she'd ever be able to forgive him.

She scooped up an armful of Rowena's clothes and threw them in the case. The sooner they were packed and on their way to London the better. She'd have to take a few toys too — the wooden bricks Tom had painted, the rag doll made out of scraps that Maureen had given her last Christmas.

At the top of the stairs she paused, listening to the murmur of voices from the kitchen. "Eat it all up, lovie. You want to be a big strong girl for Daddy."

She bit her lip. There was no doubting Tom's love for Rowena. Was she doing the right thing, depriving her child of a father? If only there was someone to help her sort out her confused feelings. But Maureen had gone and she could hardly confide in the Vicar's wife.

Through a mist of tears, she finished packing. If she hurried she'd catch the next bus into Chichester. It didn't matter how long she had to wait for a train so long as she was away from Borstall Green and the curious stares of the villagers. They'd find plenty to gossip about once she'd gone.

She checked her handbag to see how much money she had — enough to get by until she got a job. She must remember to pick up their ration books from the dresser on the way out. As she reached for the suitcase Tom spoke from the doorway. "What do you think you're doing?"

"I can't stay, Tom — surely you can understand that?"

He came towards her, grabbing her wrists and pulling her towards him. "You can't leave me, Dorothy. What will I do without you?"

"Go back to your wife, maybe?" She pushed him away, surprised at how cool she sounded, though inside she was trembling.

"Dorothy, as far as I'm concerned, you are my wife. Freda never meant anything to me."

"So, why did you marry her then?"

"She told me she was expecting. I took her at her word, although I did wonder why she picked on me when it could have been any other bloke in Shepherd's Bush."

"So you had . . .?"

"Oh, yes. I was no saint in those days and she made a play for me. I'm only human . . ." His eyes fell, then he looked up at her again. "I swear, from the moment I met you, there was only you."

Dolly believed him. But she couldn't forgive him for deceiving her. She moved to pick up the case again. He wasn't going to sweet talk her into staying.

"Please, Dorothy, don't go. Think about Rowena."

"I am thinking of her. I don't want her growing up the way I did, being called names . . ."

"But don't you see — that's what'll happen if you leave. You'll be a single woman with a child. Stay with me — please. No one will know."

"I'll know." She swung the case off the bed, gasping as a pain shot through her lower abdomen. She leaned over, clutching her stomach.

Tom was by her side in a flash. He eased her down on to the bed. "What is it?" He looked down at her helplessly. "Shall I call the doctor? You haven't been well for weeks. I told you to go and see him."

"I don't need a doctor. That case is heavy — I just pulled a muscle or something."

"No, it's more than that. I've known something was wrong for ages — you're tired, you keep being sick . . ."

Dolly clasped her hands over her stomach. Was she imagining that tiny fluttering feeling inside? Despite the turmoil of the past few hours, a slow smile spread over her face. She looked up at Tom as the realization dawned on her. "Tom, I'm not ill — I'm expecting."

He sat down beside her, enfolding her in his arms. "Why didn't you tell me before?"

"I've only just realized it myself. That's why I haven't been myself lately. I just thought it was after effects of the flu."

Tom kissed her cheek. "You can't leave now."

"I must, Tom. We're not legally married. It wouldn't be right."

"Would it be right for you to try to bring up two kids on your own — knowing that their father loved them and wanted them?"

Dolly couldn't answer. The strict moral code she'd tried to live by didn't seem so important now. She and Tom had been happy together and with two children, they'd be a proper family. And hadn't that been what she'd wanted all her life?

Tom seemed to sense her indecision. He took her hand and kissed it. "Please stay — I promise I'll try to put things right."

Knowing she might regret it, she made her decision. "I shouldn't — but, for the children, I will."

Tom jumped up, a big grin on his face. "Dorothy, I love you. You won't be sorry — I'll make it up to you."

"You can start by going down to see if Rowena's all right. Then you can make me a cup of tea, while I unpack this case."

"I'll see to it. You just rest for a while." He leaned over and kissed her cheek. "You're not the only one who wants a proper family," he said.

After he'd gone downstairs, Dolly leaned back against the pillows and closed her eyes. She still wasn't sure if she was doing the right thing. But it was too late now. By agreeing to stay, she'd accepted the situation — for the sake of her children, she reminded herself. She just hoped it would turn out to be the right thing for them. She tried to convince herself that she didn't care so much for herself. She would learn to live with the fear that one day their secret would come out.

When Tom came back with the tea, Dolly sat up and swung her legs to the floor.

He sat beside her and took her hand but she pulled away. "You've got some explaining to do."

"I told you — I married Freda when I was too young to know better really. I realized my mistake straight away but she wouldn't divorce me. I'd already left her when I met you . . ." His voice trailed away.

"You should have told me, Tom." Her voice was harsh, unyielding.

"I know, I did try — several times." He shrugged helplessly.

"Why didn't your mother tell me you were married, when I was working in the shop? I know she didn't like me and she warned me off several times."

"She thought you knew. That's why she took against you — thought you didn't care."

"You could have straightened her out. I don't like the idea that she thought badly of me. I respected your mother."

"I'm sorry. I don't know what else to say. I'd give anything for things to be different. And I wish I'd owned up and that you hadn't had to hear it from someone else — especially the likes of Derek Rose."

"However did you get mixed up with her in the first place?" Dolly leaned forward, searching his face.

He sensed a softening. If only he could make her understand. "I told you — I grew up with Arthur and Derek. We got into a lot of scrapes. But when they progressed to outright crime, I steered clear of them. I met Freda at a dance — didn't know she was their sister. It was never a serious romance or anything . . ."

"Just a bit of fun, eh?"

Tom recoiled at the contempt in her voice. "I suppose so . . . but when she told me she was pregnant and swore I was the father, I realized I had to do the right thing." Now was the time to tell her about Tony. She must realize there was a child in all this. Would it affect her decision to stay with him? Surely, if he reassured her he was supporting his son . . .

But before he could say anything Dolly gave a short laugh. "I bet you felt a right fool. It's the oldest trick in the book — telling a bloke you're pregnant. I suppose she told you she'd had a miscarriage?"

"So, I'm a fool." The words were out before he had time to think. He hadn't lied, he told himself, just let her assume . . .

Dolly was quiet for a minute and Tom took her hand again. "The most important thing for you to remember, Dorothy, is that I love you. I never loved Freda. From the minute I met you, I knew you were the one."

"I felt the same. Even when everyone was warning me off you, I just knew . . ."

He leaned over and kissed her, relaxing at last as her lips responded to his and her hands crept up to tangle themselves in his hair. She loved him, she wouldn't leave him. He wanted the kiss to go on forever, but she pushed him away.

"So, if you've left her, why doesn't she divorce you?"

"I've begged her to, time and again. She knows there's no chance we'll ever get back together. But she says the Church won't allow it. She's a Catholic, you see."

"But you're not. Can't you divorce her? She'd had other men before you were married. How do you know she hasn't been playing around since?"

"I'm sure she has. But if I try to blacken her name, I'll have her brothers to contend with." He fingered the scar on his temple.

Her hand flew to her mouth. "That's why they beat you up." Her eyes opened wide. "It was because of me, wasn't it? And you think they might do it again."

"They threatened to hurt you if they found out I was still seeing you. That's why I moved away. I tried to forget you, but I couldn't."

She leaned towards him. "Oh, Tom, what are we going to do? Now that Derek knows where you live, he'll tell her — and his brother. I could see he was dying to make trouble for you. Suppose he comes back."

"He won't be back. They're getting ready for the invasion. I don't suppose he'll get leave before they go." Tom put his arms round Dolly, soothing her. He wanted to believe that it didn't matter anyway. Now that she knew about Freda and had agreed to stand by him, nothing could hurt them again.

But deep down he knew this wasn't the end of it. He pictured Freda, holding Tony by the hand, getting off the bus at the end of the village street, the hulking figure of Arthur Rose beside them, confronting him in front of their customers. That would be the end as far as Dolly was concerned. He shuddered inwardly. He should have owned up about Tony. It wasn't too late. Hadn't he promised himself — no more lies?

He opened his mouth to speak but Dolly leaned forward, holding his hand tightly. "So, do we carry on as if nothing's happened and hope we never get found out?"

"I think that's all we can do — for Rowena's sake and the new little one."

"I don't know if I can pretend, but I'll try — for the children." She stood up. "One good thing, Tom — lucky there wasn't really a baby. I know how kids suffer in these situations. I wouldn't wish that on anyone. That's why I want to do what's best for my own children."

Tom followed her slowly downstairs. The moment for confessing had passed. He'd just have to pray that she never learned about Tony.

CHAPTER
TWENTY-SIX

After having such an easy time with Rowena, Dolly expected her second pregnancy to be much the same. But the bouts of sickness continued well into the sixth month, and she felt constantly tired and depressed. Even the excitement of the D-day landings and the knowledge that the end of the war was in sight, couldn't cheer her up.

Mrs Taylor, the vicar's wife, tried to console her. "No two pregnancies are the same, dear," she said. "But when it's all over, you'll be back to normal in no time and all this will seem like a bad dream."

"Nightmare, more like," Dolly said, with a small laugh. "Never again."

"We all say that." Mrs Taylor patted her arm. "I had four, so I should know." She looked pensive for a moment and Dolly quietly sympathized. She'd lost one son, another was a prisoner and the two girls were up north somewhere doing some rather hush-hush work. No one quite knew what they were up to and they hadn't been home for a couple of years. But Mrs Taylor never moaned about her lot, just quietly got on with her job as a vicar's wife, caring for the two little evacuees and trying to help those in trouble.

Dolly felt ashamed for whining. She managed a smile and put her hand on her bump. "Well, not too long to go now. Looks like the baby will arrive before the end of the war at this rate."

"Yes, we all thought it would be only a matter of weeks, once our boys got over there. But it's turned into a long, hard battle."

"They don't give up easily, do they? Still sending those horrible rockets over — as if that'll make any difference in the long run." Dolly couldn't believe they would lose the war now, in spite of the "doodlebugs" which were causing even more devastation than the worst months of the blitz. And poor old London was copping it again.

The shop door opened and she gave Mrs Taylor her change and turned to serve the next customer, relieved when the vicar's wife had gone. She liked the woman, but nowadays she felt tense whenever she came in. She could picture Mrs Taylor's reaction and that of the other villagers if they knew her secret. How could she carry on living here, facing their hostility if she were ever found out?

It wasn't the war dragging on and her difficult pregnancy making her so depressed. It was the constant tension. Every time the bell over the door jangled, she jumped, afraid to look up in case she saw one of the Rose brothers standing there, or worse still a strange young woman. The strain was beginning to affect her relationship with Tom, although she had long since forgiven him for his deception.

He had promised that in spite of the difficulties he would start divorce proceedings against Freda. Dolly knew it wouldn't be easy. If Freda was anything like her brothers, she'd delight in making trouble.

Dolly carried on serving, mechanically weighing and wrapping, smiling and answering the customers' comments but it was a relief when Tom came in and said he'd take over.

Rowena was playing quietly in the kitchen. Such a good child, Dolly thought, wondering how she'd cope with two. She couldn't hope the next one would be as placid and well-behaved as Rowena, especially given the trouble it was causing even before it was born.

Tom listened to Dolly's deep even breathing. She wasn't really asleep and he hated the thought that she was avoiding him. She wasn't the sort of woman who pretended to have a headache when she wasn't in the mood. Besides, she was having a difficult pregnancy and she deserved all the rest she could get. But he suspected — no, he knew — her aversion to him wasn't caused by her pregnancy.

Although she'd assured him he was forgiven, things hadn't been the same since the day Derek Rose had turned up three months ago. How he hated that man! He'd never wished ill on anyone — not even Freda at her worst. But he fervently hoped that there was a German bullet somewhere with that bastard's name on it.

He turned over in bed, his heart racing, his body bathed in sweat. Dolly was really asleep now. He sat up and swung his legs over the side of the bed. Good job she didn't know what he'd been thinking. Cynically, he thought that if he were a Catholic like the Roses he'd cross himself, go to confession next day and all would be well. But he didn't believe in all that superstitious nonsense. Dorothy did though, and he owed it to her to try and make things right between them.

He'd go and see Freda again, and this time he wouldn't take no for an answer. He'd have to wait till after the baby was born though. He couldn't leave Dorothy the way she was at the moment.

Tom cut two very thin slices of ham and wrapped them in the greaseproof paper Mrs Taylor had provided. He put the package beside the tin of beans and the bag of semolina and started adding up the total on a scrap of paper. A cry from the rear of the shop jerked his head round and he had to start again.

Mrs Taylor smiled sympathetically. "I'm sure everything is all right, Mr Marchant. Won't be long now."

Tom wiped a hand across his forehead. "It's the waiting — and not being able to do anything," he said.

"I do understand." Mrs Taylor picked up her purchases and Tom turned to the other waiting customers, trying to smile and thank them for their good wishes. He just wished they'd hurry up so he could bolt the door behind them and rush upstairs.

Dorothy had been in labour for hours and he was worried. Unconsciously he prayed, promising the God he didn't believe in that he'd do anything to make it up to her if only she was spared the pain she was going through right now.

At last he swung the sign round to "closed" and hurried upstairs. Incredibly, she was sitting up and smiling. "Another girl," she said, holding the tiny bundle close to her breast.

He sat on the edge of the bed, leaned over and pulled the blanket away from the baby's face. She wasn't as pretty as Rowena, hardly any hair and her face all red and screwed up. But Tom felt a surge of love for her and for his wife — and Dorothy was his wife, whatever the law might say. He stroked the baby's soft skin, kissed Dorothy's cheek.

"You don't mind? That it's not a boy?" she asked.

"Of course not. She's lovely."

"I know you wanted a son."

A son, if she only knew. He tried to hide the pain that thinking about Tony caused him. He forced a little laugh into his voice. "We can always put Marchant and Daughters up over the shop."

"What are we going to call her? We only discussed boys' names again," Dorothy said.

"What about Paula? I know I wasn't keen on Paul for a boy but it's OK for a girl."

Dolly had hoped that once the baby was born she'd recover her usual energy and start living normally again. But she still got very tired and Paula wasn't an easy baby. She refused the breast and grizzled constantly. Finally Dolly accepted defeat and put her on to the bottle. At least she'd know the poor child wasn't hungry.

But even as Paula grew and thrived, Dolly still felt nervy and irritable. Although she told herself she'd forgiven Tom and understood why he'd acted as he did, she wasn't happy about it. But what could she do? If only he'd told her right from the start that he was still married. She told herself that she loved him so much she'd have been willing to have her name dragged into the divorce court if only he'd be free to marry her at the end of it all.

But as she went through the mechanical actions of washing and cleaning, preparing meals and caring for her family, she had to own up to the truth: she would have run a mile from getting involved with a married man. Respectability and a good name had always been important to her, even more so after her mother had shamed them all by running off with another man.

She ran a tired hand through her hair and bit her lip. Tom had known her better than she knew herself, it seemed. And if he loved her as much as he claimed, she really couldn't blame him for keeping quiet. Understanding didn't help though.

The shop bell rang and she tensed, listening to the voices, relaxing as she recognized the butcher's wife.

She'd avoided going into the shop since Paula's birth and their customers seemed to accept that she was still recovering from a difficult confinement. But the truth was, she was terrified that one day she'd be confronted by Freda or the Rose brothers. And, if the villagers ever discovered her dreadful secret, she'd never be able to show her face again.

The bell rang again. It was busy this morning. Maybe she ought to make an effort, overcome her fears and give Tom a hand. She put down her duster and smoothed her apron, patted her hair and opened the door.

Her heart sank when she saw Mrs Taylor, but she summoned a smile. "Lovely day," she said.

"Isn't it a treat not to have those big guns banging away all day?" Mrs Taylor said. The rocket-launching site which had been sending the doodlebugs over in such huge numbers had been destroyed by the Allies a week ago and the guns up on the Downs were no longer needed.

"Maybe the end's in sight at last." Dolly sighed, thinking of the lives lost over the past five years. But she was one of the lucky ones. At least she still had her home, her children — and her husband.

With the thought it was as if the ice that had encased her heart for the past six months was beginning to melt. Tom was her husband, in every way that mattered. Yes, he'd done wrong. But he'd tried his best to make amends. And whatever he'd done, she still loved him.

She looked up to see Mrs Taylor giving her a strange look and realized that the other woman had been speaking. "Are you all right, Mrs Marchant?" she asked.

"I'm sorry, I was just thinking about the war — and everything."

"It's been hard on everyone. But it can't go on forever."

Dolly smiled. She couldn't wait for the woman to leave. It was time she and Tom had a good talk, thrashed things out. And it was time he sorted his wife out too. Despite what he'd promised, he hadn't done anything about getting a divorce — not that a trip to London had been practical these past few months. But the doodlebugs were no longer a threat and, now that she was feeling stronger, she could cope for one day.

Tom was shaken by the damage the buzz-bombs had done. It was even worse than at the height of the blitz. He'd expected to see craters in the roads and the remains of houses, as he had on his previous trips to London. But now, whole streets had disappeared. He'd had to make so many detours it was now early afternoon.

As he turned the corner leading to Freda's road, his heart started hammering. Despite telling himself he didn't care about Freda, he was relieved to find the house undamaged. He hoped she was all right — she was Tony's mother, after all. And how could he ever be happy with Dorothy if it was at the expense of his wife's life? He'd never be able to live with the guilt.

He licked his lips, realizing he'd been gripping the steering wheel. He took deep breaths, steadying himself for the coming confrontation.

He glanced at his watch. Tony would be home from school soon. Tom was longing to see him, but dreading it too, remembering how the boy had mistaken him for one of Freda's lovers. Knowing he'd have to face him sometime, not to mention the battle with his wife, he got out of the van and walked up the short path.

She took her time opening the front door, although he could hear wireless music through the open window. She was wearing a pink silk dressing-gown, the inevitable fag dangling from her lip.

"Did I wake you?" His tone was sarcastic, until it struck him that she might be on night shift at the factory. In a gentler voice he said, "Freda, we have to talk, if it's convenient of course."

"No, it's not convenient. But I suppose, now you're here . . ." She held the door open. As he stepped inside, she smirked and said, "And as it happens, you didn't wake us — we weren't asleep."

As he took note of that "we", a man appeared in the passage, buttoning his army tunic. He pushed past with an embarrassed grin.

"Oh, Bob, meet my husband," Freda said, with a screech of laughter as he scuttled away. She slammed the front door and turned to Tom. "Well, you've got what you came for I suppose — grounds for that divorce you've been on about. Anyone in the street will tell you . . ."

Tom grabbed her arm. "How could you carry on like that? What about Tony?" He didn't care how many men she went to bed with — but in her own house, with the kid liable to come in from school any minute. How could she?

"What do you care? You left us, remember. Why shouldn't I have a bit of fun?" She pulled away from him, rubbing her arm resentfully.

"I only left because of your carrying-on. You can't deny you were at it every chance you got, even when we were together, but at least you were discreet then."

"Well, there's no need for me to be discreet now. You've been gone so long, no one remembers I've got a husband. As for Tony — he's not here."

"What do you mean?" He grabbed her arm again.

"Leave off. Nothing's happened to your precious kid — though if you really cared, you wouldn't have gone off with your floozy." She laughed again. "Oh, yes, I know all about you and your so-called wife. How do you think she'd like it if everyone in that village knew you weren't really married."

"We'll get married — once I'm divorced. And you said yourself I've got grounds. You'd be rid of me for good then."

"I could still make trouble."

"I don't care. Now where's Tony?"

"Evacuated when the doodlebugs started — some place in Wales."

Tom sagged against the wall. His son was safe.

She touched his arm, gave a tentative smile. "You said you wanted to talk. Can't we do that without rowing? Come in the kitchen and I'll get you a drink."

Reluctantly, he followed her. Just like last time, the sink was piled with dirty dishes, the cooker thick with burnt-on grease. She swept a pile of clothes off one of the chairs and waved her cigarette.

"Sit down then, you're making the place look untidy."

Her harsh laughter made him wince. How could he ever have thought her attractive? He looked round the untidy room, comparing it with his own home.

"I'm not stopping. Let's get down to business."

"Now that's what I like to hear," she said, with a suggestive smile.

"The business of our divorce," he snapped.

"Well, I've been thinking about that." She paused and Tom's heart sank. This wasn't going to be easy.

"I know you've got grounds — especially after what you saw today." She put a hand on his arm and spoke in a whine. "You can't blame me, Tom. I get lonely. Besides, think of your son — you wouldn't like his mother being branded, would you?"

He shook her off. "Say what you've got to."

"It's just — if there's going to be a divorce, I should be the one doing it. After all, you're the one who left me — and you've been gone for years."

"All right — do me for desertion. No need to bring Dorothy into it." As soon as he'd spoken he realized his mistake.

Her eyes narrowed. "Oh, no — you're not getting off so easy. You've been living with that woman. Derek said she's calling herself Mrs Marchant. I can't have that."

It was no use. If Tom brought a counter-suit, everything would come out — he'd be exposed as a bigamist. And that would mean prison. He didn't care for himself. But how could he do that to Dorothy? Or his girls? It looked like he'd lost his son — he couldn't bear to lose his daughters too.

"No Freda — leave Dorothy out of it. She didn't know . . ."

"I don't care. Why should she have everything?"

"I'll send you money, Freda," he said, quickly seizing the advantage. "I've been putting money into an account for Tony. I'll do the same for you . . ."

It was blackmail. But it worked. Tom tried to hide his satisfaction at the gleam in her eyes.

"All right — a monthly cheque. But the first time you miss, I'm off to see a solicitor." She stubbed out her cigarette and stood up. "And no more talk of a divorce, right? Otherwise I'll make sure Tony knows all about you and your floozy. I'll tell him what a bastard his father is."

"No need for threats — I said I'll pay up. Now, give me Tony's address in Wales. I'll send him something for his birthday."

"Why bother — he's probably forgotten he has a dad."

"Freda — the address, please."

She scribbled on the back of an old envelope and thrust it at him. "Now get out. Go back to your precious Dorothy."

He went without another word. In the van, he stared at the address. Writing to Tony would be hard, but it would be even harder keeping it from Dorothy if the boy replied. How he wished he'd had the guts to own up when he had the chance. Too late now though. Guiltily he recalled his promise to be honest with her from now on.

As he drove away, he went over the confrontation with Freda. It hadn't gone how he'd planned. But had he really thought it would? And when he got home, Dorothy would be expecting to hear that he'd sorted out their problems. With a sick feeling in his stomach, he acknowledged he'd have to start lying to her again.

CHAPTER
TWENTY-SEVEN

Dolly looked at the clock again, twisting her hands in her lap. It had turned chilly after the rain started in late afternoon and she'd lit the fire. But she couldn't get warm.

Although Tom had told her Freda would use her Roman Catholicism as a reason not to agree to a divorce, she hoped he'd be able to persuade her. Besides, how could the woman carry on with other men and still claim to be religious? It didn't make sense to her. Still, if Tom got proof of her goings-on, he could divorce her. She didn't care which way round it was, so long as Tom was free to marry her properly and make their children legitimate.

The girls were asleep and she picked up her knitting, looked at the clock again. Surely it didn't take that long to drive to London and back? A sob rose in her throat and she clutched at her chest, feeling a physical pain as a thought struck her. Suppose he wasn't coming back? She had no claim on him — Freda was his legal wife. Could she have persuaded him to stay and give their marriage a chance?

Don't be silly, she told herself. He loved her and their daughters. And Freda had no children to bargain with. Besides, Tom would never go back to London. Here, he was a respected businessman with a wife and family. An insidious voice in her head said, "But he's not respectable is he? He's a bigamist."

She started up from an uneasy doze at the sound of the back door opening. Tom looked exhausted, the scar on his temple standing out starkly as it always did when he was tired or distressed. She leapt up and ran to him.

He rubbed his hand across his forehead, staggering as she led him to the chair she'd just vacated. "I thought I'd never get home . . ." he said.

Desperate as she was to know the outcome of his meeting with Freda, Dolly knew he was in no state to be questioned. He must have had an accident.

He shook his head. "I'm OK — it's just those other poor buggers. I kept thinking of you and the kiddies." He leaned forward, his head in his hands.

Dolly made cocoa, put the mug into his hand and closed hers round it, forcing him to drink. After a few minutes he was able to tell her. On the outskirts of London, a huge explosion had rocked the van, filling the air with dust and debris. As it settled, the full extent of the damage shocked him. This was worse than a landmine or a doodlebug.

"Secret weapon, some bloke said." Tom gave a short bark of laughter. "And we thought the war was nearly over."

Dolly put a comforting arm round his shoulder. "Don't think about it now, Tom. Get some rest. We can talk again in the morning." She urged him up the stairs, helped him undress and covered him with a blanket.

310

She bent and kissed him, her lips brushing the ridge of scar on his face.

She looked in on the girls, still sleeping soundly, tucked the blanket round Rowena, then crept downstairs. As she raked out the fire and locked the back door, she said a prayer for the victims of this terrible new bomb, whatever it was. But her most fervent prayer was one of thanks that Tom had been spared. She didn't care any more whether he got a divorce, whether they were legally man and wife. They were together, they loved each other and that was all that mattered.

Upstairs, she stood for a moment looking down at him. His face was turned away from her and she couldn't see the scar. The lines of strain had smoothed themselves in sleep, and apart from the few silver streaks in his hair, he was once more the handsome man she'd fallen in love with. She slipped into bed and snuggled up to him, kissing his bare shoulder and putting her arm across his chest in a gesture of closeness that had been missing in the past few months.

She was up early next morning but Tom was downstairs before her.

"Feeling better?" she asked.

"Surprisingly I slept OK." He poured her a cup of tea and pushed it across the table. "Aren't you going to ask me how I got on?"

"Well?"

Tom hesitated. "She wasn't there. The house was empty. It took me ages to find out what had happened."

He paused and Dolly's hands clenched round the cup, her heart racing. Was he going to tell her that Freda had been killed by a doodlebug? The bile of guilt rose in her throat. Her own family had been wiped out in the blitz and here she was wishing it on someone else. Her head was buzzing and she scarcely heard Tom's next words.

". . . don't know where she's gone, but she's left London for sure."

"Left London? But she was working in a factory. They don't let you just up and leave in wartime."

"Don't suppose she'd let that stop her. Apparently, things have been bad round her way lately what with the doodlebugs. I asked around — neighbours, people at the factory, but no one knows where she went."

The sound of the baby's crying came from upstairs and Dolly stood up. She touched Tom's arm gently. "Thanks for trying anyway."

"I'll go back again next week. We've got to get this thrashed out."

"No, Tom. You're not going back there till the war's finished. I was worried sick yesterday — and that was before I heard about these new rockets. I can't go through that again, sitting here on my own, going out of my mind . . ."

She went upstairs, leaving Tom to open the shop. She lifted Paula out of the cot and sat down on the edge of Rowena's bed to give her the bottle. As the little mouth clamped round the teat, the crying stopped abruptly.

Rowena stirred sleepily and sat up. She clambered to the end of the bed and snuggled up to Dolly, watching in fascination as the baby sucked greedily at the bottle. Thank goodness she wasn't jealous of Paula, Dolly thought. She had enough to worry about. She couldn't erase the image of Tom as he'd looked when he came in last night, and the momentary fear that Freda's brothers had had another go at him.

She lifted the baby over her shoulder, rubbing her back absently until Paula obligingly brought up some wind. Rowena had gone downstairs in her nightie to see her Daddy.

Paula sucked the bottle dry and Dolly removed the teat. She'd filled out a bit now and the fine down on her head had started to grow into a frizz of blonde curls, blue eyes stared up at her solemnly. On impulse, Dolly lifted the baby and kissed her, hugged her close. Suddenly, she realized she was crying. She couldn't bear it if her children had to suffer the stigma of illegitimacy as she had. It would be even worse if Tom went to prison for bigamy. And it would all come out if he tried to divorce Freda. Surely it was better to leave things as they were?

She dried her eyes and changed Paula's nappy, put her back in her cot, hoping she'd sleep for a while longer. She'd go and talk to Tom now — tell him what she'd decided.

CHAPTER
TWENTY-EIGHT

The whole village was agog at the news that the Marchants were leaving Borstall Green. Dolly was fed up with answering questions, the lies sticking in her throat, the smile taut on her aching lips.

Tom had taken some persuading. "I thought you were happy here," he said.

"I love the village and I have been happy — most of the time. But Freda's brother knows where we live now. He could make trouble. And what would our life here be like if anyone found out?"

"Don't worry about Derek — he's over the water fighting the Germans. We don't even know if he's still alive."

"But he's already told Freda — and there's still his brother."

"I thought you wanted me to divorce her. Wherever we go, they'll find out once I go to see a solicitor."

"I've changed my mind. I'm fed up with lying awake at night worrying about it." She clutched his arm. "Tom — you're a bigamist, you could go to prison."

She'd started to cry and that had set Rowena off. Comforting her daughter, she fought to control herself, speaking more quietly. "I couldn't live with that, Tom. The only way out is to go where no one knows us."

"I can see the sense in that — but it's going to be hard, selling this place at the moment. Look, the war can't go on much longer — I think we should wait."

In the end, Dolly had won and Tom had put the shop on the market. Despite his doubts, the estate agent thought they'd have no difficulty in selling.

"I'll be really sorry to see you go, my dear," Mrs Taylor said for the umpteenth time since hearing the news. "I'll miss your help with the church flowers and the little ones. Still, I suppose it's only natural you'd want to go back to London now that the war's nearly over. You and your husband must miss your friends and family. And country life doesn't suit everyone."

Dolly hated lying but it was better for everyone to think they were returning to the city. If the Rose brothers or any of their cronies came asking questions, they'd be put off the scent. It wasn't as if she'd made any close friends here. There was no one she wanted to keep in touch with, even Mrs Taylor.

She thought briefly of Maureen, sorry that their friendship had ended after the business with Pete Crawford. She couldn't help wondering if it would always be like this — having to move on whenever Tom's past threatened to catch up with him. Would they ever be able to really settle down and give the girls the stable home they deserved?

Dolly stood in the middle of the empty room, taking in the peeling wallpaper and dingy brown paint and almost burst into tears. She was tired after a sleepless night with Paula, worried about leaving the children for the day with Mrs Taylor, and beginning to doubt if moving from the village was such a good idea after all.

They had driven along the coast road past a beach shut off with coils of vicious-looking barbed wire and through the little seaside town that hadn't seen a holiday-maker for years. When Tom stopped the van outside the dingy, run-down grocer's shop on the corner of Holton Regis High Street and took the keys they'd picked up from the estate agent out of his pocket, her heart sank.

"Is this it?" she'd asked.

"It's not as bad as it looks," Tom said, getting out of the van.

Dolly hoped the inside would belie her first impressions. After all, everywhere looked dilapidated and uncared for after the years of war. And, as they'd entered the town, she'd seen for herself that even this quiet little place had suffered from the bombing. The shop looked all right, double-fronted with a long counter and a storeroom at the back. It was the flat above that had caused her dismay.

She couldn't believe this was the place Tom had described to her in such glowing terms. However hard she tried, she couldn't hide her feelings from him.

"There must be something better than this available," she said.

"Not with this much potential there isn't," he assured her.

"What do you mean — potential?"

"Didn't you notice the shop next door? The woman who runs it is almost ready to retire. It won't be long before I can take it over and then we can expand."

"I wasn't thinking of the business, Tom. Just look at the place. Do you really expect me and the girls to live here? I mean, it wouldn't be so bad if we could decorate it — but you know it's impossible to get wallpaper and paint at the moment. And there's no bathroom, an outside toilet . . ."

"You managed before . . ."

It was true. As a child she'd thought nothing of traipsing down the yard in all weathers, of having to wash at the kitchen sink. But she wanted something better for her girls. "That's not the point, Tom, and you know it," she snapped, her fury mounting as he started to laugh.

"It's not funny . . ." She stopped. "You're teasing me — this isn't really the place." She remembered he'd picked up two bunches of keys. "How could you?" She gave him a little shove.

"Don't get your hopes up," he warned, but she could see he was suppressing a grin.

They drove past the railway station and turned into a wide street of Edwardian houses that led down towards the sea. They were arranged in pairs, red brick with creamy yellow trim around the square bay windows. Neat little front gardens and crisp white net curtains completed the atmosphere of genteel elegance. Dolly was reminded of Mrs Crawford's house. In those days, it had been the height of her ambition to live in Carlton Road.

But this wasn't the kind of street to have a corner shop. So where was Tom taking her? The van slowed and pulled into the kerb.

"Come on then. Don't you want to see your new house?" Tom said.

"But where's the shop?" Dolly looked round bewildered.

"We've just come from there." He laughed at her expression.

"You mean we can afford to buy the shop and a house?"

"No — the shop will be rented. And it will be a struggle — these houses don't come cheap usually but I've got a bargain here."

Dolly got out of the van and shivered in the cold wind off the sea. She could smell the salt air and hear the plaintive cry of the seagulls. It reminded her of childhood Sunday School outings. She'd always loved the seaside. Suddenly her depression vanished. She and Tom and their children were about to start a new life. Surely the past couldn't reach them here?

"Let's have a look," she said, taking Tom's arm.

As they walked up the garden path of the end house, Tom explained why the house was such a bargain. Bombs had destroyed half the garden as well as the houses backing on to it. "We'll have to get it properly fenced off so it's safe for the children," he said.

"It's been empty a long time," Dolly said, wrinkling her nose at the musty smell.

"The old lady who lived here went to live with her daughter when the bombs fell."

Dolly felt sorry for the woman being forced to leave her home. It was a nice house and it would be lovely once she'd got busy with polish and scrubbing brushes. After peeping into the front room with its bay window and tiled fire surround, she followed Tom down the passage to the dining room, which had French windows looking out on to the garden. It wasn't as big as the garden at Borstall Green but, even with the bottom half fenced off, they'd be able to grow vegetables and still have space for the children to play.

"We'll have to give up the chickens," she said.

Tom laughed. "That means an extra half hour in bed in the mornings then."

"And no eggs for the children," Dolly reminded him.

"Sorry, you're right. Maybe we should look at something outside town with a bit of ground."

"No, Tom, this will do me — but are you sure we can afford it?"

"Just about — although things will be a bit tight until we get the shop running properly. But it's in a good position." He grabbed her hand. "Come on, love. You haven't seen the rest yet. You might change your mind . . ."

When she saw the kitchen, Dolly knew she wouldn't change her mind. It was big enough to eat in and, best of all, another door led through to a wash house with a copper. Beyond that was a toilet with a small wash basin. Dolly couldn't believe her eyes.

Upstairs there were three good-sized bedrooms, a box room and a tiled bathroom. Dolly had never imagined living in such luxury. But she was still worried they couldn't afford it. When she voiced her concerns, Tom pulled her towards him and kissed her. "Only the best is good enough for my Dorothy. I just want you to be happy."

"I'd be happy with you living in that horrible little flat we just looked at. I don't need all this . . ."

Tom pushed her away. "I know what it is — you still don't trust me. You think I've been up to something to get the money."

"No, of course not. I just don't want us to take on more than we can cope with. You know I'd sooner live above the shop until we get on our feet again, rather than get into debt."

"We won't get into debt, I promise. When we get back home I'll show you the figures. I worked it all out — you taught me, remember?"

Dolly had great respect for Tom's business sense. After all, he'd worked his way from being a humble market trader to running a proper shop. She remembered how impressed she'd been by his ambition when she saw his first little shop under the railway arches. And how quickly he'd picked up the post office side of things in Borstall Green. He still didn't like paperwork, but he understood the figures all right.

Yes, he'd make a success of whatever he did and she'd support him in every way she could. Besides, she liked a challenge.

It certainly had been a challenge, Dolly thought, as she pushed the pram through the streets towards her new home, Rowena clinging on to the handle. And it wasn't over yet. They still had a long way to go before she could stop lying awake at nights worrying about their finances.

And as for living in a seaside town, she'd hardly seen the sea since that day in January when they'd driven along the coast road to their new home. But despite everything, she was happy. And her heart no longer started pounding whenever a stranger came into the shop or there was a knock on the door of the house in Alexandra Terrace. For long periods of time she even managed to forget that dreadful day a year ago when her whole world had been shattered by Derek Rose's revelations.

Everyone in Borstall Green thought they'd returned to London. Dolly knew that the chances of Tom's wife or her brothers tracking them down to this sleepy Sussex resort were almost impossible. At last she was beginning to feel secure.

Tom was still at the shop. But she'd decided to walk home early and get the tea started. Since they'd re-opened it was often slack and there was little for her to do. But she liked to be involved in the business and went along every day to lend a hand. Rowena went to nursery school three mornings a week and Paula seemed content to sit up in her pram in the corner watching everything that went on. When Rowena started school and Paula was old enough for nursery, Dolly intended to take more part in the business, particularly as Tom still had plans for expansion.

Dolly urged caution, especially as it was taking longer than they'd expected to regain the custom the shop had lost during its closure. But Tom was still optimistic.

She'd already given the children their tea and bath and read them a story by the time he came home. He was late and his tea had dried up in the oven. But he didn't seem to notice, talking excitedly between mouthfuls.

Dolly picked up her knitting and listened, a small smile on her face.

"I had a chat with this bloke — Ron Clark, he runs the gent's outfitters further down the High Street. He's had a hard time of it with the rationing."

"Haven't we all?" Dolly replied.

"Well, he said he admires me — taking on a run-down business; but I know it won't always be like this; now the war in Europe's as good as over, business is bound to pick up. After the years of tightening our belts, people will want to splash out a bit."

Dolly agreed. She couldn't wait for goods to start appearing in the shops again. She counted her stitches and looked up to give her attention to what Tom was saying. "He's put my name up to join the Chamber of Commerce."

He explained that local businessmen got together to give each other help and support. "The government and the local council will be thinking about rebuilding, getting the town back on its feet. Members of the Chamber get to have a say; some of them are councillors too. It could be very useful, having contacts."

Dolly knew Tom was thinking of his plans for expansion. Sometimes councils could be a bit awkward if your plans didn't fit in with what they wanted.

"Sounds like a good idea," Dolly said, putting down her knitting and getting up to switch on the wireless for the news — a much more cheerful experience these days. The last of the silent rocket bombs — the V2s — had dropped on London in March and people were starting to talk about the end of the war with real optimism. There had even been rumours that Hitler was dead but no one knew for sure. Maybe there'd be something official this evening. As she went back to her knitting, the voice of the newsreader faded into the background, and a smile played over her lips as she planned for their future.

CHAPTER
TWENTY-NINE

The war had been over for more than five years but the rationing had got worse and Dolly was worried that Tom was over-reaching himself with his plans for enlarging the shop, as well as buying up the bombed houses in the road behind their house.

They were too badly damaged for repair, so he'd snapped them up cheaply, selling off the salvageable material, such as bricks and slates, to a local builder to help to finance the deal. The fenced-off, weed-strewn plot didn't look much at the moment but it was an investment for the future. Tom was convinced that as Britain recovered from the war, a time of prosperity would come. People needed places to live and house-building would start again. A prime building plot with room for half a dozen houses would be worth its weight in gold.

"But can we afford it?" Dolly asked when he told her what he'd done. She'd hate to have to give up her house in Alexandra Terrace.

"Things are bound to get better soon," Tom assured her. "When everything comes off ration, we'll have a nice big shop to fill with goods."

Dolly wasn't entirely convinced, but Tom had been proved right before — for example, when he gave up his market stall for a shop under the arches, and later taking on the village stores. She was proud of him, although at the moment there wasn't much to show for it. Every penny he made was ploughed back into the business.

"It's for our future, Dorothy," he said, when she voiced her concerns.

She didn't say so, but she was more worried about the woman Tom had employed. Mavis Wilcox and her two children had lost their home in the bombing and he had offered her the flat above the shop in return for a few hours work.

Although it left Dolly more time for the children and her church activities, she still spent a lot of time at the shop. Tom said there was no need, now they had an extra pair of hands. But she didn't like the idea of him spending so much time in the company of another woman — especially one who made no secret of her attraction to him.

But Dolly didn't want to think about Mavis. Since coming to Holton Regis she and Tom had recaptured the magic of their first love. They never spoke of Freda or the possibility of divorce. Dolly was terrified of stirring it all up again. No one knew them here and besides, hadn't he told her repeatedly that as far as he was concerned she was his true wife? "No words said over us in church or a register office will change how I feel about you," he said.

In a way she agreed with him, but she didn't think the staid members of the Mothers' Union would agree.

She dreaded their finding out — as much for her children's sake as her own. She would never forget what she had suffered as a child, especially when she'd begun to realize what the words *whore* and *bastard* meant.

Dolly sighed and pushed herself away from the railing, willing herself to think more positive thoughts. Today was a very special day — the day she could finally call herself a respectable member of the community. She had to go home and get ready.

But she'd call in the shop first — see what Mavis Wilcox was up to. She trusted Tom but she couldn't help feeling jealous, especially as he always responded gallantly whenever the woman mentioned that a job needed doing in her flat above the shop. He couldn't seem to see through her "poor widow" act.

Maybe she was making something out of nothing, Dolly thought. But she resolved that if they did take on another shop assistant, she'd be the one doing the interviewing.

As she turned the corner into the High Street she felt the familiar surge of pride. Marchant's, with its fresh coat of paint and elegant sign over the window was so different from the run-down place it had been in the early days. She remembered her first sight of it — the flaking paint and grimy windows criss-crossed with brown tape, remembered her heart-sinking dismay at the thought of living in the poky rooms upstairs.

Now they not only sold groceries and provisions, but items to attract the holidaymakers — buckets and spades, bats and balls, sunhats, wind-breakers, beach towels. This year they'd decided to add calamine lotion, antiseptic cream and sticking plaster — Dolly's idea. The nearest chemist was at the other end of the High Street and several times last summer people had come in the shop, usually holding a crying child by the hand, asking for first aid supplies.

The bell over the door jangled and Mavis looked up, a fleeting expression of resentment on her face.

Dolly pretended not to notice and smiled. "Hello, Mavis. Where's my husband?"

"He's gone to the warehouse." She smirked. "He said he couldn't wait for you and he was quite happy to leave me in charge."

"Well, I'm here now. You can have your break."

Mavis went through to the back of the shop and opened the door leading to the upstairs flat. "I won't be long, Mrs Marchant," she said firmly.

Dolly shrugged and sighed, turning back to the counter as the shop door opened. For a few minutes she was kept busy but when it went quiet she had time to think about Mavis Wilcox. Tom wouldn't hear of dismissing her. And Dolly had to agree she was reliable, always polite, and she worked hard.

Tom thought highly of her and couldn't understand Dolly's antipathy. "You don't have to be friends with her for goodness' sake," he'd said irritably when she'd voiced her misgivings. "She does the job she's paid for and she's reliable. What more could you ask?"

Dolly knew that if she said what was really on her mind, Tom would laugh and tell her she was being silly. Besides, she trusted him, didn't she?

But she didn't trust Mavis. It wasn't like her to take such a dislike to anyone without good reason. And, if anything, she should sympathize with the poor woman — widowed and bombed out of her home during the war. As Tom said, she needed a place to live with her two children and, being on the spot, she could open and lock up if either of them weren't available. It should have been an ideal arrangement.

Besides, Mavis had been working for them for several years now and surely Dolly would know if anything was going on.

She was serving a customer when Mavis came downstairs. "I'll take over if you like, Mrs Marchant," she said with a smile.

"It's all right, Mavis." Dolly hoped her irritation didn't show.

The shop emptied and Mavis busied herself tidying and dusting the shelves while Dolly sorted out the delivery notes and invoices.

She filed the papers away and came through to the shop. "I'm off to my meeting but I'll be back later, Mavis," she said.

"No need, Mrs Marchant. I can manage."

"I'm sure you can, but I'll come back anyway," Dolly said firmly.

She hurried down the High Street and crossed the road, fighting down her annoyance. The woman was getting too big for her boots. Not for the first time Dolly wished they hadn't given her so much responsibility when she'd first started working for them. But Tom had been involved with the renovations and the girls had been too young to leave. Since Rowena had started at the High School in Chichester and Paula was at junior school, Dolly had more time on her hands. Now that she was taking more interest in the business, Mavis clearly resented her.

Apart from the problems with Mavis, Dolly couldn't have been happier. But she wasn't going to worry about that today. She hurried home to change into her navy blue linen costume, thinking how lucky she was to be able to afford nice things. And since clothes rationing had ended, she'd been able to indulge herself. As she adjusted her navy and white hat in the dressing table mirror she grinned at herself, mocking the respectable figure that looked back at her. Respectable. If only they knew, she thought. But no one was going to find out, least of all the conventional matrons of the Mothers' Union, especially now they'd voted her in as Chairman.

She picked up her white gloves and handbag and left the house, walking briskly along the seafront to St John's Church hall, which stood at the junction of the Esplanade and the High Street. Inside, she climbed the steps to the platform and sat down rather self-consciously. Her friend Marion Russell had reassured her that there was nothing to be nervous about.

As she stood up to perform her first duty as Madam Chairman, Dolly couldn't help wondering what her audience would think if they knew her guilty secret. She'd be hounded out of the Union. They wouldn't accept her even if Tom had divorced Freda and married Dolly legally. To the Church, divorce was just as much a sin.

She stifled the thoughts and introduced the speaker, a retired missionary who'd recently returned from thirty years in China. Dolly scarcely heard a word, savouring her success. They'd lived here so long now that Holton Regis felt like home, her life in Chiswick a half-remembered dream. She was accepted by everyone — respectability attained at last.

A polite patter of applause woke her from her reverie and she glanced hastily down at her notes. "I'm sure we all found that most interesting. Are there any questions before I ask Mrs Russell to propose a vote of thanks to our speaker?" she asked, nodding towards her friend.

The meeting ended and Marion congratulated her on how well it had gone. "I told you there was nothing to be nervous about," she said.

Dolly smiled, pulling on her white gloves and adjusting her hat. "I'm glad it's over though. I must dash now — I've got to call in at the shop."

"I need a few bits too. I'll walk along with you," Marion said.

Marion's husband was a church warden and she was on the flower rota. Dolly would have said they were friends and it was true they got on well, but she could never imagine them exchanging their innermost thoughts and feelings, or giggling together over film stars as she had with Janet. Suddenly Dolly had the guilty thought that maybe respectability wasn't all it was cracked up to be. After all, she was only thirty-two, not too old to have fun.

As they walked along the Esplanade towards the pier, she only half listened as Marion grumbled about the holidaymakers and their effect on the town. "Holton hasn't been the same since they allowed that holiday camp place to open. It attracts all the wrong sort of people."

Dolly couldn't agree. "Those people probably come from big cities where there's no chance for them to enjoy fresh air and fun. We're lucky to live here all the year round and I for one don't begrudge them two weeks of it."

Marion looked taken aback but then she smiled, somewhat shamefaced. "I hadn't thought of it like that," she said.

"Besides," Dolly went on, "holidaymakers are the lifeblood of this town. Where would the shops and hotels and suchlike be without them?"

When they entered the shop, Mavis was busy so Dolly put on her overall and served her friend.

As she handed her the change, a woman came into the shop and pushed in front of Marion. She didn't recognize her until the hated voice screeched. "It is you. I thought I recognized you."

"Ruby?"

"Yes, it's me — your long lost stepsister. So this is where you ended up."

"What are you doing here?" Dolly gasped.

"On holiday, ain't I?" She smirked and looked at Marion. "Saw you walking along the front, then come in here. So, what you up to then?"

"This is my husband's shop," Dolly said, unable to keep the touch of pride from her voice. She shouldn't have said it, shouldn't have used the word *husband*.

Ruby threw back her head and laughed coarsely. Mavis turned from the bacon slicer, a thin smile playing over her lips.

Marion shifted her feet uneasily. "Maybe I should go. You and your friend probably have some catching up to do," she said.

"No. You ought to hear this," Ruby said, catching her arm. "Has she told you her *husband* still has a wife in London?"

"It's none of my business," Marion said, avoiding Dolly's eye.

Mavis's eyes were alight with the promise of gossip.

"Tom and Freda are divorced," Dolly said. Ruby couldn't possibly know the truth, could she?

But her worst fears were realized when Ruby laughed again. "Is that what he told you? Well, believe me, the last I heard, your fancy man was still Freda Marchant's husband."

Marion touched Dolly's arm. "I really must go." She hurried out of the shop. Dolly stared after her. Would she tell anyone? Maybe not, but Mavis had heard every word.

She turned to face her stepsister. "How could you?"

"And how could you?" Ruby retorted. "Bringing shame on the family? Running off with a ne'er-do-well like him? Just like your mother."

Dolly had been on the verge of tears but anger won. "You never treated me like family in the first place. If it hadn't been for Annie . . ." The tears welled again and Dolly swallowed them back with an effort. "Well, she's gone. And I've made a new life for myself — a good life . . ."

"Until I came along and spoiled it," Ruby said. Satisfaction gleamed in her dark eyes. "Just wait till I get back home."

"You won't say anything?" Dolly hated herself for pleading and she could see it wouldn't do any good. "Look, Ruby, she knows about us. She doesn't care about Tom, only about the money he sends her. And it's not as if there were any children . . ."

Her voice trailed away as she noticed the triumphant look on her stepsister's face. A cold hand clutched at her stomach.

"You didn't know, did you? He's a fine strapping lad, young Tony — the spittin' image of his dad —"

"I don't believe you." Dolly could scarcely get the words out. She clutched the edge of the counter. "Get out — go on."

The shop door banged shut, only the whirr of the bacon-slicer piercing the sudden silence. Mavis carried on working as if the exchange of the past few minutes hadn't happened. But Dolly knew she was digesting Ruby's revelations, wondering how she could turn things to her advantage.

When her legs stopped shaking, she took off her overall, picked up her handbag and said, "When Mr Marchant comes in, tell him I've gone home."

Dolly scarcely remembered the walk back to Alexandra Terrace. This really was the end. Ruby had no reason to lie, but Tom . . . How many times must she forgive him?

He'd know she'd found out of course. Mavis was sure to tell him. He'd have time to think up his usual plausible excuses. Well, she wouldn't be here to listen to his smooth talk.

She began packing as soon as she reached home. When the girls got in they'd be off. She couldn't stay now. She was so angry she couldn't even cry.

As she threw things into a case, she calmed down and tried to think where they'd go. She had no friends or family now. And, although she had some money of her own, it wouldn't last long. She'd have to get a job.

She sank down on the edge of the bed, her head in her hands. What a mess. If only Ruby hadn't chosen to holiday in Holton Regis of all places. But wasn't it better to know the truth? Dolly didn't think so. She'd been happy until now, had even managed to bury the truth about her relationship with Tom deep down where she never needed to think about it. So she tried to tell herself. But it was always there, wasn't it — the fear that someone would find out? And now that both Marion and Mavis knew, it would be all over Holton. She had to get away, should have gone when she'd found out she and Tom weren't really married all those years ago.

She went into Rowena's room, opened the top drawer and started to sort through her daughter's clothes.

Was she doing the right thing? Was it fair to make the children suffer? They loved their father. Maybe she should put a brave face on things, hope that they'd keep quiet? But the respectable Mrs Russell would waste no time informing the vicar that the new Chairman of the Mothers' Union wasn't fit for the post, let alone being allowed to remain a member of the organisation.

And as for Mavis . . . well, she was welcome to Tom Marchant. She'd soon find out he wasn't to be trusted.

As she slammed the lid of the suitcase, she heard the back door open. He pounded up the stairs and charged into the room. "Mavis told me Ruby's been here. What did that bitch say . . .?"

Dolly looked at him, her eyes cold. "She told me you had a son — it's true, isn't it?"

His guilt-stricken face said it all.

"How could you, Tom? You had a duty to your son —"

"And to you and the girls," Tom interrupted. "Don't you see, Dorothy, I had to make a choice. And I couldn't go back to her, leave you and the kids to cope alone. I didn't want to lose you."

He reached out a hand but she leapt away from him. He'd never know how hard it was not to let him touch her. She'd made the right decision, she told herself. He wouldn't get the chance to betray her again — and she did feel betrayed. This was even worse than when she'd discovered he was still married. He'd lied by omission. And who knew what else there was in his past, waiting to leap out and hit her?

"Dorothy, please — let me explain." Tom was running his hands through his hair, the scar standing out vividly on his temple as he pleaded with her.

Funny, she thought, I haven't noticed that scar for ages. It's part of Tom, so dear and familiar. She longed to reach out and touch it, smooth his hair back, to have him hold her, tell her everything was going to be all right. Yes, to have everything back as it was when she'd woken up this morning, singing.

You couldn't turn the clock back though, and dear and familiar as her *husband* was, Dolly had always known there were things he hadn't told her or that he'd skimmed over as being unimportant.

She straightened her shoulders and smoothed her skirt, willing her hands to stop trembling. "There's nothing to explain. I've made my mind up. I'm going — and I'm taking the girls with me."

"Dorothy, please . . . Surely we can work something out. We could sell up, move somewhere else, far away where no one knows us, make a fresh start."

"It wouldn't work, Tom. I'd always be looking over my shoulder, wondering when someone else from your past was going to turn up. You can't keep running away." The anger had gone and the words came out almost sadly. She pushed past him and picked up the suitcase.

He grabbed her arm. "You can't take the girls."

"Why not? I can hardly leave them here."

"Please, Dorothy. I've lost my son. I can't lose Rowena and Paula too."

"You should have thought of that."

He sat down on Rowena's bed, his head in his hands. "I know you're angry — you've every right to be. But won't you let me explain?"

"What's to explain, Tom? You abandoned your wife and child, bigamously re-married, fathered two

336

illegitimate children . . ." She clutched the door frame, sure her legs wouldn't hold her up much longer.

She started downstairs, still carrying the suitcase. His voice followed her. "You accused me of always running away, but isn't that what you're doing?"

She reached the bottom step and put the case down. The girls would be home soon and she must be ready to leave as soon as they came in. As she opened the hall cupboard to get her raincoat, Tom appeared on the landing.

"You're really going then?"

"I don't have a choice."

"Well, at least leave the girls here till you're settled. We can make up some story . . ."

"You're good at that — making up stories," Dolly snapped.

"I only meant I don't want them upset." He came downstairs. "Let them stay, please. Mavis will give me a hand with them . . ."

Mavis Wilcox — never. She thrust a finger in Tom's face. "You'd love that, wouldn't you? She's been after you ever since she came to work for us."

"Don't be ridiculous."

"You can't see what's under your nose, Tom Marchant. I'm not letting that woman get her claws into you." She took a deep breath, her decision made. "I'm staying."

A smile broke over his face and he tried to put his arms round her. "I'll make it up to you, Dorothy, I promise."

She shrugged him off. "You can wipe that grin off your face. I'm doing this for our daughters."

He looked tired, defeated, and for a moment her heart went out to him. She wanted to touch him, stroke his hair, see that so-familiar smile which could still turn her legs to jelly after all these years, to feel his arms holding her and telling her that everything would be all right. But it wasn't that easy. They couldn't just carry on as if nothing had happened.

He ran his hand through his hair. "How can I make things right, Dorothy?"

"First of all, you're going back to the shop. You can tell Mavis Wilcox if she so much as breathes a word of what she overheard, she'll have no job and nowhere to live. I'm sure she won't want to see her children homeless."

Tom was about to protest but Dolly stopped him. "And then you've got to sort out your marital status. Until then — it's the spare room for me."

"Anything you say, love."

He looked so wretched that Dolly almost gave in. But she wasn't going to let him off the hook so easily. The shock had receded a little and in some ways she understood. She truly didn't think he'd meant to deceive her, but once you started lying, things snowballed and then you couldn't go back and tell the truth. Looking back, she realized he had never actually said he and Freda had no children; she'd just assumed it.

Tom went out and she heard the van start up. Had she done the right thing, sending him to see Mavis?

338

Even more, was she right to stay? Until now, her lifelong search for respectability had left no room for compromise. She'd tried that when she'd first discovered how Tom had deceived her, even managed to convince herself that there were extenuating circumstances. For a long time she'd managed to suppress the guilt. What was the harm — especially when there were no children involved?

But, as a Christian and a churchgoer she should have known right from wrong — and it was wrong to live with a man you weren't married to. Now she was being punished for her sin — and her children would be punished too.

She sighed and took the suitcase upstairs. As she unpacked, the girls came in from school, chattering and strewing their things around as they always did. She smoothed her hair, plastered a smile on her face and went down to get their tea ready.

Tom came in a few minutes later and Dolly asked, "Everything all right at the shop?"

"Yes, I spoke to Mavis. We've sorted out that problem."

"Good," Dolly said and dished up their meal.

They were quiet as they sat at the dining table, any tension masked by the children's chatter about their day.

When the girls were in bed, Dolly knew she couldn't put off their discussion any longer. She still wasn't sure what to do for the best.

Tom stretched a tentative hand across the table. "Dorothy, I want to put things right. I know I've behaved badly. But you've known about Freda for years — I thought you'd accepted that situation."

"I had, but it's always been at the back of my mind. You can't keep that kind of secret forever."

"I did try you know — to sort Freda out. But with the war and everything . . ." he trailed off helplessly.

"I'm just as much to blame," Dolly said. "I should have insisted. But I was terrified you'd go to prison. Bigamy is a crime, you know."

"It's not too late to put things right," he said.

"That's not the point right now. You should have told me you had a son. How are you going to put that right?"

"I don't know, Dorothy. But I will try."

Dolly's heart softened at the hopeless expression on his face. But she wouldn't let him see. She stood up abruptly, too tired to carry on arguing. "I'm going to bed — we'll carry on this discussion in the morning."

She climbed between cold unused sheets that had never known a visitor. Now I know why we needed a spare room, she thought, tears welling as she forced herself to try to sleep.

CHAPTER
THIRTY

Tom sat at the kitchen table smoking one cigarette after another, scarcely noticing the overflowing ashtray at his elbow. He'd never known Dorothy to be so cold, her blue eyes glittering, her voice was like splintered ice. This was far worse than when she'd found out about Freda.

If only he'd been brave enough to tell her about Tony then, but she would have left him for sure, she'd only stayed because she'd been pregnant.

He thought about his children — his two beautiful daughters whom he loved as much as he loved their mother. And his son — the boy he'd abandoned, telling himself it was better that way. Suppose it came to a choice between them. What would he do?

There was no contest. Dorothy meant more to him than anything. He would do whatever it took to keep her with him, even if it meant never seeing Tony again. But first he had to try and put things right.

He was still sitting there as dawn broke and, before he could change his mind, he wrote Dorothy a note. By late morning he was crossing Kew Bridge towards Chiswick.

★   ★   ★

As he reached the house where he and Freda had once lived, he noticed the fresh curtains at the windows, bright new paint on door and windows. The hedge had been clipped and the path was free of weeds. Either Freda had latched on to a bloke with money or she didn't live there any more.

He hoped she was there — he couldn't keep putting things off, but the woman who answered the door said, "She moved years ago."

"Any idea where?" Tom asked.

"Sorry." The woman closed the door.

Tom turned away, not sure whether to be relieved or disappointed. He'd have to go home, tell Dorothy he'd done his best. But that wouldn't do. He must sort things out. Her brothers would know where she was.

Bracing himself for a confrontation, he decided to start at the market. Pushing his way through the crowds, he saw that nothing much had changed.

The fish stall was still there. But it wasn't Big Sid Pearson manning it.

Tom stopped, gasping as if from a physical blow. The youth behind the stall could have been himself twenty years ago.

"Tony?" The word came out in a harsh whisper and the young man swung his head round, eyes widening in shock. The lips which had been stretched in a laugh, narrowed to a thin line. Then he looked away and carried on serving the customer.

Tom took a step towards the boy, his heart thudding. Tony gave the woman her change and turned to the next customer, ignoring Tom.

342

He couldn't bear it. He grabbed the boy's arm. "Tony, don't you recognize me?"

"Course I do — but as far as I'm concerned, you ain't my dad," he said through clenched teeth. He shook Tom's hand off and faced the customer. "Haddock, Mrs? There's a nice bit — just right for hubby's tea." The twinkling smile was back as he deftly wrapped the fish in newspaper and took the money.

Tom watched, his heart aching. A real chip off the old block, his lad was, and no mistake. But the boy didn't want to know, and who could blame him? After a few minutes, he mooched away, wondering if there was anyone around he knew from the old days.

The smell of frying onions tempted him and he realized he hadn't eaten since setting out early that morning. He pushed open the door of Bob's Café where a buxom woman he didn't recognize stood behind the counter cutting thick doorsteps of bread.

Sitting by the window with a plate of bacon, eggs and fried bread and a thick mug of strong tea in front of him, he found himself immersed in the past. He recalled those two girls, one fair, one dark, arm in arm, faces flushed with the cold, giggling over some film star as they used to in those far off days before the war.

Giving himself a mental shake, he slurped his tea, almost choking as someone slapped him on the back.

"Tom Marchant — thought you was dead, old mate. What you doin' round here then?"

Tom looked up into Big Sid Pearson's beefy face. "I'm havin' a cuppa tea. What's it look like?" He grinned, pumping Sid's hand up and down. "Good to see you, mate. How've you been?"

"Not so bad." Sid looked at Tom's smart suit, white shirt and blue-striped tie. "Looks like you're doin' OK too." He pulled out a chair and sat down. "Young Tony told me you'd been by the stall. Gave the poor kid quite a shock, you did. We all thought you was dead — least that's what Tony was told."

"I s'pose that was Freda's doing. And how is my ex-wife these days? Still shacking up with anything in trousers — provided it can keep her in the style she wants to be accustomed to?" Tom asked bitterly.

"I wouldn't know. Haven't seen her for years. She took up with an American GI at the end of the war. Gone off to the States, she has." He broke off as the buxom woman approached the table, plonking a plate of chips and a mug of tea in front of him. "Thanks, Vi," he said, leaning towards Tom confidentially. "Didn't you know? But then, none of your business if you was already divorced."

Tom pushed his plate away, bitter bile rising in his throat; a swig of tea did nothing to take away the taste of Freda's treachery. "But she's been cashing the cheques I sent."

"I expect her brothers sent them on to her."

"But that money was for Tony." Trust Freda to get her hands on it, Tom thought.

"Looks like you need to talk to a solicitor, mate," Sid said.

"That can wait. Tell me about my son. How's he been living since his mother went off with her Yank?"

Tom knew his wrath was unfair. Hadn't he deserted his son too?

"Well, first off he stayed with Arthur. Derek was killed in the D-Day landings. Tony hung around the market, running errands, earning a few bob here and there. But Arthur's still up to his old tricks and I didn't want to see the lad getting into trouble. So I gave him a job on the stall. My lad joined the Navy and I needed a spare pair of hands. He's been lodging with me for a coupla years now too."

Tom was grateful to his old mate for looking after his son. The lad had turned out well. And he couldn't blame Tony for rejecting him. It must have been a shock, him turning up like that. He barely listened as Sid chuntered on about all that had happened over the past few years. He was re-living the confrontation with his son, hearing again his bitter words, *"as far as I'm concerned you ain't my dad."* Was he being punished for the mistakes of the past? And what's more, would he ever be able to put things right?

He took a swig of the now cold tea, his thoughts swinging between his son and Dorothy. He drained his mug and stood up, shaking Sid's hand. "Nice to see you, mate. And I'll take your advice about the solicitor." He hesitated. "Try to explain to Tony. It wasn't my fault . . ."

"I'll do me best, but if his mum's poisoned his mind against you . . . anyway, keep in touch, mate."

Tom scribbled his address and phone number on an old envelope, handed it to the fish merchant, and hurried away. All he could do now was go back to

Holton and hope that, somehow, Dorothy would forgive him. But he knew things would never be the same again.

Tom's hasty departure to London had given Dolly time to think. She was sure Marion Russell couldn't have worked out the whole story and, besides, she wasn't the type to gossip. And Tom had dealt with Mavis.

Dolly would have to resign from the Mothers' Union of course. But, despite the church's attitude, being a divorced woman no longer carried such a stigma. She would make the excuse that she wanted to spend more time helping with her husband's business. Surely any gossip would die down eventually.

But that didn't solve the problem of her relationship with Tom. She felt she could no longer trust him and, if it weren't for the girls, she would definitely have left. But they needed a father. She never wanted them to suffer as she had.

It would have to be separate rooms from now on — at least until he was legally divorced. And maybe even after that. It was easy to make such a decision when he wasn't there, but would she have the strength to stick to it when he got back?

For, despite everything, she still loved him.

The girls were in bed and she had almost decided to go up herself when she heard the van pull up in the drive.

Tom seemed startled to see her sitting at the kitchen table and he made to walk past without speaking. She stood up and put her hand on his arm. "Did you find her?" she asked in a whisper, almost afraid to ask. A cold finger of apprehension touched her. Was Freda dead, had she been killed in those last raids of the war? Despite her hatred of the woman who had helped to ruin Tom's life, she couldn't regain her own happiness at the expense of someone's life.

"She's gone," Tom said, sinking wearily into a chair.

"Oh, no." Dolly's hand went to her mouth.

Tom shook his head. "No — not that. She went off to America with some GI after the war. Big Sid told me."

"What about the boy?"

"She left Tony behind." The bitter twist to Tom's mouth eased into a smile. "He's practically grown up now — working on Big Sid's stall."

"Did you speak to him?"

The bitterness returned. "He doesn't want to know me — said he hasn't got a father." Tears gleamed at the corners of his eyes. "She told him I was dead."

Dolly couldn't help herself. Her arms went round him and she pulled his head against her bosom, stroking his hair. "Oh, Tom. What a mess. What are we going to do?"

He looked up, hope flaring in his eyes. "Can we sort things out? Is there a chance for us, Dorothy?"

"I can't say at the moment. Anyway, you need to rest if you're going to open the shop in the morning." She walked towards the door and he stood up to follow.

"I told you I'm sleeping in the spare room, Tom," she said, hurrying upstairs before she could change her mind.

Tom lit a cigarette. He couldn't blame her. The fact that he'd done what he thought best made no difference. Right was right and wrong was wrong in Dorothy's eyes. He'd seen signs that she might relent though, and he clung to the hope that things would eventually go back to normal. He knew she really loved him. Her scruples were on behalf of their daughters who must never be made to suffer the taunts of illegitimacy as she had.

Tom stubbed out his cigarette and went to bed. But despite his exhaustion he couldn't sleep. There was too much to think about. And even as he finally succumbed his dreams were filled with images of two of the people he loved most in the world — Dorothy and Tony, both looking at him with contempt in their eyes.

CHAPTER
THIRTY-ONE

It was six months since that awful encounter with Ruby. Dolly had gone back to working full time in the shop — anything to stop her brooding on her relationship with Tom. She still loved him, could even understand why he'd behaved so badly, but she couldn't forgive him.

Hypocritical, she knew. If her own moral code was really so strict, she'd have left him when she first discovered he'd committed bigamy. But she had stayed and pretended to herself it didn't matter so long as they loved each other. She had even joined the church and its organisations, knowing she was going against their teachings.

Then there was Mavis Wilcox, who'd had her eye on Tom from the start. Although she'd found another job, she still lived above the shop. The connecting door had been boarded up and the Wilcoxes now used the side entrance. Dolly no longer had anything to do with her but she was acutely conscious of her presence overhead. As landlord, Tom had to make sure the flat was maintained and Mavis was quick to use the excuse of something wrong with the boiler, a gas leak, or anything else to lure him up there. Dolly wished they could get rid of her, but much as she hated the woman, she couldn't turn her and her children out.

As Dolly tried to explain the workings of the till to Sally, the new shop girl, her mind just wasn't on the job.

Tom had verified that Freda had actually divorced him for desertion four years ago. He'd returned from London a few days before Christmas waving a copy of the decree, a big grin on his face. "Now we can get properly married, all legal. That'll make things right, won't it, Dorothy?"

She had shrugged and carried on stirring the stew. His shoulders drooped and he crumpled the vital document in his hand as he sat down. "I thought you'd be pleased," he said.

"You think that's all it takes — a piece of paper?" she asked, turning from the stove. It wasn't what she'd intended to say, but the words were out and she couldn't take them back. All the hurt and bitterness she'd suppressed for years welled up and she began to scream at him, terrible hurtful words. She couldn't stop herself. At last she ran out of steam and sank into a chair, covering her face as she broke into noisy sobs. Tom had tried to hug her, but she stiffened and he let go immediately.

Now, as she set Sally to tidying the shelves of tinned goods, Dolly realized she had handled it all wrong. Although they'd sat down later when the girls were in bed and tried to talk things through, she'd stubbornly refused to accept that Tom had done his best.

350

How she wished she could throw herself into his arms, tell him she loved him no matter what. Instead, she lost no opportunity to remind him of the wrong he'd done them all — including his son. Tony was at the centre of all their arguments for, as she said, if he could so easily abandon one child to pursue another woman, what's to say he wouldn't abandon her daughters in the same way?

That fear dominated everything Dolly said and did and the sight of Mavis Wilcox and her superior smile did nothing to set her mind at rest. But it wasn't Mavis she should be worried about, she now realized. It was her own actions that were pushing Tom away. Trouble was, she didn't know what to do about it.

Christmas had been a nightmare, although they'd both put on a good front for the girls. It should have been their best Christmas ever, with more goods in the shops and more money to spend too. But however many presents she bought, nothing could make up to them for the disintegration of their former happy-go-lucky lives. Rowena was sulky and difficult, sensing the tension between her parents and Paula was clingy and tearful.

Tom thought everything would be all right if they legalized their marriage, but Dolly couldn't see how they could do that without people knowing they'd lived in sin all these years. And worse still was the thought of the girls finding out. She couldn't bear it if they had to put up with the taunts she'd endured as a child.

So far there'd been no hint of gossip, so maybe it was better to keep quiet. The thoughts whirled round in

Dolly's head as she sliced bacon and wrapped cheese, supervised Sally giving change and smiled politely at the customers. Sometimes she thought it would have been easier if she had run away.

But that wasn't the answer and, as Tom's van pulled up at the kerb, she realized that despite everything, she loved him as much now as she had when she'd first laid eyes on him all those years ago. His hair might be greying at the temples but he was still the same handsome man who had smiled at her from behind his stall and set her heart fluttering. No matter how much she might try to convince herself that she stayed with him for the sake of the children, she couldn't deny that he still aroused those feelings in her. Even now, just a look from those brown eyes, a touch of his hand, could reduce her to quivering jelly.

As he unloaded the van he looked up and smiled. She couldn't help smiling back and in a second she knew she'd almost reacted as she would have before Ruby had turned her world upside down. Was the ice melting a little?

She was still smiling when Sally told her she was wanted on the phone, until she realized who was calling.

"It's Miss Skinner here, St John's junior school. I'm afraid there's been an accident. Paula's had a nasty fall . . ."

"A fall? Is she all right?" Dolly's hand shook and she gripped the phone more tightly. "I'll come straight away."

"I'm phoning from the hospital," Miss Skinner said.

"Hospital?" As she swayed against the wall, the phone was snatched from her hand. She was dimly aware of Tom speaking, helping her into her coat, urging her towards the van.

She huddled in the passenger seat, too numb to protest when Tom said to a frightened Sally hovering on the pavement, "You're in charge, Sal."

They were met by Miss Skinner and the Ward Sister. Dolly gripped Tom's arm, until the Sister smiled reassuringly. "She's fine — sitting up and asking when she can go home."

Paula was propped up by pillows, her face almost matching the sheets except for the purple bruise above her eye. Her wrist was bandaged as well.

"Sweetie, whatever happened?" Dolly put her arms round her, terrified that her daughter had been bullied.

"I was skipping and my foot caught in the rope. I tripped and banged my head on the wall." The child's voice was ragged, choked with tears.

She looked up at Tom, who had followed her in. "The teacher saw her fall," he said. "Lucky she was there."

"Can we take her home?" she asked.

"They want to keep her overnight. When the doctor's seen her in the morning . . ."

Tears of relief welled up and Dolly let go of Paula's hand to fumble in her bag for a hankie. Tom patted her shoulder awkwardly and shuffled his feet, saved from saying anything as the Sister came in and bustled them away.

"You can come back later if you wish," she said. "Let her rest for now."

Miss Skinner, who was hovering in the corridor, hurried towards them, saying, "I'm so sorry. We try to keep the children safe but accidents do happen."

"We're not blaming the school, or you, Miss Skinner," Dolly assured her. "I'm just thankful it wasn't more serious."

"I was so worried, seeing her lying there unconscious . . ."

"It wasn't your fault. Thanks for looking after her," Tom said.

He took Dolly's arm, steering her towards the van. "We'd better get back. Rowena will be home from school and wanting her tea."

When they got back to Alexandra Terrace there was no sign of Rowena but a note on the kitchen table said "gone to shop". Dolly ran upstairs, snatched Paula's doll off the bed, grabbed her best red hair ribbons — they'd help cheer her up.

"I'll pick Rowena up from the shop and lock up. Poor Sally will wonder what's going on," Tom said as she came downstairs.

"Can you drop these off at the hospital too?" Dolly held up the bag.

"Why don't you sort things out at the shop and I'll go to the hospital. It's too far to walk," Tom said. "I'll pick you up later."

Dolly wanted to see her daughter and set her mind at rest. But it made sense. Not for the first time she wished she could drive, but this wasn't the time to be thinking about that.

354

Sally was waiting anxiously. "Mrs Marchant, thank goodness you're back. Is your daughter all right?"

"She's fine. Be home tomorrow, just a bump on the head. Where's Rowena? I thought she was here."

"She's upstairs. She was a bit upset when she heard about the accident. Mrs Wilcox said she'd look after her," Sally said.

"All right, Sally, you can go now. I'll lock up." Dolly kept her voice even although she was furious. She was about to go and bang on the side door when Mavis came in.

"Rowena's doing her homework. I thought I'd let you know she was all right. She's had her tea."

"You'd better tell her I'm here," Dolly said, tight-lipped.

"I will, but I intend to say what's on my mind first." She took a deep breath. "Mrs Marchant — Dolly — Tom's a good man and he . . ."

"It's none of your business," Dolly snapped. "You just keep your hands off him."

Mavis uttered a short laugh. "Huh, chance'd be a fine thing. I would if I thought he'd even look at me. But you can't see what's right under your nose, can you? Tom loves you, you stupid cow."

Dolly stepped back as if she'd been slapped. Tears welled up in her eyes. "It's nothing to do with you," she faltered. "It's between me and Tom."

Mavis's harsh features softened. "Look, I know things aren't right between you two and it's eating him up. I've never seen a bloke look so miserable."

"Don't worry, we're working things out," Dolly said, wondering why she was trying to justify herself to this woman.

"Working things out? But he's still unhappy, isn't he." Mavis wagged a finger. "I tell you, Dolly, if you're not careful you'll lose him. And I'll be waiting to pick up the pieces." She turned away abruptly. "I'll fetch your daughter." She slammed the shop door and disappeared through the side entrance.

Dolly's legs were still shaking when Tom came in.

"I thought you'd be all locked up and ready to come home by now," he said. "Was that Mavis just leaving?"

"Yes, she's gone to fetch Rowena. She's upstairs doing her homework."

"Good of her to help out."

Dolly, still reeling from Mavis's accusations, ignored his remark. "How was Paula?" she asked.

"She was asleep. I sat with her for a bit in case she woke up but the nurse said they'd given her a sedative. I tucked Arabella in beside her so she'd see her when she wakes." Tom smiled and reached out to touch Dolly's hand. "Don't worry, love, she'll be all right. She'll be home tomorrow."

Dolly smiled in reply, feeling guilty that he attributed her strained looks to worry over their child. The truth was that both her children were very far from her thoughts at that moment.

Anyone looking through the window at the cosy kitchen scene later that evening would have seen a very normal family, Tom thought. He was sitting at the table with

Rowena, checking her homework and complimenting her on her spelling and neat handwriting. Dorothy was at the sink washing up their supper things and telling Rowena it was time she was in bed.

She still looked pale. Their younger daughter's accident had shaken her up more than he realized. He wanted to comfort her, to take her in his arms and tell her everything would be all right — not just Paula, but their relationship, too.

Over the past months he'd tried so hard to talk to her, to thrash things out, but each time she would go cold on him, shrugging him away, closing the door of the spare room in his face.

He kissed Rowena goodnight and shooed her out of the room. Perhaps he should try again. After all, this mess was his fault. He should be the one to put things right. But he dreaded another row, or worse still, her cold indifference.

He fingered the letter in his pocket. Paula's accident had driven it out of his mind. He'd felt such a surge of joy when he'd opened it that morning, the first step towards healing the breach between him and his son. He'd wanted to share the news with Dorothy, but any mention of Tony or his past life only raised the barrier between them again.

Should he broach the subject now? Better not. She'd had enough to put up with for one day. She looked tired — more than that, defeated somehow. It wasn't just the accident. These last few months had been a strain on her too. He hadn't noticed — too busy being angry at her stubbornness, her refusal to accept that their love for each other was more important than her notions of so-called respectability.

Now he studied her intently, noting the tiny lines under her eyes and at the corners of her mouth, the few silver threads in the fine blonde hair. But to him she was still the laughing girl who'd captured his heart, whose smile could chase the clouds away when he was at his lowest ebb. He remembered how she had leaned against him at the hospital; it was the first time in months that she hadn't shrunk away from his touch. Was it too late? Could they recapture what they'd had at the start?

He stood up and sighed. Tomorrow. He'd definitely tackle it tomorrow. Right now, he was just too tired. "I'm off to bed, love."

She didn't turn round, just carried on with her cleaning. He shrugged and left the room.

Dolly gave a last wipe of the draining board, passed the cloth over the taps and rinsed it out. Although aware of Tom's scrutiny, she hadn't dared turn round. As he stood up and cleared his throat, she tensed. Had Mavis been right? Had he reached the end of the road? If he told her he was leaving could she swallow her pride and beg him to give her another chance?

Yes, of course she would.

But when he just wished her goodnight and left the room, her shoulders sagged and her throat closed up. She wouldn't cry. This situation wouldn't be solved by tears. She went slowly upstairs into the bathroom. Maybe a hot soak would ease some of the tension.

358

As she lowered herself into the scented water and closed her eyes, she replayed the conversation with Mavis. She'd been angry, partly because she didn't want to admit the truth of the woman's accusations, but it had made her think. Did she really care so much what other people thought?

The most important person in her life was Tom, she realized, closely followed by her daughters. They ought to sit down as a family and decide what they should do. If Tom and the girls wanted to move away where they could start afresh, so be it. And if they decided to stay and face people, she would cope with that too.

She stood up and grabbed the towel, dried herself and pulled her satin nightdress over her head. "*Tomorrow is another day*," she whispered, echoing the words from one of her favourite films. But unlike Scarlett O'Hara, she wouldn't let her stupid pride lose her the man she loved.

She quietly opened the bedroom door — not the spare room. In the faint light from the streetlamp outside, she could see Tom hunched under the blankets. He seemed to be asleep and Dolly lifted the covers and slid in beside him. He stirred and mumbled, threw an arm across her. She leaned over and brushed the hair away from his face, kissing the scar that, to her, had never marred his handsomeness.

His eyes flew open and she drew back, uncertain of his response. But he grabbed her and pulled her to him. "Dorothy, my sweet, I've missed you so much," he whispered, raining kisses on her eyes, her nose, her lips.

She clung to him as joy surged through her. It wasn't too late after all. He still loved her.

And through that long night he proceeded to show her exactly how much — and she responded in kind. They didn't get much sleep between their bouts of passionate lovemaking and whispered promises, explanations and apologies.

Dolly sang as she prepared breakfast next morning and laughed when Tom playfully grabbed her from behind. Their happiness must have been infectious because Rowena lost her sulky expression and smiled for the first time in weeks. Her smile grew broader when Tom said she could skip school and come with them to fetch Paula home from hospital.

Once back home Tom explained to the children what had been wrong these past few months. No details — there was no need for them to know that their father had committed a crime. It was a mistake, he said, one which meant they weren't properly married and that they'd have to have another wedding.

"Can we be bridesmaids?" Rowena and Paula asked in unison.

"Don't see why not," Tom said, taking Dolly's hand and grinning all over his face.

"We'll be a proper family then, won't we?" Paula said, her little face creased in a serious frown.

"We always were," Dolly said. She looked at Tom and nodded encouragingly.

He took the letter out of his pocket and cleared his throat. "I explained to you that you already have a brother — from my first marriage," he said tentatively.

The girls nodded eagerly.

"Well, he might be coming to visit us soon. He wants to get to know his other family."

Paula looked excited but Rowena's sulky expression appeared again. Dolly sighed. It looked as if they might have trouble there. But she held on tightly to Tom's hand and decided not to say anything. Dealing with a pouting fourteen-year-old would be child's play after the storms of the past few years.

And, as Dolly had discovered, most problems could be solved with a little understanding and a lot of love.

Also available in ISIS Large Print:

Death's Dark Vale

Diney Costeloe

London 1937. When Adelaide Anson-Gravetty discovers she is not who she thought she was, her search for her true family leads her to the convent of Our Lady of Mercy in St Croix in northern France.

The defeat of France brings German occupation to the village, the nuns are caught up in a war that threatens both their beliefs and their lives. Involved with the resistance and British agents, Adelaide and the sisters truly walk in the shadow of death as they try to protect the innocent from the evil menace of the Nazi war machine.

ISBN 978-0-7531-8356-4 (hb)
ISBN 978-0-7531-8357-1 (pb)

Muddy Boots and Silk Stockings

Julia Stoneham

It's 1943 and the country is at war. Yet on one remote Devonshire farm the days are not so dark. An unlikely group of land girls are finding out about life, love and loss, forming surprising friendships along the way.

When Alice Todd's husband runs off with another woman, she is forced to find a means to provide for herself and her young son. Accepting a position as a hostel warden at an old Devonshire farmhouse, Alice finds herself looking after a group of ten volunteer land girls.

The job is not as easy as it first seems. Not only does Alice have to deal with the uncompromising farm owner and her resentful and unhelpful assistant Rose, but as her young charges arrive at the farm, she discovers every girl has a story — and some have rather dark secrets.

ISBN 978-0-7531-8186-7 (hb)
ISBN 978-0-7531-8187-4 (pb)